A Slight Hangover

A Slight Hangover

Ian Ogilvy

Writers Club Press
San Jose New York Lincoln Shanghai

A Slight Hangover

Published by Writers Club Press
an imprint of iUniverse.com, Inc.

For information address:
iUniverse.com, Inc.
620 North 48th Street
Suite 201
Lincoln, NE 68504-3467
www.iuniverse.com

ISBN: 0-595-01007-5

Printed in the United States of America

To Emma and Titus, who actually read my books—and to Sam and Lee who, on the whole, would really rather not.

Contents

Acknowledgements

Grateful thanks to Graham Payne, for allowing me to write the play on which this book is based—and profound gratitude to the late Sir Noel Coward, for giving me the idea in the first place.

Chapter 1

She was remembering the time when Lewis had brought them some hashish and, later, when they were as high as kites, all three of them had got into the same bed—this bed, now that she thought about it—and they'd rolled around like puppies for a bit, nobody being quite sure what to do to whom, until she'd suddenly found herself sandwiched between them, Orson in front and Lewis behind and then everybody just stroked everybody else, for hours it seemed, until Lewis started to laugh; and, when they asked him what he was laughing at, Lewis had said that while the stroking was perfectly agreeable there was a limit to his patience and, if they weren't going to do anything more erotic than this then on the whole he'd rather read a good book—and Orson had said that it would have to be a goddam great book and Lewis had said that the one he was reading was rather goddam good, actually and Orson, who was shivering with lust, said that perhaps he ought to go and read it then and Lewis had replied that perhaps he ought.

He'd managed to get out of the tangle of sheets with most of his dignity intact; then he'd smiled down at them with a lot of affection on his bony face. A moment later he'd left the room and she'd turned to Orson and they'd gone at it hammer and tongs, blissfully, for hours and hours.

It was the only time they'd tried a threesome and the outcome had resolved so many unspoken questions that, leaving out the blissful hours and hours with Orson, the exercise (and goodness, what a workout he'd given her) had been well worth doing. Of course, everybody had always thought they did it all the time, which was idiotic of them but amusing for her and Orson and Lewis. Such fun, to be thought wickeder than you actually were. Of course, they had been dreadfully wicked in lots of different ways. They'd drunk too much and smoked too much and experimented with far too many drugs and spent far too much money on themselves and not nearly enough on other people and, generally, had lived life to the hilt, which was what you ought to do with your life, since it was the only one you had.

Living to the hilt had been such a huge lark and they'd all had the most marvelous time imaginable but now it wasn't fun anymore, at least not for her; it was just terribly tiring and painful and boring—so bloody, bloody boring and tiring and painful and, quite honestly, she'd had enough of it.

Writing that letter had been exhausting. So idiotic, really. In the past, she'd written tons of letters. It was what you did back then. You wrote letters to your chums. And telephoned them, of course. The dear, darling telephone. Sweet Mr. Bell for inventing it. Such fun, sitting there, chatting away for hours and hours, about nothing at all. Smoking a secret cigarette and twisting the wire round your fingers and chatting and shrieking with laughter. Muriel had been marvelous on the telephone. You could spend hours on the telephone with Muriel.

Of course, telephoning the girl would have been quite wrong, so she hadn't; she'd written the letter instead.

But, perhaps she oughtn't to have sent it. Perhaps she oughtn't to have written it, either. Her hand had ached so horribly when she finished it and her eyes had been so sore and she'd drifted off into one of her little zizzies and when she'd awoken the pen was still in her hand and the letter was still resting on the New Yorker and she'd heard one of the boys lumbering up the stairs—Orson, of course because Lewis didn't lumber—and she'd just had time to slip the letter between the pages of the magazine and then slide down under the sheets and pretend to be asleep.

She'd heard Orson come into the room and then pad, like an old Labrador, over to the bed. She'd felt him looking down at her and she'd wondered if he'd started crying again. Best not to wake up. Best to stay in her pretended sleep. If Orson was going to cry like this every time he looked at her, then it was best not to let him know that she knew. He'd stood there for a few moments; then he'd stroked her hand for a moment and gulped a couple of times and then she'd heard him tiptoe away.

This dying business was so tiresome. No drama to it at all. It was like being all alone in Dr Beale's waiting room with only golfing magazines to read—waiting for the doctor to see you with some awful news which you already knew. All so slow. Where was the plane crash when you needed it—or the bullet from some gangster's gun? That Sammy man had been a gangster and he'd probably got a gun—why couldn't he walk into her bedroom and plug her right now? He was probably dead by now, of course. What was his name? Orson had picked him up in Sardi's one night and had brought him back to the Algonquin Hotel so proudly, like a fisherman with a record trout. What was the man's name? Sammy Something—something Italian, anyway. How could she possibly remember a something Italian name? It was forty, maybe fifty years ago, for heaven's sake.

Giuliani. Sammy Giuliani. Orson had said that he'd killed at least four men and the man had laughed and shown his gold tooth. Nonsense, probably. Still, if was funny that she'd remembered his name.

The letter. Had it made any sense? She'd been in such a hurry to get it done—perhaps it had ended up a bit incoherent. And Bella had been so stupid with it, not understanding for such a long time that the boys weren't to know about it.

"No, Bella—you can't just leave it with the postman. You have to go to the Post Office and mail it yourself, or else the boys might see it." When Bella had looked doubtful, she'd explained it all again, slowly, until Bella nodded and had turned to go, still clutching the envelope in one huge hand.

"You have to hide it Bella, dear—all the way, you see. Stuff it down your front, darling. God knows there's room in there."

Later, when she'd brought her supper on a tray, Bella had hissed that the letter was at now the Post Office, just as Miss Giselle had asked, and that the gentlemen hadn't seen a thing.

What fun it would be if she could watch the girl's face when she read it—which was out of the question, unless she managed to die before the letter reached its destination. And then it would only work if you became a ghost and she wasn't sure you did; she wasn't sure what happened after you died but, if you *did* become a ghost, then perhaps she'd get the chance to watch the reading. She could hover up in one corner of the ceiling and watch the envelope being torn open. Of course, she'd have to take the address with her, otherwise she wouldn't know which ceiling to hover under. Could you do that when you were dead? Perhaps you didn't need address books when you were dead? Perhaps you just knew, by supernatural means, where everybody lived—but, to be on the safe side, she'd have to remember to look in her little book, just before she slipped away.

It was somewhere in Hampstead. A ceiling in Hampstead. She hadn't been to Hampstead for years. There was a heath, wasn't there? It was up on top of the hill and there was a little pond where children sailed model boats. The woman lived somewhere around there. Not to worry—she'd be sure to find it and, if she got lost, she could always ask a spectral policeman.

What was the girl's name again? Or *woman*, rather—she'd be too long in the tooth now to be a girl anymore. Whitehall. Olga Whitehall. Whitehall was her married name. The Olga bit was clever. She'd never have thought of Olga. Olga wasn't a very pretty name but it was clever.

The pain was starting up again. It was so frightfully unfair, this dying business. Surely men were supposed to go before women? And yet, there they were, Orson and Lewis, the pictures of health (Orson, she decided, was a Rembrandt and Lewis an El Greco, or perhaps an Alberto

Giacometti)—and here she was, quite a few years younger than both of them and sinking fast. No, not fair at all. Well, they'd both be sorry they outlived her. With any luck, the nest she had stirred up would have hornets in it. No—Lewis was frightened of hornets. Perhaps just some unassertive wasps would do. Just a bit of mild stinging was all she asked for.

She'd been so clever with the clues she'd left—particularly the clue stuck in the relevant diary, and the diaries themselves, of course. And she'd been clever with that private detective—just *organizing* him from this great distance without the boys finding out had been bordering on genius—the detective had been very effective, really, finding out all sorts of things for her, although there was that one thing that had been a bit upsetting, although it shouldn't have been upsetting at all, really, because lots of women her age were grandmothers (horrid word, summoning in Giselle's mind images of crones and hags and awful old witches) and they didn't seem to mind at all.

Of course, nothing might happen at all—but, if it did, well it was too delicious to imagine. She'd have to find her way to and from the Hampstead ceiling somehow, if she wanted to enjoy all the consequences. Could one haunt the first class section of a 747, she wondered—or would one be relegated, by some sort of ectoplasmic air stewardess, to coach, or worse, to the luggage compartment?

The pain was getting worse. It was deep in her stomach and it felt as though somebody was twisting something down there. Horrid. Really horrid.

Below her window, somebody coughed.

Orson tried to stifle the cough but it came out anyway. It was all those cigars, smoked in all those restaurants in the days when nobody minded—and Giselle had sat there with them while they smoked and had, no doubt, breathed in the fumes, which may or may not have had something to do with her illness—but at least the cancer wasn't in her lungs. If it had been in her lungs, the burden of guilt on him and Lewis would be intolerable. Of course, she'd smoked in the old days—everybody did—but they'd made her stop years ago, when she'd had pneumonia and the doctor had told her that cigarettes were bad for her.

"Aren't they bad for Orson and Lewis too?" she'd asked.

"Yes, of course they are," the doctor had said. "Only, they're much worse for you."

He was good, that doctor. Orson tried to remember what he'd looked like. He was Dr Beale's predecessor—or even the predecessor to the predecessor. It was years ago, anyway. Giselle had given up her cigarettes—she'd made a terrible fuss, but she'd given them up—and he and Lewis had carried on smoking their Havanas and now Giselle was the one who was dying of colon cancer—but at least it wasn't in the lungs, which was something—and perhaps the cancer had nothing to do with their Havanas and was just happening all by itself.

Orson wondered how many more days he had left in which to tiptoe into her room and look down at her and try to remember how she had been. She was always asleep nowadays. Practically every time he went in there, she was asleep. Looking at her asleep made him cry. Funny, that. It was Lewis who cried at things usually but now he was the one doing it. Boo-hooing all over the place. He ought to pull himself together, get on with things. This flower bed, for a start. Everything else in the garden was fine but these begonias looked diseased—as though Giselle's sickness had become contagious for nearby plant life and had drifted down in a miasma, infecting only the flowers directly under her window.

They weren't the most cheerful of plants, Orson decided—even when healthy. Their dark leaves and their small, fussy petals and their tendency to cling close to the ground in a misguided attempt to avoid detection made them, in his eyes, at least, seem chicken-hearted—they liked to cower in the shade. The flower bed got hardly any sun at all because Giselle hated the sun coming into her bedroom.

Orson looked up at her window. The shutters were closed and he knew that, on the other side of the glass, the cotton nets were drawn as well and the room was cool and dim. He looked back at the flower bed. What he ought to do, he decided, was to plant some new begonias. Get rid of these sick little guys and plant some good strong ones and then, maybe, some essence of their rude health might float up, somehow, driving back the mist of sickness and scattering it on the wind—and then the victorious molecules might slip through the little gaps in the windows and settle over Giselle's poor, thin body and then she'd start getting better and then soon they'd all be back to normal again— Ridiculous notion.

All the same, he ought to plant some new stuff here. Maybe something different, though. Something a bit more lively. Something Impressionistic, perhaps. A patch of California poppies would be good—but they'd never grow in this damp, shady place. Impatiens would work here and they were brightly impertinent little flowers. Cheerful, too. Lewis called them Busy Lizzies and had always said he didn't like them.

Busy Lizzies it would be.

Lewis was sitting on the terrace under the big green sunshade, with the letters and the Sunday Times. He'd put the letters into two piles; those that addressed him as Sir Lewis Messenger and those that didn't. Those that didn't, he threw in the waste bin. He always picked them out of the bin later, so the gesture was symbolic. All the same, there were standards. The knighthood had been a long time coming and, now that he'd got it, the least his correspondents could do was acknowledge it.

Meanwhile, a quick look through the newspaper. No point bothering with the news, since it was several days old and he'd seen all the latest events on television. No, just straight to the arts section to see if any old friends might be working at something he might be interested in seeing, then on to the book reviews to see if any old friend had written something he might be interested in reading—the lightest of skimming over the pages, in fact, before tackling the crossword puzzle, which was the real reason for having the thing delivered in the first place.

One across. Nine letters. *Monster's makeshift cremation.*

Oh, bugger it—to be reminded about the awfulness of everything by one of the few divertissements designed to take your mind of such things. But here it was, a reminder of the question of cremation. Giselle had always wanted to be cremated—she was adamant about it—but, when he'd asked her a few days ago where she wanted to be scattered, she'd grinned like the Cheshire Cat and said that it was all in her will and that they'd find out in due course. The grin spelled trouble, Lewis knew. It had always spelled trouble for them in the past and, just because Giselle was dying, it didn't mean that it wouldn't spell trouble for them in the future. Giselle, of all people, would be more than capable of a piece of posthumous mischief-making.

Her will. Where was it? He'd never seen it and Giselle had only said that she'd made one when he'd asked her about the ashes. It was hard enough to ask about the ashes—asking about the will implied a nasty-minded interest in the thing, as though you were keen to get your hands on whatever legacy you might have been left. Not that Giselle had anything to leave them, apart from her jewelry and her clothes and neither he nor Orson had any use for them. And where was her jewelry? He couldn't remember seeing her wear any of her necklaces or bracelets for years and the only ring she wore was that cabochon ruby they'd bought her just before the war—that year when Orson had sold those four paintings to that demented Texan and when the royalty payments on his musical *The Seersucker Suite* had been pouring in—their best year, in fact, when a good cabochon ruby represented about half a week's income for them—so, the long and the short of it was, if she wanted to be cremated and have her ashes scattered in some specified location (rather than just being dumped over the cliff) then she'd better stop being coy about it and tell them where her bloody will was.

Monster's makeshift cremation. Obviously an anagram of *cremation.* Ah—MANTICORE. Oh, very clever—the old brain was still there, at least enough of it to handle one across. Of course, quite what a Manticore was—beyond being a legendary beast—he couldn't for the life of him remember. Wasn't it one of those patched-together creatures—a head of something, a body of something else and a tail which had nothing to do with either? A trio, certainly, of unrelated body parts. Rather like the three of them, really. He'd ask Orson. Orson would be sure to know. And Orson would want to know why he wanted to know and then he could show off his cleverness.

MANTICORE. So, one down starts with M. Eight letters. *Playwright cooked greens after I left back half.* Shouldn't be too difficult.

Was Dr Beale coming back today or tomorrow? Not that he could do much for her but at least he was generous with the painkillers. Thank God for that nurse. Nurse Clap. That was what Orson called her; he said he broke out in a rash whenever she came near him. A severe woman, with no detectable sense of humor but with a fairly decent moustache. At least she stayed in her room most of the time, only emerging to perform the unpleasant tasks—tasks which he and Orson had wanted to do at the beginning but Giselle had pleaded and pleaded with them not to, so they'd hired Nurse Clap on Dr Beale's recommendation and had been glad that they did, because the unpleasant things were really very unpleasant indeed and, much as they both loved Giselle, he knew that neither he nor Orson could have coped.

Playwright cooked greens after I left back half. Anagram of *GREENS*, perhaps? Half could be *SEMI*—back half would be *IMES*—take out the I, leaves us with *MES*—Good God Almighty—of course. *MESSENGER.* Well, well. Fame had come in many forms but never before in a crossword clue. Dear old Sunday Times. This was going to irritate Orson no end. Lately, he'd been finding a certain, perverse pleasure in irritating Orson.

When she woke up, the pain wasn't there any more, which was nice of it. Taking a little holiday from her body, perhaps. She couldn't blame it—she'd like a little holiday from her body, too. It used to be such a good one and now it wasn't. Now, it was all thin and wasted and wrinkly, with horrid little sags and tucks and droopy bits—but once (actually, not that long ago) it had been awfully nice. So many people had told her how nice it was. Mostly men, of course, although once, in the South of France, on the terrace of that apartment, Freda Helfinger had made a pass at her, which had been exciting if only for the novelty.

Nobody would make a pass at her now. All her lovely hair gone. She looked like Lewis' agent, little Tolly Utteridge. Tolly had been bald for as long as she'd known him, which was ages and ages, so he must have got used to it. That wasn't going to happen to her—she wasn't going to have the *time* to get used to it.

Here came Nurse Clap with her little plastic cup of joy. She wouldn't tell her that the pain had gone for the time being. The stuff in the plastic cup was far too good to miss. A bit like the hashish they used to get sometimes. It didn't taste nice but that was all right—the hashish hadn't tasted nice either. Both were dreamy.

Had poor Nurse Clap never heard of depilatory cream? Or even a razor? She must remember to have a little chat with the poor woman. There was no reason why even a woman as plain as Nurse Clap should have to clump about the world with a moustache.

But she was so tired. Too tired to worry about other women's moustaches. Just before she drifted away into the lovely velvet blackness, she thought that, on the whole, the letter had been a good idea. Quite *why* it was a good idea was out of reach but it didn't matter. Nothing mattered anymore, because here came her dark cloak of painless, dreamless sleep and, if that was what death was like, then it was exactly and absolutely up her alley.

Orson had been irritated by one down and Lewis felt sorry for him and made up by asking him all about one across—and Orson knew a surprising amount about manticores, which put him in a better mood. They had dinner together and talked practically about Giselle and what they would do afterwards. Dr Beale came and looked in on Giselle and then he joined Lewis and Orson for coffee.

"Are you sure you wouldn't rather have her in the hospital?"

"It's not up to us," said Lewis.

"It's up to her," said Orson. "Always has been. How much longer?"

Dr Beale shook his head slowly. "Not long, I'm afraid. A couple of days at the most."

Lewis watched as Orson poured himself a brandy. He said, "I'd like her not to have any pain."

Orson said, "So would I."

"Then she won't," said Dr Beale. "But it might be less than two days."

Then Nurse Clap came in and, in a hushed voice, said that she thought Dr Beale ought to come and take another look at her.

The funeral service was as secular as an Anglican bishop could make it without being openly derisive of his own religion. Both Lewis and Orson had begged Bishop Winston to keep God out of it as much as possible and, with good humor, Bishop Winston did his best.

He spoke about her warmth and Muriel muttered to Neville that he made Giselle sound like a radiator. He extolled her vivacity and her charm and her wit and stayed away from any suggestion that her life might not have been as pure as the Christian Church would have liked, emphasizing instead her many good works.

"She did good works?" whispered Muriel in an audible hiss.

"I once saw her give a beggar a five pound note," muttered Neville.

"Just once?"

"She never did anything twice."

Orson twisted irritably in his seat and stared at Muriel and Neville, and Muriel dimpled and fluttered her fingers at him. He put one finger to his lips and Muriel nodded seriously and made a zipping gesture across her mouth.

Orson stayed twisted in his seat for a few more moments, taking the opportunity to look around the small church. There weren't many of the old gang left. Actually, it was something of a miracle that anybody was there at all—it was such a long way for them all to come, except for Muriel and Neville, who lived in Florida now. Old Swifty was there, looking more like a bloodhound than ever—and Edie too, still looking like a llama (a moth-eaten one too, Orson thought—but then she *had* come all the way from California) and dear old Peter and Robert, both of whom had aged almost beyond recognition—and several more scattered here and there in the pews—but there were so many faces not there that should have been there. Of course, most of the missing faces were missing because they were dead, weren't they? They'd been dropping like flies, recently. Hardly surprising, with everybody in their seventies and eighties. What could you expect? All the same, it was tough, losing people.

Orson felt the weeping coming on again and he turned back in his seat, wincing at the small stab of pain in his back. He stared blindly ahead, his vision blurring. He closed his eyes and felt a tear slide down his cheek.

Oh, Christ, thought Lewis, sitting at Orson's side. He's blubbing again. Would he never stop? He'd wept buckets in the car on the way here and, before that, almost non-stop for the past two days. Americans were so emotional, compared to the English. And it wasn't just the tears, either. Orson had become helpless, like a child, getting himself dirty and not bothering to brush his teeth and eating only ice cream. There had been sudden bursts of temper, followed by wild crying of the Russian kind, all tremendously Chekhovian and tremendously embarrassing and thank God none of the funeral guests was staying in the house, so nobody but him and Bella had to witness all the drama. The decision to put everybody up at the Regency had been a wise one.

The coffin was moving now, on its rollers, through the curtained rectangle. Lewis felt a tightening in his chest and he closed his eyes to stop his own tears from flowing, letting his mind drift to other times, better times—like the early days in Paris when they'd first met Orson at one of those parties where the room smelled of oil paints and garlic and Gauloises cigarettes and where the girls didn't shave their armpits.

Orson had been wearing an enormous Bohemian hat, he remembered. It was black felt, with whimsical bends around its wide brim, turned up here, bent down there and, underneath, there was a boyish face with a curly mouth and a broken nose and green eyes that glittered with amusement. Giselle had been instantly fascinated. He knew she was fascinated because she stopped stroking his bottom and stared so hard at the Bohemian that Lewis had felt jealous and had started to sulk.

The room was full of students all pretending to be artists and, to Lewis, it seemed that the Bohemian was just one of many, but pretending rather harder than the rest. He said this to Giselle.

"Ignore the hat, darling," she'd said. "The nose! Look at the nose! It's marvelous!"

"What's so marvelous about it?"

"Don't be obtuse. The *shape*! It's a marvelous shape."

"Is it better than mine?"

'It's *exactly* the same as yours but in an *utterly* different sort of way."

Later, they discovered that the Bohemian wasn't Bohemian at all but was, in fact, an American from Buffalo, New York. His name was Orson Woodley and he was studying art in Paris and had no money at all, which was odd, Lewis thought, because surely all Americans had money? Particularly the ones who could travel all the way to Europe?

Even later, when they all went back to Orson's poky flat on Rue Maldarmier, Lewis and Giselle discovered that, far from merely pretending to be an artist, Orson was actually a very good one, although nobody important knew it yet. His paintings were stacked round the walls. They were mostly bits of Paris in close-up—a corner of Les Halles, one leg of the Eiffel Tower, a pissoir from the inside. There was a bold, original vigor to his pictures—at least, that was what Giselle had said, using her breathy, art critic's voice.

Lewis had recognized the voice. The art critic part was the one she used when she didn't know what she was talking about but wanted people to think she did. The breathy part was the one she used when she wanted to impress a man. Both together, and the effect was overwhelming.

The poky flat on the Rue Maldarmier was being pushed out of Lewis' memory by the taped strains of the Moonlight Sonata and Lewis opened his eyes, blinking against the light in the little church. Not his favorite piece, the Moonlight but Giselle had liked it.

He felt a jab in his ribs. Orson was frowning at him.

"What?"

Orson lowered his head and whispered, "Were you asleep, Lewis?"

"Of course I wasn't asleep. I was thinking."

"You looked like you were asleep."

"I wasn't."

"Because, if you were asleep, it's a goddam shame."

"Oh shut up. I wasn't asleep."

"It looked like you were asleep."

"*Jesus.*"

After the service, everybody went back to the house and drank champagne. Muriel and Neville got into their swimming costumes and lay by the pool, looking like two pieces of beef jerky. Since going to live in Florida, they had taken up sunbathing and golf and had become numbingly dull, which was a pity, Lewis thought. In the old days they had been such fun. Muriel, admittedly, had always had the mind of a house plant but Neville had been quite a funny young man until he'd gone to Hollywood and become a film star. Then he'd started taking himself seriously and that was the end of that.

Lewis glanced round at the scattering of guests on the terrace. It looked, he decided, like a garden party at an old people's home. Everybody was sitting about on the patio chairs, as though waiting for something to happen. Robert had a stick leaning against his knees—a black one with a silver handle in the shape of a dog's head.

The wake didn't last too long and, quite soon, everybody was demanding taxis to take them back to the Regency and a line of island cabs came coughing up the hill, belching blue smoke from their exhaust pipes. People started to bend themselves into the back seats. Robert came up to Lewis and Orson to say goodbye.

"Probably won't see you again, old things," he said, shaking them gently by the hands. "Peter's not too well, I'm afraid and I don't think I'll want to make the trip on my own. Of course, if you're ever in London, give us a tinkle. In fact, Lewis—aren't you coming over for your show?"

"No," said Lewis. "I'm not."

"But it's going to be at the National, isn't it? Surely you want to be there for that?"

'No, I don't. Apparently that stinker Finlay's running the place now and wild horses wouldn't get me within hailing distance of the man. The bugger had the cheek to write to me, would you believe? A lot of self-important garbage. I couldn't finish it. It was practically a royal summons. To hell with him."

Robert laughed and said that the only reason Lewis didn't like Finlay was because Finlay had got his knighthood years before Lewis and, to make matters even more intolerable, had recently been elevated even further with a seat in the House of Lords.

"Exactly," said Lewis, who disliked Finlay for quite a different reason. "can you imagine it?"

Robert gave them both a hug and climbed into the back seat of the taxi, squashing his bulk next to little Peter. Then they both waved like a matched pair of Queen Mothers and the taxi coughed asthmatically and took its place in the convoy that was beginning to free-wheel down the driveway.

Later, at dinner—a mostly silent affair—Orson said, "When will we get them, do you know?"

"When will we get what?"

"The ashes. When do we get them?"

"I don't know. When they've cooled down a bit, perhaps?"

"You're so goddam callous, Lewis."

"No, I'm not. I don't know when we'll get them. Why do you need to know when we'll get them?"

"Because Bella found the will, that's why. Under her pillow. I had a quick look. We get everything, as we expected, including the responsibility of disposing of her ashes."

"Ah. Right. Well—where does she want to end up?"

"You don't want to know, Lewis. You really, really don't want to know."

Chapter 2

It was a lovely, sunny morning. Skippy Squirrel jumped out of his little bed and looked out of the window.

"Hello sun!" he cried. "I'm coming out to play! Don't go away!" But when he went to his chest of drawers, he couldn't find any clothes to put on! He looked in his laundry basket. It was full of dirty clothes. "It's time I did some laundry!" he said.

Skippy went hippity, hoppity down the road until he got to the launderette. He put the dirty clothes into one of the big, shiny machines. Then he shut the door, clang, and switched it on.

Chuggety chug, chuggety chug went the machine. His clothes went round and round and round. Skippy Squirrel watched them go round and round and round. Splishety splosh, splishety splosh, went his clothes.

Round and round and round went the clothes. Round and round and round.

Skippy Squirrel kept watching them going round and round and round.

Skippy Squirrel began to feel a bit sick.

Suddenly, he was sick all over the floor! Hewarrrghhh, went Skippy Squirrel.

Hewwwaaarrgh, hewwaaargh.

Olga pulled her fingers off the keys and glared at the screen. This had been happening all morning. Perhaps it was time to take a break. Perhaps it was time to take a break from the sodding squirrel and write something grown-up for a change. Perhaps, on the other hand and rather more dramatically, it was time to take a break from the whole bloody thing and come up with an alternative way of making a living. She stared at the screen and then pressed the backspace button until the screen was clear. Then she swiveled round in her chair and looked glumly at the easel in the middle of the floor. There was a water color pad with a half-completed picture of Skippy Squirrel standing by an overflowing laundry basket resting on it. He looked, she thought, quite extraordinarily stupid. And dull. And unadventurous. An insipid little beast, with all the dash and bravado of a glass of water—he didn't deserve this string of biographical novellas she'd labored on over the last ten years. All those words, all those pictures. Skippy getting up. Skippy going to bed. Skippy on the bus. Skippy on the train. Skippy at the greengrocer's. Skippy at the fishmonger's. Lately, she'd tried a story about Skippy going to France in a hot air balloon.

"Not too sure about this one, love," Simon had said. "Lovely story, super illustrations—but are we straying a bit, do we think, from the spirit of the series? They are, after all, for very young kids. General feeling is that we ought to put this one on the back burner for the time being. Marion had such a nice idea—lots of kids not actually having a washing machine in their family, how about if Skippy goes to the launderette? That would make a good one, Marion thought."

Of course, what was messing her up was the letter and it was going to go on messing her up until she did something about it. There it was, on her writing desk, hiding in its blue airmail envelope. The writing on the envelope was thin and spidery and somehow uncertain, as though the writer was not only unsure of the name and address but also whether to post the thing at all. The stamps had pictures of tropical flowers on them. Olga thought they might be hibiscus.

She picked up the envelope and took out the two flimsy sheets of blue paper.

'*Dear Mrs. Whitehall,*' it began, '*you don't know me and I hardly know you but the fact remains, whether we like it or not, that I am your mother.*'

It was, Olga thought, the most eye-catching opening sentence to a letter that she'd ever read. She scanned the rest of it again, more quickly now that she'd deciphered some of the scrawled words and sorted out the arbitrary punctuation and the odd phrasing and the obsessive underlining of almost every other word. When she reached the end, with its scribbled signature—and, under the scribbled signature, the printed words 'Giselle Palliser'—she read it all over again.

What the hell was she supposed to do with this?

She got up and went to the tall window that overlooked the back garden. The lawn was grayish, with little bald patches here and there. Most of the trees were bare, except for the big rhododendron down at the end, and the fallen leaves that she raked together yesterday had been blown out of their neat piles and had clumped themselves all along the edges of the flowerbeds. It looked cold out there and depressing. There was something about Hampstead in the winter that was more depressing than say—Putney, or Pimlico. Perhaps it was being that much closer to the bottom of the clouds. Of course, winter was depressing all by itself. At least the bloody squirrel had the sense to sleep through it, which explained the endless bloody sunniness of her books. It never rained, or snowed, or hailed on Skippy Squirrel. It was permanent summer in Skippy's world. Perhaps he could get skin cancer.

"*It's fatal, Skippy,*" *said the kind doctor.* "*You're going to die.*"

Skippy Squirrel started to cry. Ploppity plop went his tears on the cold hard floor.

"*You're a fucking crybaby, Skippy,*" *said the kind doctor.*

She really ought to talk to somebody about this letter. Harry would be good at sorting out her feelings for her. She dialed his number. Serena answered.

"Olga, how lovely. Harry's not here at the moment. Anything I can do?"

Serena was pleasant enough and absolutely the right person for Harry and they all got on swimmingly, which was wonderfully civilized of them all but she was a little too pragmatic to give advice on matters of the soul.

"No—it's not important. I'll try later. Thanks, Serena. Bye."

She put the phone down and stared at the blue envelope again. Amanda would have to be told, there was no getting away from it. Before Harry, actually. Of all people, Amanda should be the first to know.

She met Amanda for lunch. The restaurant was in Greek Street and it was very crowded and Olga had to raise her voice against the din.

"I got this letter!"

"What letter?"

Olga took the two sheets of airmail paper out of her handbag and held them up. Amanda reached for them and Olga said, "Did you bring it?" Amanda nodded and held up a newspaper clipping and, simultaneously, they   passed the papers across the table to each other. Amanda turned the pages of the letter this way and that and then looked at the bottom of the second sheet. Olga saw her lips moving as she deciphered the name and then Amanda looked up at Olga and raised an eyebrow and, pointing her chin towards the piece of newsprint in Olga's hand, said, "*That* Giselle Palliser?"

Olga glanced down at the newspaper clipping. It was from the obituary age of the Times. There was a picture of a woman in forties' dress and makeup, very posed, with careful lighting. The words 'Giselle Palliser' were in heavy type and there were two columns of print beneath them.

Olga nodded. Amanda's eyebrows were pulled down and together into a small frown. Then she looked down at the first page and began to read. Olga turned away and stared round the restaurant. It wasn't very appealing, she decided. Chianti bottles with straw bottoms hanging from the ceiling. Fish nets and green glass floats on the walls. All these impossibly young business men in their suits, all talking so loudly and with such confidence—surely, when she was their age, she didn't have this noisy brashness? She glanced back at her daughter. Why would she like a place like this? How strange that one's child should be so different and in so many ways. To be so remarkably beautiful—Olga examined each feature in turn, the high forehead—dented at the moment with a small vertical crease—the straight nose, perhaps a little long, the high cheekbones and the almost ridiculously full lips—where on earth had they come from?—but most of all she looked at Amanda's eyes that were flicking backwards and forwards at a furious rate, which was impressive, given the scrawly writing and the bizarre punctuation but then, she supposed that in her job Amanda would have to be able to read quickly and efficiently, no matter how bad the writing or how startling the contents—the eyes were green, like a cat's and a little overwhelming at first—one of Amanda's early boyfriends had said they were intimidating—and then the eyes came to a stop, staring at the signature at the bottom of the page and Olga noticed that the vertical furrow was deeper and the corners of the mouth were pulled down. Olga reached forward to retrieve the letter and, when their eyes met, she started to say something but Amanda shook her head and said, "Aren't you going to read yours?"

Olga looked down at the clipping again. She read through it quickly. Then she put down on the table top and sighed.

"She really did so little, didn't she? And yet, she warrants this bloody great obituary. Why, do you suppose?"

"Some people are just famous," said Amanda. "Is there anything there that you didn't already know?"

"No."

Later, when they left the restaurant, Amanda took Olga's arm and walked her up to Soho Square. They sat on a bench in the gardens. Pigeons wandered at their feet.

"Don't you have to be back at the office?" asked Olga, shivering a little in the cold air.

"No. I'm the boss, remember?" Amanda leaned back, her arms spread across the back of the bench. "Do you believe it?"

"Yes."

"So do I. What are you going to do?"

"I don't know. What would you do?"

"Well—I think I'd be sad for a bit, suddenly discovering who my mother was but not being able to meet her at last because, before I can, she goes and dies on me—"

"That's what you'd feel. That's what I feel. What would you *do*?"

"I haven't the faintest idea. You?"

"I thought of going over there."

"Where? The Caribbean?"

"Mm."

"What for?"

"Oh, come on, Amanda. Think about it. Here's this extraordinary, almost legendary creature, claiming to be my mother in a letter full of remorse and regrets but, at the same time, she carefully omits any mention of who might be the father."

"Ah."

"Exactly. Ah."

"And you think—?"

"Well, yes I do. Wouldn't you?"

"Well, you've had the letter longer than me. You've had more time to absorb it all. But yes, I would think the same. I think I would. So—who do you think it was?"

"Well—one of them."

"Of course one of them. Which one?"

"I don't know. But, look—narrowing it down to two is pretty good, isn't it? Given that I only got this at nine this morning and, in that time,

I've discovered who my mother is—or was, rather—and have a pretty good idea that my father is one of two unbelievably famous old men–"

"There's a book about them, you know. I think it's called '*Jeunesse Dorée*.'"

"God. It would be, wouldn't it?"

"That came out a bit acid."

"Well, they were much discussed in the fifties, you know. Endless articles about them. Lots of speculation, none of which was ever either answered or refuted. We all got rather bored with them, to be honest. I mean, it was either the Dockers or the Ménage à Trois—you couldn't get away from them."

"Who were the Dockers?"

"Vulgar rich couple. They had yachts and gold-plated cars and things. They were flashy but sort of fun. An antidote to the austerity of the fifties. Anyway, it was either them or the Ménage à Trois. That was what papers like the Daily Sketch called them. It was just showing off that they knew a bit of French, I think."

Amanda shivered. "I'm freezing. Walk me back to the office."

They got up from the bench and made their way up towards Oxford Street. When they got to the crowds, Amanda said, "What would you do when you got there?"

Olga shrugged. "I don't know. Go and see them, I suppose."

"What—just like that? All the way to Saint Marta's without a word of warning? Shouldn't you write to them first?"

"I don't know. Maybe."

"Have you talked to Dad about this?"

"I called this morning but Serena answered and I really didn't feel up to explaining it all to her. She asks so many questions along the way, it takes forever to tell her anything."

They walked on in companionable silence, dodging the knots of people coming from the opposite direction. Then Amanda said, "Look, if you do go—and I think you're completely mad, by the way—"

"Thank you."

"Well, I just don't think you can march in unannounced, that's all—but, if you must, then I'd rather like to come too. May I?"

Olga felt a wave of relief wash over her. It would, she thought, be so much less frightening with Amanda along. Amanda could do all the confrontational stuff so much better than her—assuming that there was going to be some sort of confrontation which was, she thought, going to be unavoidable if she stuck to her instincts—which were looking more and more irrational with every step she took—

"I wish you would."

"Then I will."

"Maybe I ought to write."

"I think so. Of course, we don't know what they know, do we? I mean, do they know that she wrote the letter? Do they know about you at all? She didn't say—in fact, she left out everything that might help us with this, which was dreadfully irritating of her and completely irresponsible, if you ask me. So—what we ought to do—"

"We?"

"Of course—we're talking about my grandparents remember—"

"So we are. I hadn't thought about that."

"We write a letter and say we have to meet them on a matter of personal urgency."

"Personal urgency?"

"Yes."

"That sounds as though we've been caught short and need a lavatory."

"All right—we'll work something out—but, whatever, we're vague about our purpose. That way, if they know all about it, then they're prepared for us and if the don't know all about us, then at least they'll know we're coming."

"What if they flatly refuse to see us either way?"

"That's why 'personal urgency' sounds good to me. Like there's the possibility of a law suit. They'll see us."

Olga smiled. Amanda had always had this confidence. Another mysterious genetic attribute that neither she nor Harry possessed. Sometimes she wondered why she'd felt the need to divorce Harry. At other times, she wondered why she'd felt the need to marry him in the first place. He was a perfectly pleasant man, nice-looking, with excellent manners and rather better taste than hers. There was really nothing wrong with him at all—other than his inability to get excited about things. She'd never known Harry to raise his voice—or his eyebrows, come to that—about a single thing. Nothing was wonderful to Harry— or marvelous or smashing or any of the other hyperbolic words that made life if not fun then at least sound like fun. 'Not bad' was the most you could ever get out of Harry.

Tolly Utteridge's head was bald and brown and covered in little splotches of darker skin. His face was a mass of thin criss-crossing wrinkles. His mouth was lipless and his chin hardly existed at all—what skeletal structure he had under his mouth simply falling away and disappearing in the wattles that hung from his neck. Michael Corbo thought he looked like a tortoise.

Tolly was sitting on his leather sofa, his immaculate knees crossed and a small cigar held between his fingers.

"You know this big revival the National Theatre's doing in London? Of *The Seersucker Suite*? Well, they want Lewis to go over and be there for opening night. Apparently they intend doing a very lavish number on it—make some sort of obeisance, I think. A bit of a ceremony for the old man. They want us to approach him—well, Julian wants us to approach him. Apparently, Julian has already tried and Lewis turned him down flat. Julian gave up after that. So much for our London branch—sometimes I wonder if Julian is really up to it. Anyway, in desperation, he's asked me to use our old friendship—that was the phrase he used—and sound him out. That was another phrase. What do you think?"

Michael sniffed. "I think it's pathetic. I think it's too little, too late. They've ignored him for years and all of a sudden they discover him and want to do one of his musicals and they expect him to come running."

"I don't think they expect him to run, Michael. Hobble, perhaps."

"Well, whatever—I think Lewis will be rather angry and rather cynical. I think he'll eat them up and spit them out—"

"But do you think he'll go?"

"No. No, I don't."

Tolly sighed and re-crossed his legs. He stared at the twinkling light on one polished toecap and sucked at his cigar.

"When I say 'they', I actually mean Finlay, you know."

"Finlay?"

"The Lord Ferguson himself. Called me up ten minutes after Julian had made his plea and tried to climb up my ass. Kept calling me love. One of the more unpleasant aspects of our profession, I'm afraid— having to do business with the sort of Brits who call you love. Mind you, he's probably busy right now bemoaning the unpleasant aspect of his profession that forces him to deal with godawful Yanks like us. Let alone profess affection towards."

"But we're lovely, Tolly."

"Are we? Well, I am. Never been sure about you, Michael. Anyway, Finlay climbed off his throne and got on the phone and lowered himself to talk to an agent. He's come to us, so he must want Lewis awful bad. And all of a sudden—because he's got involved with it—it's become— significant. It would be quite a coup, you understand."

Michael wandered over to the window and looked out onto 5th Avenue. Another gray day. Even the taxis looked less yellow than usual, as though they'd been bleached somehow.

"He won't go."

Tolly coughed delicately. "How much influence do you have there?"

Michael turned round in surprise. "What do you mean?"

"Well," said Tolly, waving the cigar in small circles, "you do know them, don't you?"

"Yes—but so do you. And for rather longer, I should think."

"Oh, for ever. We all go back to before the war, would you believe. But that doesn't make us close. I'm his agent, not his friend. Business—always business. That's the way to do it. No broken hearts when a client leaves you, that's the trick. But you've got a relationship, haven't you?"

"Sort of, yes. Through my mother. Apparently they all knew each other way back."

"Lovely woman. I met her a couple of times. Never looked after her, of course."

"No, well—she wasn't an actress or a writer, was she?"

"No, but such a lovely voice, I'd have bent the rules. You've actually been there, haven't you? To Gladstones."

"A few times, yes."

"That's a couple of times more than I have. Do you think you could get another invitation?"

"I've got a standing one."

"Have you really? Well, well. What do they see in you?"

Michael laughed. "Orson likes me because we're both New Yorkers. And I once said to Lewis that I thought he was probably the most influential playwright of this century and, ever since then, he's liked me too. And, of course, I kinda blend into the ethnic scenery. They're inclined to use me in their dealings with the local authorities—as though my color gives me some sort of passport to places and people that might bar them entry, although of course they're not barred anywhere. Well, maybe Orson is. But look—I don't know what the situation is down there at the moment, with Giselle gone. There's been no word from them. Maybe they're so plunged in grief that asking either of them for anything wouldn't be appreciated at all."

Tolly nodded. "Giselle. Another lovely woman. Crazy as a loon but lovely with it. Listen—why don't you write a letter of condolence and ask to visit and then you could fly over and—in amongst the condoling—you could use some of your charm to persuade Lewis that being fêted by the National Theatre is a good thing and much to be desired. Particularly since Finlay's offered to pay for the whole thing. First class all the way. He said Orson could go too. Got any idea what two first class round tickets from Saint Marta's to London cost?"

"He hates Finlay, you know. I don't know why."

"I do but I won't tell you. It might affect your powers of persuasion, and ignorance is bliss in this matter."

"Thank you. You'd give me some time off for this?"

"All the time in the world, kiddo. In fact, I want you to go to London first. Take a good look at Julian and find out if he's up to the job. Then, when you've found out that he probably isn't, you can fly to Saint Marta's from there. When you arrive, you could even visit some relatives."

"I don't have any relatives on Saint Marta's, Tolly."

"Sure you do—the brothers. The bros. You can give them high fives, or whatever you do when I'm not watching. I'm joshing you, you know."

"I know, Tolly."

"Go away now. I want to sleep."

"Yes, boss."

Freddy was being teased by some of the maids. He liked being teased by them, it made him feel wanted and useful, which was nice, really because, ever since old Ma had popped off, he'd felt a little *de trop* here and there.

They were all in the room that Freddy called The Green Room. It wasn't green but Freddy liked the theatricality of the name. It reminded him—and anybody else who knew of his younger days—of the short time he'd spent hoofing it around the country. All the maids called it the Green Room now.

"So, Meester Fraidy—where you go for your holiday?" asked Conchita. She was fat and jolly, always laughing at something or other, which was funny, really, given her job. How any of them could even crack a smile was beyond him, it really was. All that endless bed-making and sheet-changing and towel-picking-up awfulness—and for complete strangers too—and precious few tips, either. He'd had enough of that with old Ma, thank you very much.

"Yais—where you go, Meester Fraidy?" said Maria One.

There was a chorus of interest from the rest of them. "Where, Meester Fraidy? Where you go thees year? You gonna be bad boy in Freenton again, like las' year?"

Freddy brushed away the little brown hands that were prodding him playfully.

"Now, girls—you stop that. I won't have it. You're all wicked, you are really. I don't know what I'm going to with you. I don't really. Send you all back to Barcelona, quick as a wink, if you don't behave."

Maria Two said that she came from Valencia and the rest chimed in with where they all came from and none of them came from Barcelona, it seemed. Freddy said, "Well, I don't care—I'll send you there anyway and then you'll be sorry," and they all squealed at this witticism and stroked his hands and said they were sorree, so sorree, Meester Fraidy and where was he going for his holidays?

Freddy paused dramatically. It was ever so exciting, his news and he wanted it to have a big effect on the girls. He looked around the little room—not much more than a closet really, the shelves stacked with the sheets and the towels and the little wrapped-up bars of soap and the little bottles of shampoo and shower gel—and then he looked at each of the girls in turn, making them wait for it and they understood the game and leaned forward, their brown eyes sparkling with the fun.

"You'll never guess," said Freddy slowly.

"Freenton?" said Conchita and the rest of the girls laughed and the ones sitting behind her pushed Conchita gently between her shoulder-blades.

"No, Conchita—not Frinton. Not this year. Frinton will have to do without me this year. They'll all have their hearts broken by my absence but I don't care. I don't. I'm breaking out this year. Out of the rut. I'm screwing up my courage—pardon my French—and taking the plunge. This year, I shall be turning my back on the rain. This year, I'm for sunnier climes."

"You gonna climb, Meester Fraidy?"

"No, you silly you, I'm not going to climb. What an idea. Me—half way up Mount Everest? Please."

That made them scream. They were nice girls. Good friends. The only ones, really, now that old Ma had gone and now that he was getting on a bit himself and the boys no longer flocked (not that they ever had *flocked*, really—sometimes he'd thought boys must be an endangered species). Besides, nowadays it was ever so dangerous, wasn't it? Thank God he was past all that. Still, a friend would be nice. Comfortable, sort of. Well, if wishes were horses, we'd all be in the Household Brigade.

"I am going, girls—I am going to—wait for it—"

"Queek, queek, Meester Fraidy—"

"I am going to where the palm trees hang over the water's edge, where the steel drums go boinkety boinkety boink, where a flower behind the ear is a definite fashion statement—the land of calypso and rum and a jolly good time being had by one and all. I am going—wait for it again—I am going—hold your breath—to—Saint Marta's."

"Saint Marta's?" This was from Theresa, the quiet one, who didn't giggle as much as the others.

"Yes, Theresa, Saint Marta's. It's in the Caribbean."

"I know. Why?"

"What do you mean, why? Why not?"

"Why not Freenton?" asked Theresa seriously.

"Because," said Freddy, loftily. "Just because."

He couldn't tell them the real reason. The real reason was so feeble and silly and unrealistic and so unlikely to come to anything that they'd never understand how he'd come to think of it in the first place. If it came to that, he was having a hard time understanding it himself. All

those years ago, it was. And so casual, for both of them. Memorable—
at least for him, it was—but still ever so casual. Just one of those things.
So what he thought he was doing, he couldn't imagine and nor could
the girls if he chose to elaborate. In fact, if he thought about it at all,
there was a danger that the whole adventure would look so ridiculous
that he'd give it up and go to Frinton instead. He didn't think he could
bear Frinton again. Those lonely walks along the front. The way people
looked at him, their eyes showing that they knew all about him just by
the way he walked and by the tilt of his little felt hat and perhaps by the
touch of mascara he'd worn for goodness knows how many years,
except when he was on duty, of course, when a touch of mascara
wouldn't do at all.

No—bugger Frinton. Besides, if he didn't do it now, he never would.
And it didn't matter—really it didn't—if nothing came of it. Just the
sunshine would be nice. "I need a change. That's why." He stubbed out
his cigarette in the hotel ashtray and Conchita took the ashtray from
him and dropped the stub end into one of the rubbish bins. Then she
wiped it clean and put it back on its stack.

"When you go, Meester Fraidy?"

"Next month. I've bought some lovely togs to go away in. Even some
shorts. I shall be exposing the knees, dears. You won't recognize me. I
shall look like a film star."

"Ooh, Meester Fraidy."

Chapter 3

After a week, Lewis decided that it was time to cope with the letters. They had been arriving in sackloads every day and he and Orson had transferred them to cardboard boxes in Lewis' study.

He sat at his desk, staring hopelessly at the pile he'd arranged on the blotter in front of him. There were perhaps twenty letters in the pile and they represented a mere skimming off the top of just one of the boxes. He looked down at the floor—there were five boxes, filled to the brim. Did they actually know this many people?

He couldn't do this on his own. Orson was no help. He never was when it came to correspondence. "Goddam letter," Orson would growl, brandishing a page of affectionate phrases from an old friend. "Why can't the bastards leave us alone?"

Perhaps they ought to hire a secretary. Although, where one got a secretary on this island was anybody's guess. Perhaps the employment agency could help. He looked up the number and dialed. The same woman he'd spoken to last time replied. He recognized her voice—she was one of a number of impoverished members of middle class English gentility, left behind after Saint Marta's got its independence. Her name was Miss Wilkes.

"Hello, Miss Wilkes. It's me again."

"Sir Lewis—what a pleasure. May I say, straight away, how sorry I am."

"Thank you, Miss Wilkes."

"She'll be sorely missed."

"She will indeed."

"Oh dear—I'm afraid, Sir Lewis, I don't think I'm going to be able to help you this time."

"How do you know, Miss Wilkes?"

"Oh, Sir Lewis—I do find this so difficult but—well—it's Mr. Woodley, you understand. He's not the easiest of gentlemen, is he?"

"No, indeed, he isn't Miss Wilkes. In fact, I don't think I'd be overstating the case if I said he was one of the most difficult old sods on God's green earth."

"Oh, Sir Lewis—I wouldn't say that—"

"I would, Miss Wilkes."

"But he is a tiny bit difficult, shall we say—we're both agreed on that—and his reputation with our members is not terribly helpful when we try to persuade somebody to take a post at Gladstones—"

"Too true, Miss Wilkes but we don't need a domestic servant, you see. Bella is still with us and I actually believe she'll stay. She doesn't seem to notice, you see. Not like the others."

"Well, that's a relief and no mistake."

"Isn't it, Miss Wilkes? No, what I'm looking for is a temporary secretary. We have a veritable Kanchenjunga of letters and I cannot handle them. She would be dealing with me and with me alone. The whole time would be spent in a room as far away from Mr. Woodley as possible."

"Well, Sir Lewis, we don't actually handle secretarial positions. Not as such."

"As how, then?"

"Well, we don't actually handle them at all. We're purely domestic, you understand. However, I would personally be delighted to help you out."

"You, Miss Wilkes?"

"It would be a pleasure, Sir Lewis. I could come up in the evening and we could put our heads together and zip through them in no time."

"Well, that's very good of you, Miss Wilkes," said Lewis, thinking that the last thing he'd care to do was put his head together with Miss

Wilkes and zip through anything. "I have no idea what sort of fee would be involved—"

"Oh, Sir Lewis—there wouldn't be a fee. It would be an honor."

That evening, Miss Wilkes drove up to the house in her neat little Mini Minor. Lewis took her to the study and Miss Wilkes made small exclamatory noises at the cardboard boxes, picking letters out of them at random and turning them this way and that, as if trying to guess the identity of the senders by the weight of the papers and color of the envelopes. Lewis gave her a sherry and she took a few, bird-like sips. Then they started.

It was soon apparent that Miss Wilkes wouldn't do. She was so distracted by the celebrity of many of the writers that, far from zipping through, they were crawling along at a snail's pace.

"Oh, Sir Lewis—here's one from Lord Claridge! He says—oh my goodness—he says that Miss Palliser reminded him of the entire cast of Macbeth, including the witches and he's miserable that she's gone. What a very odd thing to say."

"Not odd at all, Miss Wilkes—a fair description—"

"Oh—and here's one from Gregory Peck! The handsomest man in the world, I've always said."

"Have you really, Miss Wilkes?"

"Such a wonderful actor. He extends his warmest sympathies—Oh good heavens, Sir Lewis—this is from Princess Alexandra! Such a properly royal person, don't you think and so unlike some of the others, who really behave rather commonly, I always say."

"Do you, Miss Wilkes?"

"So serene, the Princess. She's my favorite. This is from a Michael Corbo—we don't know a Michael Corbo, do we Sir Lewis?"

"I can't speak for you, Miss Wilkes but I do know a Michael Corbo, as a matter of fact. May I see it?"

"Oh—and dear Dame Maggie's sent you the loveliest little poem— shall I read it to you?"

"Perhaps a snippet Miss Wilkes—but after I've been the bathroom. Do excuse me for a moment."

Lewis stuffed the letter from Michael into the pocket of his dressing gown and hurried from the study. He found Orson sitting moodily in the dark living room, staring at the portrait of Giselle that was hanging over the fireplace.

"Have you got a moment?" Lewis asked, standing in the doorway.

Orson didn't turn round. "I have too many. What do you want?"

"I'm going mad. Do you think you could come and be mildly offensive to this woman? I mean, just enough to get rid of her but not so much that I'm duty bound to punch you on the nose. Do you think you could manage the subtlety of such a thing?"

Orson pulled himself to his feet. "Lead me to this harridan."

"I can't lead you, you fool. That would be too obvious. Give me five minutes and then come."

Lewis went to the downstairs lavatory. He put the lid down and sat on it and read Michael's letter twice. How charming of the boy to offer help and how excellent his timing. It would be good to see him again.

When he returned to the living room, he found Miss Wilkes frowning over an airmail letter.

"I think this person wants something, Sir Lewis—though for the life of me I can't discover what. It's from a Mrs. Olga Whitehall."

"Never heard of her."

"No, well—her address is Hampstead, although that doesn't mean a thing nowadays, does it? She says she needs to see you and Mr. Woodley on a matter of personal urgency and would you please write back to her and tell her you will and then she'll fly out and visit—"

"No, no, Miss Wilkes—that's one of those letters that goes straight in the bin. We get several every year. They're all from raving lunatics. We never reply to them. People who write letters like that shoot rock stars as a hobby."

"Heavens."

The door flew open with a crash and Orson stood bulky in the opening. There was a pause while he surveyed the room, then—

"Who is this woman, Lewis?"

"This is Miss Wilkes, Orson. I think you've met before. She's come to help me with the letters."

"A likely tale. You can't fool me, Lewis. This is some doxy you've picked up in the harbor, isn't it? No, don't speak to me. You'll only lie. You disgust me. You have the mating instincts of a gerbil. You're a tramp, Lewis and you, madam, are no better. Try to break up a family, would you? Well, you won't succeed. He loves me, do you hear. Me, me, me! Oh, hateful! Hateful!"

Orson collapsed sobbing on the sofa and Lewis said, "I'm so sorry, Miss Wilkes. Mr. Woodley isn't himself—" and Orson groaned and said that he certainly wasn't anybody else and Lewis said that perhaps it would be better if she left now and Miss Wilkes, who was terrified, hastily gathered up her glasses and her handbag and her scarf and hurried from the room. Lewis followed her out to her car. She got in and started the engine. Then she looked up at Lewis and shook her tight gray curls in bewilderment.

"Oh, Sir Lewis—how could Mr. Woodley think such a thing?"

"Stress, Miss Wilkes. All Americans suffer from it. Don't take it personally. I'll have a word with him. There'll be flowers from him in the morning, you'll see. Good night—and thank you so much for your help. We've broken the back of it, I think."

Miss Wilkes drove off down the drive and Lewis waved until she was out of sight. Then he went to the living room. Orson was sitting on the sofa. He had a half-filled brandy glass in his hand.

"Has she gone?"

"Ossie—are you completely mad?"

"What do you mean?"

"I asked you to be mildly offensive. I didn't ask you to barge in here like an hysterical catamite and accuse the poor woman of dockside prostitution."

"She's gone though, hasn't she?"

"Yes, she's gone and so has any chance of us ever finding any sort of domestic staff in this or any other universe. What is the matter with you?"

Orson sighed. "I'm grief-stricken, Lewis. It's making me irrational."

"I'm grief-stricken too, Orson."

"Really? It's so hard to tell."

"Why? Just because I'm functioning, for Christ sake?"

"It would be more attractive if you couldn't."

"Yes, well—I'm not like that, Ossie. I'm as heartbroken as you are but I keep going. It's in my nature to do so. All I ask is that you make an effort. Don't you think it's time you pulled yourself together? We can't go on like this, we really can't."

"Go on like what?"

Lewis shook his head gloomily. "I don't know. We seem to be getting on each other's nerves dreadfully."

"Yes, well—perhaps it's time we parted. I mean, without Giselle to hold us together, what's the point, really? Two old farts like us, living together—ridiculous."

Lewis lowered himself into one of the armchairs and stared into the black rectangle of the fireplace. Then he pulled Michael's letter out of his pocket and extended it towards Orson. Orson took it, gingerly, between thumb and forefinger.

"What's this?"

Lewis waved impatiently at the letter and went back to staring at the empty fireplace. Orson took the pages out of the envelope and read the letter quickly. When he got to the end, he said "Ah."

Lewis glanced at him and was pleased to see that Orson's face had brightened a little, the muscles tightening in a small show of enthusiasm losing, in the process, some of the jowly, hangdog look of misery that he'd adopted over the past week.

Lewis said, "Shall we have him down?"

"Why not? He could help us with all this." Orson waved grandly at the cardboard boxes.

"Us?"

"Yes—and with the will and everything. He could deal with all that, couldn't he? And it would be good to see him again. I shall call him now."

Orson struggled out of the sofa, holding carefully to his brandy glass. He went to the telephone on the desk and dialed a long number. Lewis was impressed.

"You know his number?"

"Of course I do. Don't you?"

Lewis slapped both his hands down onto his knees. "There you are, you see—that's what I mean. All this endless, petty sniping at each other, all these pointless little verbal skirmishes that get us nowhere—"

Orson held up his hand, his face suddenly animated.

"Hello? Michael? You sound ill, what's the matter?…Oh good. Now look, Michael, you're to come at once, Lewis needs you, he simply can't cope, he's completely at sea, poor old bugger—no, no, it's all the letters. Thousands of them. He tried to do them with some godawful woman but I chased her off. So, you get on the first plane—we'll pay, of course…*who's* paying?…Good God, why?…He must be crazy. Oh well, if he's paying, all the better. Yes, well…we look forward to seeing you…yes…goodbye."

Orson put the telephone down. "He's coming. And you'll never guess who's paying for it—paying for Michael and a lot more, it seems."

"You're being opaque, Orson. Who's paying?"

"Lord Finlay-fucking-Ferguson, that's who. First class air tickets fluttering about like Fall leaves. And you know why, of course?"

Lewis rolled his eyes. "Yes, of course. Well, it won't do any good but it'll be nice to see the boy. When?"

"I don't know. Soon."

Orson was fiddling with the small pile of letters that Miss Wilkes had managed to process. She'd written the name of the sender on the front of the envelope and Orson squinted at each in turn. "Anybody say anything interesting?"

"Maggie wrote one of her poems, apparently. I haven't read it yet."

Orson sorted through the pile and found the letter. "Oh, this is good. Listen to this:

'A peacock's feather, glistening with semi-hidden steel,
fanned in knowing splendor and laughing at the world
for admiring it—blue iridescence hinting at things that
may not be as they seem and yet they may, which is
the joke of course—or at least one of them—'"

"Oh, do stop," said Lewis. "I'm getting a headache."

Orson dropped the letter onto the desk and yawned. "I'm going to bed." He hobbled slowly out of the room.

Lewis sat still, holding tight Michael's letter. Suddenly, there was something to look forward to and that hadn't happened in a long while—but, as usual these days, he found he wasn't looking forward at all but backwards, his mind wandering into the lanes of the past. Lately, he could remember, with startling clarity, events and conversations that had taken place over half a century ago—like the time when they all went to stay at the farmhouse just outside Neuilly—

He'd rented the house. He was the only one with any money and, since the money was an unearned allowance, remitted monthly by his fond father, he didn't mind being the one to foot most of the bills. Besides, it had been his idea to have somewhere in the country— somewhere quiet, where he could write his plays and his songs—so he'd looked around with Giselle and they'd found this small jewel of a house, set in Van Goghish farmland—all corn fields and cypresses and populated by Van Goghish peasants in blue smocks and white poke bonnets—and Giselle had pleaded with him to take it and so he had, for the whole summer.

Their new friendship with Orson Woodley had become passionately strong and for the rest of the week—after that first meeting at the party—they went everywhere together as a trio, arms linked, with Giselle in the middle. When Friday came, Lewis and Giselle asked Orson to come down with them for the weekend and they drove to the farmhouse in Lewis' car, which was a two-seater with a dicky seat in the boot. Orson sat in the dicky seat, his long scarf blowing behind him and his black hat pulled down over his eyes, so that he looked like an anarchist. He'd brought a bottle of wine and he drank most of it during the drive.

They'd eaten a scratch supper round the kitchen table. Giselle had appointed herself the caterer which, they all agreed later, was a mistake, because Giselle's idea of food was different from everybody else's, in that she'd brought a tiny jar of caviar, an onion, a hard-boiled egg and some salt and pepper in twists of newspaper. It wasn't enough, Orson said, to feed a dieting pygmy and he'd borrowed the car and some money and had gone off for half an hour, during which Lewis and Giselle ate the caviar and the onion and the egg. Orson came back with a baguette of bread, a salami, a small camembert and several more bottles of wine and they sat round the table and got pleasantly drunk.

"I shall paint you," Orson said at one point, grinning crookedly at Giselle.

"All right," said Giselle. "Naked or dressed?"

"Naked," said Orson. "You're relatively uninteresting dressed."

"What about me?" said Lewis.

"I don't want to paint you," said Orson.

"No—I mean—what about if I don't want you to paint her? Naked or otherwise? What about that, then?"

It was a stupid thing to say and he realized it was stupid as the words came out but, for some reason—possibly the wine—he was unable to stop them in time. Giselle turned and looked at him. Her eyebrows slowly rose up her forehead, until they seemed to be reaching for her hairline and her eyes got very big and she opened her mouth as wide as she could, dropping her lower jaw in mock amazement. Then she turned her head and stared at Orson and Orson stared back and raised *his* eyebrows and opened *his* eyes wide and dropped *his* jaw onto his chest and they stayed like that for twenty seconds, gazing at each other in feigned astonishment and Lewis realized that he'd lost her.

It didn't happen immediately. Lewis and Giselle went to bed that night and made love in a satisfactory way, although Lewis thought he detected a hint of kindness from Giselle, where before there had been only passion. The next day they all went for a long walk and picked blackberries and, in the evening, they drove back to Paris and dropped Orson off at his squalid flat and then went back to their rather nice one on Saint Honoré and Giselle went on being kind to him for the rest of the week. They saw Orson every day, eating with him in restaurants and going with him to small, dark clubs on the Left Bank. Lewis paid for everything.

On Friday, they drove down again to Neuilly—with proper food this time and even more wine—and Orson brought some of his painting equipment. They got drunk again in the evening.

"Indoors or outdoors?" said Giselle suddenly and Lewis frowned in puzzlement, because they'd been in the middle of a conversation about the books they were reading.

"Indoors," said Orson.

"Where indoors?" said Giselle.

"Your bedroom. All tangled up in the sheets. A post-coital look, I think."

"When?"

"Soon."

They were talking over his head, as though he wasn't there and worse, they were talking in the sort of shorthand that takes months to develop. He and Giselle had only just begun their version because it had taken him all this time to discover that a simple train of thought was an alien concept for Giselle—and here was this newcomer, an American, understanding immediately how Giselle's mind worked, with its dragonfly dartings—here one minute, there the next and even slipping backwards and forwards in time—and he was joining in with an ease that was irritating.

Lewis knew, when he first met her, that he'd never be able to keep her—at least, not for very long. She was so lovely, in every way, that it was inevitable that somebody more attractive than him would come along sooner or later and steal her from him—and an odd little satisfaction at being proved right stole over him and he began to take a wry pleasure in the transfer of affections from him to Orson. Giselle still kissed him on the corners of his mouth and she still jumped into his arms at the oddest of moments—and even still presented bits of herself to be stroked by him whenever she felt like it—but now she did all these things with Orson as well. It was almost as though she was quite deliberately sharing her affections—and her libido—as equally as she could between them both, parceling herself out in balanced measures, like a sensitive sultan with a small and jealous harem.

It was just a matter of time and place, Lewis knew that and, somehow, it didn't seem to matter so terribly, as long as she went on loving him as well. Her generosity with herself set such an example that it seemed churlish to be jealous, so he began to give Giselle and Orson opportunities. He made excuses—they needed some milk, he'd just walk to the village for some, the exercise would do him good—and when he returned from these absences he would look at them surreptitiously, trying to determine if anything had happened between them.

On the third Sunday Lewis went out after lunch to pick the last of the blackberries and when he came back, an hour and a half later, Giselle and Orson were no longer sitting opposite each other at the kitchen table, which was where he'd left them. He stood in the middle of the kitchen and listened. Silence.

"Hello?" he called.

"We're upstairs," shouted Giselle.

Lewis put the basket of blackberries down on the table. He took a deep breath and then walked out of the kitchen into the small hallway and up the stairs.

Orson and Giselle were in his bedroom. Rather, they were in the bedroom that he shared with Giselle. *Their* bedroom.

Orson's torso was bare and so were his feet. He had on his old trousers, the ones stained with paint and they were held round his midriff by a knotted cord through the belt loops. Lewis noticed that Orson had some real muscles on his chest, quite sculptured really, which was surprising since, as far as he knew, Orson never took any exercise. Orson had a brush in his right hand and he was standing by his easel. There was a canvas on the easel and on the canvas were a few strokes of terra cotta paint suggesting, if you looked very hard at them, a supine, human form of indeterminate sex. It was a painting in its infancy, perhaps only twenty seconds old.

Giselle was on the bed. She was naked, lying on her stomach, one leg drawn up to her side. Her upper body was raised, her chin propped on the heels of her hands. Her hair was a tangled mess and there was a soft, bruised look in her eyes and a slackness in her lips and Lewis knew that they had done it, that they had been doing it ever since he left the house and had only just stopped doing it, probably at the moment when he'd called out to them.

He raised one eyebrow and said, "Been at it long?"—leaving a second for the double entendre to register with them before jerking his chin at the canvas.

"About twenty seconds," said Orson cheerfully. He dabbed a bit more terra cotta onto the canvas.

"And before that?"

"You're not going to be horrid about this, are you, sweet?" said Giselle, in a small voice.

"This is the post-coital look you wanted, I suppose?" said Lewis, turning on Orson and trying to make his voice drip with sarcasm. "Of course, it was always my understanding that the coitus would be half mine. Silly me."

Orson fiddled with his brush and looked out of the window. Lewis turned back to Giselle.

"Don't you think you ought to get dressed?"

"Whatever for?" said Giselle, sitting up and making no effort to cover herself. "You've both seen it all now, haven't you? Besides, I rather like it. I shall never wear anything again—at least, not around the house."

"How could you?" said Lewis, limply.

"Are you very cross?" said Giselle.

"Very. Very cross indeed. Furious, in fact."

"You don't look very cross. In fact, you look a bit smug. I can't think why—you haven't done anything clever."

"This was clever?"

"Well, the way Orson does it, frightfully clever."

How odd that he should remember this conversation. The last bit had hurt his pride dreadfully, until he found out that Giselle hadn't meant it at all—the remark had been nothing more than a quip, without any intent to hurt him. He found it out four months later, when Giselle had come back to him. Orson had been terribly angry about that. He had some old-fashioned, Yankee idea that if you took somebody away from somebody else, the first somebody stayed put with you and didn't, after a month or so, go back to the one she'd deserted so easily. Lewis pointed out that, since desertion obviously came easily to somebody like Giselle, he didn't expect, for a moment, that she would stick with him for very long either.

"All I can hope for," said Lewis, "is that if she leaves me again—"

"*When* she leaves you again"-said Orson.

"Yes, all right—when she leaves me, she leaves me for you."

"That's handsome of you," said Orson. "In a cold-blooded way, I might add."

"Not cold-blooded at all. I just think she ought to stay with us, that's all and not go gallivanting about the place causing all sorts of havoc, which she would if we weren't around to stop her. That's the main thing, really. Which one of us she happens to be sleeping with at the time is relatively immaterial, I think."

"Ha! Easy for you to say—she's sleeping with you at the moment."

"At the moment, she is. We don't know about tomorrow, do we?"

They'd been so young then—in their early twenties, all three of them. He was the oldest, then Orson, then Giselle. Giselle was the most beautiful, which was proper of her. Orson came second, with his bumpy nose and his curved mouth. Lewis was definitely the last; he was almost ugly, with a bony face and a long jaw and ears that stuck out a little—Giselle said he looked intellectual and terrifically clever and if she wanted a pretty boy she'd go look for him in the chorus at the Folies Bergere.

Giselle was supposed to be studying Art but she didn't. Her paintings were terrible, or so Orson told her and Lewis agreed, although he admitted that he knew little about the subject—but just enough to know that Orson was good and Giselle wasn't. Giselle didn't seem to mind that her paintings were terrible. She would cock her head to one side and look at the picture leaning on the wall and say, "Well, it's supposed to be a tree, you see, in the Luxembourg Gardens. There's a little fence round it—that's those brown splodges."

"It looks like somebody's thrown up in a circus ring," Orson said.

"It does, doesn't it? All right, that's what it is. Somebody's vomit. Verlaine's Vomit. Better?"

"Much better."

The picture would be slung under the bed and, a week later, Giselle would produce another for Orson and Lewis to look at and, quite soon, there was a stack of small canvases under the bed, with titles like Rimbaud's Road Accident and Maupassant's Miscarriage.

She had almost no money at all and, for a while, tried to be a waitress at a café but she couldn't get the orders right and undercharged everybody, particularly her friends, so she was fired after a month. She was a model for a short time but walking up and down the catwalk made her shake with laughter at the absurdity of it all and the couturier thought she was frivolous so he fired her too. Giselle sat on the bed and cried and Lewis and Orson sat down on either side of her and tried to cheer her up.

"You don't need a job," said Lewis. "You're with me. I'll pay for everything."

"I can't just live off people," sniffed Giselle. "I have to have a job. I'm useless, that's all there is to it."

"You're not useless. You're wonderful," said Orson.

"I can't paint for peanuts," said Giselle.

"Well—no, you can't paint—"

"There! See, I'm useless."

"There are other things besides painting," said Lewis.

"What?"

"Well—" He couldn't think of a thing that Giselle was useful at, other than companionship and sex, both of which she was wonderful at—which meant that the only trade for which Giselle was obviously suited was prostitution and he certainly wasn't going to suggest that.

"You speak French," said Orson suddenly.

"Yes!" Lewis cried. "Marvelous French. Far better than ours."

This wasn't really true. Giselle's French was fast and fluent and accented like a Parisian but it was riddled with bad grammar and worse slang, filled with phrases translated literally from English and peppered with words that she'd made up. When she couldn't think of a noun, she would substitute her French version of 'thingy' and say "Je veux acheter cette chosey la," and then be surprised when the shopkeeper claimed not to understand her. "The silly man can't even speak his own language," she would whisper to Lewis and Orson.

"Far better than our French," said Orson.

"Well, and what if I do?" said Giselle, wanly.

"You could interpret for us." said Lewis.

"With all the shopkeepers and the landlords and things." said Orson.

"Yes—whenever we—um—need something, wherever we might be, you can do it for us," said Lewis. "I'm hopeless at all that," he added.

"So am I," said Orson. "Utterly hopeless."

They persuaded Orson to leave his horrible flat and come and live with them. Orson was spending every weekend with them at Neuilly, so it seemed pointless that he didn't spend the week with them as well, so they asked him and he agreed. There was a spare bedroom, with a big window that faced, according to Orson, in exactly the right direction. Orson pushed the bed against the wall, strewed his paints and canvases and easels all over the rest of the room and, stripped to the waist and with bare feet, painted furiously all day long. Occasionally he would sell a piece, making enough from the sales to pay rent money to Lewis once a month.

Lewis was writing steadily, pounding out articles and short stories and songs on his typewriter. He, too, sold something every now and then and, when that happened, he would take them all out to dinner and they would have champagne and caviar until all the money was gone, which was fun, because it didn't really make much difference to their finances if he sold anything or not.

When he got tired of writing, he would climb the stairs to Orson's bedroom and watch him paint. He looked at Orson more than he looked at Orson's canvases and, one day, Orson turned and caught him staring.

"What are you looking at?"

"You."

"Why?"

"You're rather magnificent. Your body. I'm not surprised Giselle likes sleeping with you. What does surprise me is that she still likes sleeping with me, too. I mean, with you around. If I were Giselle, I'd pick you."

"If you weren't Giselle, would you pick me?"

"If I was another girl, you mean?"

"No. If you were a man."

"What *do* you mean?"

"You know what I mean."

"Oh. Well—no, I wouldn't. We're friends."

"And if we weren't?"

"No. It wouldn't work. You're not queer. At least, I don't think you're queer."

"I'm not. Are you?"

Lewis searched Orson's face for any trace of animosity. There was none, so he said, "I have been. Occasionally. At school, mostly. Once or twice afterwards."

"Recently?"

"Not recently, no."

"Oh. Does Giselle know?"

"No. And I'd rather you didn't tell her, actually."

Orson gazed at Lewis for five silent seconds. Then he smiled and said, "Lucky for both of us that we're friends, isn't it?"

Lewis felt better now that Orson knew. Not that there was much to know, really. He'd only done it a few times, with boys at school and then later with boys in Paris; and then he'd met Giselle and most—if not all—thoughts of boys left his head. Orson never mentioned it again and now, when Lewis climbed the stairs to Orson's bedroom, he did his best to stare at the canvas Orson was working on and averted his eyes—as much as he could—from Orson's painfully beautiful body. Sometimes, Orson caught him staring though and, when he did, he would smile and shake his forefinger and say, "OK, knock it off."

Before long, something happened that broke the fragile magic of their threesome. One of the plays that Lewis had been working on—*View Hollow*—had been picked up by an impresario in London and, quite suddenly, Paris and Neuilly no longer seemed the center of the universe. Suddenly, London seemed the place to be and Lewis packed up everything very quickly and made plans to go to London and Giselle went with him because they were the couple at the time and it seemed the right thing to do. Orson took their departure well—or so they thought. He was his usual cheerful self when it was time to say goodbye. There were still several months to go on the Neuilly lease and Orson said that he'd stay on at the farmhouse, if it was all the same to them and Lewis and Giselle, feeling guilty about leaving him, said that that was fine by them.

"What will you do when it runs out?" asked Giselle.

"Go back to my old place, I suppose," said Orson.

"Why don't you come and paint in London?" said Giselle—and Lewis, standing next to her in the hallway, their suitcases piled around them, nodded firmly, to show Orson that the invitation was his as well as Giselle's.

"No," said Orson. "I won't do that. I can't stand the fucking English."

Then he'd kissed Giselle on both cheeks and given Lewis a bear hug and had then turned rather abruptly and walked out of the front door and down to the bottom of the garden and hadn't even waved when they drove away.

Chapter 4

Freddy almost didn't go.

It happened at the last minute. He'd packed everything the night before and the next morning he decided to repack it all because he remembered something about putting all your lotions and toiletries in the middle of the soft things, like your undies, so they wouldn't break— and he was pretty sure he hadn't done that and it was better to be safe than sorry. So he had a hurried breakfast and started all over again and he was half way through—looking every now and then at his alarm clock, because the taxi was coming at eleven—when, all of a sudden, he got an awful attack of nerves. He knew what the trouble was: he'd bought everything new and it was this newness strewn all about him that brought it on. New, brightly patterned Hawaiian-type shirts, still with their pins and their cardboard, new nylon socks and new underpants and three pairs of stiff white polyester shorts and three pairs of stiff white polyester slacks, all still with their tags on—and all of a sudden everything looked too bright and too colorful, like it had come from a fancy dress hire shop and the sheer waste of money (he'd never wear any of these things again) and the sheer silliness of what he was doing suddenly swamped him and he sat back on the Candlewick bedspread and buried his head in his hands and had a small crisis.

Ma would have been so cross with him, he thought, dabbing at his eyes with a corner of the bedspread. She hated him being silly and she was right, of course. There was no point in being silly. It got you nowhere fast. But which was sillier—having a crisis just because everything was new and bright and shouted *yoohoo, look at us, we're a TOURIST*—or embarking on this daft odyssey in the first place? It was sure to come to nothing and he'd be just as lonely as he'd been when he went to Frinton all those times, only a lot poorer. And, whatever happened, he'd be stuck there, on Saint Marta's, for the whole two weeks. At least, at Frinton, he could come home if it got too awful. He'd done that once—come home before he was due. That time when he'd been chased by the yobbos, all along the sea front, his fish and chips flying all over the place. He'd just made the front door and he'd burst into the Bellevue Guest House dining room and everybody had been there and they all looked at him, panting and weeping and generally being in an awful state and he'd packed up and taken the first train home in the morning.

And then there was the cost of it all—the new clothes and the hotel and the air fare and thinking about it made him sweat with shame and he buried his head in his hands again and moaned softly.

While they were powerful as long as they lasted, these little hiccups of emotion never lasted long and, quite soon, Freddy lifted his head from his hands and wiped his eyes again and took a deep breath and said, "Right, that's enough of that, Mr. Waterworks. Get a grip. You're going and that's the end of it," which was exactly what Ma would have said.

The mood passed as quickly as it had arrived and he packed all the stuff back into the new suitcase, carefully stowing his bottles right in the middle so that they'd be cushioned against the shocks.

"Pity I can't be cushioned as well," he said to the Candlewick. "Wouldn't that be nice?" It was lucky, he thought, that the crisis hadn't come upon him when the taxi was drawing up. He'd have sent it away and that would have been that and nobody on Saint Marta's would ever have seen the glory of his bright Hawaiian shirts and his white, white shorts and his white, white knees and that would have been most definitely their loss—and here was the taxi drawing up outside, he could hear the clatter of the diesel engine—another shocking extravagance but, as Ma had always said, you can't take it with you.

On the way to Heathrow, the taxi driver half turned his head and said, "Where are you goin', then?"

"Saint Marta's. It's in the West Indies."

"Yer. I bin there an' all. Very nice. Staying at the Vacation Inn, are you?"

"Yes."

"Very nice. They do a lovely breakfast."

Freddy felt disappointed. People were supposed to be impressed he was going to Saint Marta's in the West Indies—they weren't supposed to have heard of it in the first place and they certainly weren't supposed to have been there before him in the second place. Least of all, on both counts, the taxi driver that was taking him to the airport.

Heathrow cheered him up. There were lots of little shops, where you could buy scarves and perfume and watches and magazines and books and just about everything. He bought a Jackie Collins to read on the plane and a blow-up pillow that you put round your neck when you wanted to sleep. It came in a pouch and had a picture of a handsome man sitting bolt upright with his eyes closed, the pillow round his neck and a happy smile on his face. He also bought a money belt and he took it into the Men's Room and locked himself in a stall and put the belt round his waist and transferred all his money and his travelers checks into the pocket in the belt and felt much more secure about everything once he'd done it.

He had some coffee in the restaurant and read a bit of his book but he couldn't concentrate at all. Then, all of a sudden, they were calling his flight and he found the gate and was swept along with all the other passengers—ever so many there were, it seemed that they couldn't possibly all fit on the plane—and then they squeezed through an oval opening and he realized that now he was actually inside. Of course, he'd been on a plane before. To the Channel Islands, on an old propeller-driven Viscount, he remembered. This plane was much bigger and had jets. His seat was right in the middle, nowhere near the window and he'd specifically asked for a window, so that travel agent lady was going to get a piece of his mind when he got home.

There was a pleasant-looking, youngish woman on his right and a fat man, in a tan safari suit, on his left and he nodded to both of them in a friendly way. Quite soon the engines started and Freddy felt the plane moving under him, so he closed his eyes, because he was a little frightened and, when he was a little frightened, he always closed his eyes because that seemed to make the fear go away. They bumped along forever and then they stopped for a bit and then there was a tremendous roaring noise and a pressure against his back and a nasty vibration which seemed to go on forever—far longer in time, Freddy thought nervously, than the runway was in yards—and then a dramatic uptilting and a sudden absence of vibration and Freddy opened his eyes and swallowed once at the extraordinary steepness of the airplane's angle and then turned to the woman on his right and said, "Well, off we go then—up up and away, into the wild blue yonder."

The woman nodded politely but without warmth, so Freddy decided to give Jackie Collins another go. Jackie Collins always cheered him up if he was a bit low. All her characters led such interesting lives. All that travelling and parties and going to bed with each other. A far cry from Dollis Hill and Ma and all those years just being Freddy Millsap, hotel employee. No travelling at all, if you didn't count Frinton (and he didn't), precious few parties and not much going to bed with anybody either, because he'd always lived at home with Ma and Ma wouldn't have cared for that sort of thing going on under her roof, so actual nights spent in someone's arms had been few and far between—and never at 27 Dresden Street, Dollis Hill.

The best times—and those closest to the spirit of a Jackie Collins book—had been on those tours doing The Desert Song with the lovely John Hanson. Freddy had only been in the chorus, third brigand from the left in the back row (always in the back row, because neither his voice nor his dancing were all that good, really) but Mr. Hanson liked him enough to ask for him whenever the occasion arose. Mr. Hanson thought he was ever so funny, so Freddy repaid the great man's kindness by being the life and soul of the party all through the tour, a sort of campy Court Jester, which was completely exhausting and cost him far more effort than either the dancing or the singing—and there was always an affair too, with one of the boys and usually they'd break up messily half way through the tour and that was fun, too, what with all the drama and tears and general carrying on. He'd done three of those tours and several bits and pieces in regional pantos at Christmas as well. The pantos hadn't been as much fun as the tours and he stopped auditioning for them after four seasons and went and got a job selling ties at the Christmas rush at Harrods. That was fun, too—more fun than the panto, really and better paid. You met all sorts of interesting people at Harrods. He'd once sold a silk paisley to Ted Heath, before he was Prime Minister, of course.

The tours dried up and Freddy didn't want to struggle with the pantos—and, what with the tours and the pantos being the entire extent of his professional career—he retired from the business and got a job as a waiter at the Park Place Hotel, which was quite old when he started there all those years ago, and now he was something of a fixture there these days. Almost part of the furniture, really.

Ma had been pleased when he'd stopped the hoofing. "A proper job—that's what you want," she said and Freddy got the job at the Park Place as much to please her as anything. And it had been a good job, too. He'd had to butch up a bit but management all knew, really and turned a blind eye, which was nice of them. Well, he made them laugh and he'd discovered years ago that if you make them laugh, they didn't mind you at all.

The maids came and went—this new lot all seemed to be Spanish—and he always made chums of them because it was somebody to talk to during the breaks and it could be pretty lonely if you had nobody to talk to. And they did like his little jokes, even if they didn't understand half of them. All he had to do was pull down one corner of his mouth and roll his eyes and they'd all scream. He should have been a comedian, like that Larry Somebody on the telly. Come to think of it, he'd been acting all the time, really—ever since he'd left the Profession. He'd been acting being a waiter because being a real waiter was something that he had no idea how to be, so he put on a performance every day and had quickly discovered that the better you acted being a waiter, the bigger the tip and he'd acted being a waiter for years now and had enjoyed every minute of it. Just so long as he remembered that it was a performance and not the real thing, it was quite fun really.

Of course, it was even more fun when you recognized one of your own. He could spot them a mile off and, when he did—and if he liked the look of them—he'd put on his queeny voice—or at least a hint of it, you had to be careful—and he'd flap his hands a bit more than usual and be ever so bright and perky and, occasionally—very occasionally because it could be dangerous—it had paid off and he'd had a little flingette with the guest and, when the guest left after a few days stay, the tip would often be so generous that he could regard it more as a farewell present than an appreciation for services rendered. That's what had happened with Mr. Messenger—or Sir Lewis as he was now and not a moment too soon, as far as Freddy was concerned. He should have been knighted—for the plays alone—ages before he was; and then there were the novels, too and the lovely songs, all of which Freddy could sing and often did. A great man, Sir Lewis. A lovely man. Should have been a Lord by now, except he didn't live in England and you were supposed to if you wanted to be a Lord.

They'd only had the one night, of course and Sir Lewis had been a bit squiffy but still, it had been one of the highlights of Freddy's life, if not of Sir Lewis', who had probably forgotten all about it and Freddy couldn't blame him if he had. If you live with Orson Woodley and Giselle Palliser and throw parties for the likes of Montgomery Clift and

Gore Vidal, then you don't, on the whole, remember a perky little hotel waiter called Freddy Millsap, no matter what—and with those thoughts, and with the plane's engines humming efficiently and the coast of Southern England slipping away beneath him, Freddy's eyes started getting heavy and his head was nodding like one of those toy dogs in the rear windows of cars—

Jackie Collins slid off Freddy's lap and thumped onto the floor.

"They haven't written back," said Olga cradling the telephone between her head and her shoulder.

"A bit soon for a reply, don't you think?" said Amanda, her voice sounding surprised and a little severe.

"Well, no—not really. I mean, if my letter was just half the bombshell to them that Giselle's was to me, I think I'd have had a reply by now."

"Write again."

"I can't go on writing, Amanda."

"Then what are you going to do?"

"Well, I thought I'd just go, actually."

"When?"

"I don't know, next week maybe—"

"Tomorrow."

"What?"

"Let's go tomorrow."

"Tomorrow?"

"Yes. Leave it to me. Just pack."

Olga packed and later on that day Amanda telephoned with a note of triumph in her voice to say that she had managed to get them not only the last two seats on the only flight but also the last two rooms at the only hotel on Saint Marta's that was bearable.

Their seats were at the back of the plane, by the lavatories. They passed through the Club section and Amanda noticed a beautiful man sitting by a window. He was staring out through the Plexiglas, his chin propped on his hand, his long brown fingers cradling his face and stretching up into his hair line.

"Did you see that?" muttered Amanda in Olga's ear as they inched their way towards the back of the plane.

"See what?"

"The beautiful man by the window. Back there in Club."

"You mean the black chap? Well, blackish."

"Mm. Very nice, don't you think?"

"Well, certainly nice enough for both of us to notice him."

Hours later, when they stepped off the plane and into the hot, soft darkness of a Caribbean evening, Amanda looked for him again but he was nowhere to be seen. At the rickety luggage carousel, where the crowd pressed tightly together, she searched for him but all she saw were tired and pale English faces.

"He's not here," said Olga, slyly.

"Who isn't?"

Olga grinned. "He probably just had a carry-on. Scarpered when he saw the predatory look on your face."

It was almost midnight when they got to the Regency Hotel. There was a bowl of tired fruit in their rooms and they ate two bananas in silence, sitting together on Olga's bed.

Michael Corbo sat in the back of the taxi and watched the headlights sweep between the familiar gates. He felt the taxi tilt backwards and heard the engine begin to labor as they started up the steep incline of the drive They drove between banks of bougainvillea, the tires crunching on the gravel, the driver handling the three hairpin bends with the practiced ease of one who had made the trip many times before. Then the backward tilt leveled off, the engine raced momentarily and they slid to a stop at the front door. Michael got out and was about to pay the driver when he noticed that the house was dark. There were no welcoming lights in the ground floor windows and none upstairs either and he paused uncertainly, looking up at the house. Had they perhaps forgotten he was coming? He looked at his watch; 11:45.—a bad time to be arriving. He stood irresolute for a moment, then got back into the taxi.

"The Regency Hotel, please."

The taxi driver snorted. "You be lucky," he said into the driving mirror.

The tired clerk at the Regency desk was polite but immovable. "I'm sorry, sir but there simply isn't a room left. You might try the Vacation Inn. It's a couple of miles down the road."

The same taxi driver took Michael down the road to the Vacation Inn, where an equally tired but not quite so polite desk clerk gave him the same bad news—that it was the height of the season and there wasn't a room to be had at the Vacation Inn and, quite possibly, not one to be had on the island.

The taxi driver took him to a small motel on the depressing outskirts of town. The room was clean and the bed was small but Michael didn't care. He'd be sleeping in Zeboiim tomorrow—or, if that was taken, then probably Gomorrah, which was nearly as nice. He hoped it would be Zeboiim—if only as a reward for his tact and consideration in not banging on their front door in the middle of the night.

Orson sat on the edge of his bed, staring morosely at his feet. The hands on his old alarm clock showed 6:30, which meant he'd been awake for two and a half hours at least, if not more. There was no hope that he'd be able to get back to sleep now, so he might just as well make a start on the begonia bed. He rocked forward, transferring his weight to the balls of his feet and slowly straightened up until he was standing. The pain in his hip was fierce and he hissed on an intake of breath at the first step.

"Oh, shit," he muttered. He started to dress, taking clean clothes out of the wardrobe. Last on were his old gardening trousers. They were clean too, hanging on a wire hanger and they felt stiff when he touched them. He took the hanger off the rail and pulled the trousers off it and, inexplicably, they stayed bent double at the crease where the metal cross piece had been. He shook them and they unbent slowly, with a stiffness that seemed to mock the stiffness in his own joints. He pulled at them, twisting the fabric backwards and forwards but the cardboard-like rigidity stayed in the cloth.

"Shit, shit, *shit!*"

He banged out of the bedroom and stumbled down the stairs, along the corridor and into the kitchen. The kitchen was dark. Bella must still be asleep. Somehow, the image of Bella comfortably asleep, while he had lain staring at the ceiling unable to sleep himself, enraged Orson even more. He stamped out of the kitchen and down the passage to Bella's room. He pounded on the door panels.

"Bella! Bella! Wake up, you frightful creature! Wake up!"

There was a pause and then the door opened a crack and Bella peered out at him.

"Wha'?"

"What have you done to my pants? Come on, come on! Don't just stand there, gaping like a flounder. Answer me! What have you done to my pants?"

"Haven't done nuthin'," said Bella.

"Yes you have! Yes you have! Look at them!"

Orson shook the trousers in the narrow gap between the edge of the door and the frame. "They're ruined! Ruined!"

Bella put her hand through the opening and patted the fabric. "They clean, that's what they is."

"But they're all stiff!" roared Orson. "Stiff as a board. They're unwearable, for Chrissake!"

"You rude man," said Bella, firmly.

"You put starch in them, didn't you?"

"Mebbe I did and mebbe I didn'."

Orson breathed heavily through his nose for five seconds and then spoke with icy calm. "You, madam, are a fat, black, elephant seal—a useless, fat, black elephant seal—"

The door slammed in Orson's face.

Freddy had been there a week now and still hadn't managed to pull himself together and get on with what was, after all, the whole point of the trip. He'd put it off every day since he'd been there, which was a whole week wasted, although he'd had quite a good time really, sitting about by the pool, drinking rum and cokes and getting the beginning of rather a glamorous sun tan, which was something you didn't often get in Frinton. And the Vacation Inn was ever so much nicer than the Bellevue Guest House. At Bellevue you had to mingle with the rest of the guests and sit all together round the big dining table for meals—which wasn't too awful really because Freddy was a social sort but, all the same, endless bonhomie could get dreadfully tiring and, once or twice, there'd been the odd, quite unpleasant character there, which had been horrible.

Of course, the Vacation Inn couldn't compare with the his Park Place Hotel but then again, Freddy couldn't claim that he'd ever actually stayed at the Park Place. It didn't count working there but there was no doubt about it, the Park Place was a superior establishment all round. It was the little things that Freddy noticed. The napkins were folded in a different way—he thought the Park Place way was much more elegant—and the Vacation Inn cutlery wasn't so heavy and the ashtrays were made of a very inferior glass and the rooms were smaller and the furniture rather cheap-looking—but the staff were friendly and the food wasn't half bad and the other guests kept themselves to themselves and didn't bother Freddy at all. He'd sat by the pool every day, under a real palm tree and had finished his Jackie Collins and had read two more books since then; and, every day, his awareness of his own craven procrastination became more acute until now, over his solitary breakfast, when the shame had mounted to such a pitch that Freddy knew he would have to do something about it or just get on the next plane home and forget the whole daft business.

He swallowed down the last drops of his papaya juice (now, that was something even the Park Place Hotel didn't run to) and took a deep breath. It was now or never. He waved at Jackson and Jackson hurried over to the table and Freddy signed the bill and, flush with his determination, added rather more tip than he usually did, although the usual—in Jackson's experience—was a lot more than any of the other guests in the Vacation Inn ever contributed. But then, Mr. Millsap had said that he too was a waiter, in London, and therefore Mr. Millsap understood all the problems that being a waiter entailed, like not being properly tipped. Mr. Millsap's tipping was generous. Jackson hoped little Mr. Millsap would stay at the Vacation Inn forever.

Freddy went to the front desk and asked for a taxi and, five minutes later, he was climbing gingerly into the back of a dirty old car. The driver had a shaved head and a big gold hoop earring in his right earlobe. Freddy thought he looked like a pirate.

"Where to, man?"

"I want to go to a house called Gladstones. It's where Sir Lewis Messenger lives. And Mr. Oscar Woodley. It's a big house and I think— only think, mind you—that it's somewhere out on the road to the mountains—"

"I know it, man."

"I do wish you'd change your mind," said Olga. She was sitting on the edge of Amanda's bed, fiddling with the strap of her shoulder bag.

Amanda came out of the bathroom. She had a towel wrapped around her head.

"Much better for you to go alone," she said. "At least the first time. If we both turn up, they might be intimidated."

"But I'm going to be intimidated on my own."

"You'll be fine. I'll do the follow up visit, I promise. I just think that it might be a bit much for them, suddenly being faced with a daughter and a granddaughter and all before breakfast."

"Do you think it's too early?"

"Don't take me so literally." Amanda stood and looked at Olga, her head on one side. "You look very nice, Ma."

"Sufficiently daughterly?"

"In a mature sort of way. The headscarf and the dark glasses are a bit Garbo but the rest is very good."

"Thank you."

Amanda rubbed her hair with the towel. "Why don't you call for a taxi? That way, it'll be waiting for you when you go downstairs."

"I thought I might walk, actually. Apparently it's only half a mile up the hill."

"A procrastinating walk."

"It's a lovely day."

"You're just dragging it out, Ma."

Olga stood up decisively. "No I'm not. I'm off. See you later."

She was at the door when Amanda said, "What will you do when you get there?"

Olga turned and smiled bravely. "I haven't the faintest idea."

Michael was in the motel office, paying his bill. His neck was stiff—the pillow had been thin—and he felt grit in his eyes.

"Can I get a taxi here?"

The old woman behind the counter sighed. "What you think—we behind the times? Sure you can get a taxi. I telephone."

Michael waited outside. The motel was painted purple and there was a huge, copper, happy face sun, with bulging cheeks and a toothy smile stuck on the flat roof. As far as Michael could see, he was the only guest. There were no cars on the dusty forecourt—nothing, in fact, other than a nervous chicken that strutted backwards and forwards, one red eye fixed on Michael.

The old woman poked her head out of the office door. "Taxi comin'", she said and then withdrew.

Michael waited for ten more minutes, watching the chicken peck self-consciously in the dust. Then a taxi turned off the road and slid to a stop next to Michael. Its locked tires raised a small cloud of dust and the chicken squawked and fled. Michael climbed in and began to give the driver directions and the driver held up his right hand and said, "Gladstones, right?"

"Right."

The driver half turned in his seat. "Ever'body knows dat place, man. Dey famous, dose guys. Lotta parties in the old days. Not so much now. One big one the other day. When the old lady died. I drive two old English guys dere." The driver flapped his right hand twice, leaving it bent at right angles to the wrist. "Dey was like that, know what I mean, man?" He laughed. "Hey, I don't care. Live and let live, dat's my motto."

"Mine too," said Michael.

Freddy told his driver to drop him at the gate.

"You don't wanna go to the house?" asked the pirate, turning and looking hard at Freddy.

"Well, yes, eventually. By Shank's Pony, though, thanks very much."

The driver shrugged and pulled the taxi over to the side of the road. "Here you are, den, man."

Freddy stared out of the window. The road stretched ahead, climbing towards to the top of the hill. On either side of the road there seemed to be a wall of impenetrable jungle, with no sign of a gate anywhere. Then he saw a woman, standing by the side of the road on a patch of deep red asphalt that broke the ribbon of green verge. She was looking up at something and Freddy craned over the back seat to see what was holding her attention. This new angle revealed a brick pillar that supported one half of an open iron gate—presumably there was a twin pillar supporting a matching gate just out of view—and an opening in the jungle, paved in the same red asphalt that the woman was standing on.

"Is that it?" asked Freddy. "Gladstones?"

The pirate grunted. Freddy paid the fare and got out and the taxi sped away down the hill, leaving a plume of blue smoke in its wake.

Freddy wasn't sure what to do next. He'd always known there would come a moment when he wouldn't know what to do next and he'd always assumed that he'd be able to improvise something, rather like when he'd forgotten a dance step or the words to one of the songs, so he walked with as much confidence as he could muster towards the woman, who had turned and was watching him approach. She was pleasant-looking, about fifty, well-dressed in the sort of clothes women might wear to a summer garden party; there was a scarf over her head, tied under her chin and a pair of sunglasses hid her eyes.

"Hello," said Freddy, putting his head on one side like a robin.

"Hello," said the woman, smiling tentatively. "Is this Gladstones, do you know?"

"Yes," said Freddy, authoritatively. "Yes, you've come to the right place. Gladstones it is. In all its glory."

"I walked, you see," said the woman. "There's no sign, is there? So I wasn't sure."

"Mm," said Freddy, agreeing that there was, indeed, no sign. They stood together, in an awkward silence, staring up at a point on the brick pillar where a sign might be expected to be positioned.

A moment later, during which they both searched their minds for something to say to the other, they both became aware of an approaching figure that was stamping its way down the driveway towards them. Like rabbits caught in the headlights of a car, they froze. As the figure neared them, they saw that it was a big black woman in a flowered dress. The woman was carrying two large suitcases and hefting them as though they weighed ounces. She stared fixedly at the ground six feet in front of her and she muttered to herself in a furious undertone. Olga and Freddy stepped slowly to one side, to give the woman a clear path just in case she failed to look up and see them but, as she marched through the gates, she raised her eyes and stared crossly at them.

"Hah!" she said, her gaze darting between them. "What you want?"

"Well—" said Olga and Freddy echoed her almost immediately and said, in a squeaky falsetto, "Well, the thing is, you see—"

The black woman pushed her way past them in a cloud of patchouli and then turned.

"You wanna see the gennelmen, you go on up. You welcome to dem. Dey welcome to you. You go on up there an' make yourselves at home. One ting the gennelman like, it's visitors. You just bang on dat old door an' say Bella sent you. That's me—Bella. You tell 'em—Bella said for you to have a good time."

The woman cackled unpleasantly and then turned away and stamped off down the road. Olga and Freddy watched her go and then turned uncertainly to each other.

"Well—" said Freddy again, only not falsetto now that the threat of the big black woman was receding down the road. "Well—shall we?" And he bent a little at the waist and extended his right hand in the direction of the drive and Olga thought he looked like a bell boy at an hotel, ushering her into her room. She said, "Yes, let's," and, together, they walked between the brick pillars and into the jungle.

The red asphalt drive meandered from side to side, climbing steadily up the hill in a series of hairpin bends and, by the time it leveled off and revealed the house, Olga and Freddy were hot and tired. Neither had said anything during the five minute walk except Freddy, who had pointed at the red asphalt at about the half way point and said, "Ooh, look—it's just like outside Buckingham Palace—the Mall, you know? That's red too. Very regal, I must say."

This revelation that the little man was as unfamiliar with Gladstones-beyond-the-brick-pillars as she was, made Olga feel a little less nervous and she smiled warmly at Freddy. He looked, she thought, like a nicer sort of weasel—or a mongoose perhaps, given the unpleasant nature of weasels and the rather nicer reputation of mongooses.

The red asphalt continued to the main door of the house, widening there so that several cars could be parked in the front. There were no cars parked there now. As Olga and Freddy neared the door, they instinctively slowed their pace to a crawl, each willing the other to take precedence. Ten feet from the door, they stopped altogether. Neither could think of anything to say or to do, so they stared in silence up at the house like a couple of architecture students appraising a colleague's design.

The house was painted a brilliant white; there were dark green shutters at the windows, the whole overhung by a red, Spanish tile roof. Magenta bougainvillea clung in great swatches to the walls and all around the base of the house, in neat flowerbeds, were masses of yellow snapdragons.

There was the sound of a car engine behind them and they turned and saw a taxi coming towards them. The taxi stopped a few feet away and a man got out, pulling a carry-on bag after him and Olga saw that it was the beautiful, Club Class man from the airplane. They watched him pay the taxi driver and then the beautiful man walked up to Olga and Freddy with a smile on his face and said, in a soft, American accent, "Hi. I'm Michael. Are you here to see the guys?"

Freddy said, "Ooh—well, Sir Lewis, of course."

Olga said, "And Mr. Woodley too,"—and Freddy said, "Well, yes, Mr. Woodley too, that goes without saying, doesn't it?"

Michael glanced towards the front door and said, "Have you rung the doorbell?"

"No," said Olga.

"Not as yet," said Freddy.

"We just got here, you see," said Olga.

Michael's eyes narrowed. "Really? I didn't see a taxi."

"We walked," said Olga.

"Shank's Pony," said Freddy, rolling his eyes.

"Ah," said Michael, wondering who they could be. "Well, let's roust them out, shall we?"

Michael went purposefully to the front door and pressed the doorbell. They could hear it ringing in the distance. Freddy sidled close to Olga and whispered, "He's taking charge. Thank the Lord for small mercies, that's what I always say."

They waited for a minute and then Michael rang the doorbell again. Another minute went by and Michael said, "Bella must be going deaf."

"Bella?" said Olga.

"Yes. She's the housekeeper. Scary great woman."

Freddy laughed uncomfortably and Michael said, "Have you seen her?"

"Well, possibly. One can't be sure, can one?"

"Big fat woman. Big fat black woman."

Freddy wriggled his torso in a strange undulating movement. "I think she was black, yes," he said.

"Well, you'd know with her," said Michael. "I mean, there's no question about it."

Freddy said, "Ha," again and then lapsed into an uneasy silence.

Olga said, "I think we might have seen her. She was leaving as we arrived. Down there." She waved back down the driveway.

Michael said, "Leaving?"

"She had two suitcases and seemed rather cross."

"Ah, shit. Sorry. But that means trouble. Cross and carrying suitcases means big trouble. Well, there's nothing for it—we'll just have to barge in."

"Oh dear," said Freddy. "Do you think we ought?"

Michael didn't reply. He took hold of the doorknob and twisted it and pushed the door open. Then he turned and smiled conspiratorially at Olga and Freddy and led the way into the house.

Chapter 5

For several weeks, Lewis had been having a difficult time getting to sleep and Doctor Beale had prescribed him some strong sleeping pills, which Lewis had been taking regularly every night. The pills worked well, putting him under within an hour of swallowing one and keeping him unconscious for the better part of eight hours, so the shouting and the banging of doors as dawn was breaking only just nudged against his awareness and did nothing more to him, other than cause a small and meaningless blip in his otherwise undisturbed sleep. But now, at nine thirty in the morning, the sound of a car drawing up at the front door triggered his slow climb out of the well of sleep.

Orson had a small pile of dying begonias at his side and the flowerbed in front of him now looked satisfyingly naked. He sat back on his haunches and pain flared in his hip and he hissed and squeezed his eyes closed until the pain went away. He was warm from the exercise but he could feel the chill in the air around him. The sun never reached this part of the garden and it was always cool here, even at high noon, which was why Giselle had picked this side of the house for her bedroom.

"But I *like* a cool and gloomy room, darling," she'd said. "Sunlight is all very well in the garden or on the beach but it has no place in a bedroom. Certainly not in mine, at any rate."

He opened his eyes and looked up at her window. The shutters were still closed. Perhaps they ought to open them? Let the light in, dispel the darkness and put the room to some use. Somehow, thought Orson, that would never happen.

He'd heard a car driving up to the front door a short time ago. It sounded like a taxi. Bugger whoever it was. Thank God he was round the back and couldn't be seen.

Olga had expected a hallway of some sort, with doors leading off it to the ground floor rooms but the area they stood in was open plan and multi-leveled. The room extended for fifty feet in front of her and at least twenty five feet on either side. Immediately in front of them was a well, with fat sofas and fat armchairs and a black grand piano with lots of silver photograph frames covering its lid. Beyond the well there were two steps up and then an obvious dining area, with a long refectory table in some sort of dark wood, surrounded by matching Windsor chairs. There were French windows beyond and Olga could see that the ground outside the windows fell away in a gentle slope, revealing a small patch of sea far below. To the right and the left of the two main areas were more alternating wells and raised sections, some with book-lined walls, others covered with pictures but everywhere the same emphasis on comfort and well-being. It was, Olga thought, the perfect house for parties.

There was a staircase against the wall at her right, with wide, shallow steps that led up to a gallery that overhung part of the ground floor. Michael stationed himself at the foot of the staircase and put his hands on either side of his mouth.

"Hello!" he shouted up the stairs. "Anybody around? Lewis! Orson!"

Freddy snickered. "Wake the dead, that would," he whispered to Olga. Then he gulped and looked worried. "Not that I mean to pass any kind of remark that might cause offence, you understand, madam. There having been a recent one, of course. Death, I mean. Oh dear."

Olga didn't reply. She felt suddenly uncomfortable and a desire to be somewhere else—anywhere else, it didn't matter—swept over her. She touched Michael on his sleeve.

"Do you think perhaps we ought not to be here?"

Michael stared at her. "I'm expected," he said. "I was expected last night. Aren't you?"

"Well—" Olga began and then Freddy stepped forward.

"The lady said we were to come up, sir. She said we'd be welcome."

"That might have been a sort of joke," said Olga.

Michael folded his arms and looked down at Freddy. "You do know these guys, don't you?"

"Well, Sir Lewis, yes. I've known Sir Lewis for, ooh, ever such a long time. Not actually had the pleasure of making Mr. Woodley's acquaintance. That's a treat yet to come and very much looked forward to as well, I don't mind admitting. But Sir Lewis? Oh yes." Freddy nodded mysteriously and stared hard at the ground near Michael's feet. Michael looked at Olga and she felt herself blush.

"Well—I suppose you could say I've known them—well, all my life," she stammered. "Although they probably wouldn't—" she trailed off and shrugged her shoulders. "It's rather complicated."

Michael stared pensively at her for a moment. Then he said, "I don't want to sound rude but you're not fans, are you?"

"Oh, no," said Olga quickly. "No, it's not that at all. Of course, I think they're wonderful but that's not why I'm here. No—um—well, it's personal. And terribly complicated."

"So you said."

"I'm sorry."

Michael shook his head. "Don't be." He looked at Freddy. The little man had taken off his straw hat and was still staring at the floor and looking mysterious. Michael turned away and cupped his hands round his mouth again and called, "Lewis! Orson! You've got company!"

A door at the top of the stairs burst open and Lewis came out. He wore a long, silk paisley dressing gown and his thick, white hair was spiky. He strode to the balustrade and planted both hands on the railing.

"What, in the name of all that is holy, is the meaning of this banshee wailing? Sleep is almost impossible under normal conditions and utterly out of the question when selfish shits decide to amuse themselves by shrieking at the tops of their voices, mere feet from one's bed, in the middle of the fucking night! Oh—hello, Michael. It's you. Weren't you supposed to arrive last night?"

"I was, yes. But I got in so late, I thought I'd let you sleep. I stayed in a motel."

"How thoughtful of you. I take back some of what I said. Now, what the hell is going on? Must we put up with all this row practically at the break of dawn?"

"It's almost ten, Lewis."

"And your point is?"

Lewis became aware that Michael wasn't alone—there was a woman there too and an odd little man next to her who was gaping up at him and breathing heavily. Lewis smoothed down his hair.

"I beg your pardon," he said. "Inexcusable language. I do apologize."

"Please don't," said Olga.

"No, no," said Lewis. "No, unforgivable rudeness. Regrets all round. Where's Orson, Michael? Have you seen him?"

Michael shook his head. There was a pause and then Lewis said briskly, "And your friends? Won't you introduce them?"

Michael turned accusingly to Olga and Freddy. "I thought you said—" he began but Olga had stepped to the foot of the stairs.

"I'm Olga Whitehall," she said, her voice ringing off the walls. "I wrote to you."

There was something vaguely familiar about the name but, for the life of him, Lewis couldn't remember where he'd heard it; so he did what he always did when this happened and said, "Ah," politely and inclined his head in a gracious but formal gesture of acknowledgement.

"Oh, Sir Lewis," said the gaping little man, twisting his straw hat in his hands. "I must say what a very great pleasure it is. I'm over the moon, I really am."

Lewis transferred his gracious inclination of his head to Freddy and smiled distantly. There was something about the man that was familiar but, again—and to Lewis' growing dismay—he couldn't put a finger to the face. Perhaps, he thought, this is the beginning of dementia and I shall be doomed, for the rest of my life, not to remember people's names and faces at the precise moment when it's most important that you do.

Freddy stepped forward, twisting his hat harder than ever and stood next to Olga. "Frederick Millsap, Sir Lewis. Freddy to my friends."

"Of course," murmured Lewis. "Freddy. Well, how lovely to see you again. To see you both. What a long time it's been."

Olga laughed suddenly and Lewis joined in, out of politeness and then Freddy gave a squeaky giggle and then they all relapsed into silence again. Lewis coughed behind his hand. Then he said, "Has Bella been looking after you all?"

"It seems Bella might have left," said Michael.

"Left? What do you mean, left?"

"They saw her leaving," Michael said, pointing with both his hands at Olga and Freddy's backs. "She was carrying two large suitcases. They were large, weren't they?"

Freddy half turned. "Ever so big, they were."

"She's *left?*" said Lewis, his voice rising in pitch and volume. "*Left?* What the hell did you do to her?"

Freddy quailed under Lewis' furious gaze. "I didn't do anything to her, Sir Lewis. We never said a word—did we?" He turned to Olga with a pleading look on his sharp little face.

"Not a word," said Olga.

Lewis' rage subsided as quickly as it had risen. "Of course, you didn't," he said. "I should have known. It was Orson. It's always Orson, goddammit. Where the hell is he?"

Freddy felt unaccountably guilty, as though he had, indeed, had something to do with the woman's departure and his eyes dropped from looking up at Lewis and shifted uneasily round the room. There was a movement at the French windows; Freddy saw an ancient peasant, in mud-caked boots and work-stained canvas trousers, limp slowly past. The peasant had an old straw hat on his grizzled head and he was carrying a trowel in one hand and a basket with green stuff poking over the lip in the other. He looked, Freddy thought, ever so picturesque—and then the old laborer was gone round the corner.

Lewis started down the stairs. He shouted, "Orson! *Orson*! Where is he, dammit?"

Freddy said, "Perhaps the gardener might know, Sir Lewis."

Lewis stopped on the staircase. "Gardener? What gardener?"

Freddy pointed towards the windows. "Out there. I saw him. He went that way."

Lewis said, "Well, if we *had* a gardener, I daresay he would. Ossie! Ossie!" He trotted down the remaining steps and walked briskly to the French windows and opened them. He stepped out into the sunlight and looked in the direction that Freddy had indicated.

"Ossie! Come back here! On the double!" Then he turned and stepped back into the room. "Michael, dear boy, Orson is either ignoring me or he's deafer than usual this morning. Be an angel and fetch him back, would you. Have you got a gun?"

Michael laughed. "Not on me, no."

"It's just that, if you did, I'd encourage you to use it on him, that's all. Oh, do hurry up. The sooner we get to the bottom of this, the sooner we can work out the hospitality problems."

Lewis walked back across the room, patting Michael encouragingly on the shoulder as Michael passed him. He came up to Olga and Freddy and smiled, his long, lean face crinkling into fine wrinkles. It was a famous smile and Olga recognized it at once and she felt some of the unease leave her, which was the effect the smile had on everybody at whom it was directed. Lewis said, "If you'll excuse me for just a moment?" Then he crossed to the far left of the room and opened a door and went out.

Freddy lowered his face into his hands. "Ooh," he moaned. "I'm suffused with shame."

"Why?" said Olga.

"I can't believe it. I can't believe I did that."

"Did what?"

"Confuse Orson Woodley with a common gardener. I've never been so embarrassed in my life. Jamais dans ma vie. Ooh."

"You weren't to know."

"But, he's hardly a nobody, is he? Hardly a nonentity. He's the great Orson Woodley and muggins here thought he was the gardener. I wanted the ground to open up."

Lewis came back. He crossed to them, shaking his head. "Well, it's a disaster. The woman's gone. There's not a stitch of her clothing in the room, the bathroom is stripped—it's as if she was never here. I don't know what we're going to do."

Freddy said, "I hope you don't still think that I was in any way to blame for the lady's departure, Sir Lewis?"

"No, no. My dear fellow. Of course not."

Where had he seen this strange little face before? He recognized the expression—he'd seen it a thousand times, on a thousand adoring faces and it never failed to touch him—but it was usually plastered across the faces of awed strangers and not worn by acquaintances, among whom this little Freddy man must surely be counted, for there was something familiar about his features.

Lewis said, "I expect you'd like some coffee, or something but it could be difficult, since I haven't the faintest idea where everything is and, even if I did, I wouldn't have the faintest idea how to use it—so, we're all out of luck, it would seem."

"I could do it, if you'll permit me, Sir Lewis," said Freddy.

"Do what?"

"Make the coffee."

"How? I mean, could you really?"

"Oh yes. Just point me in the direction of the kitchen and I'll follow my nose. It would be a pleasure."

"But, do you know how to do it?"

Freddy laughed. "I should coco, Sir Lewis. It's my job, isn't it? Well, not the making, as such, although it has been known—but the serving, well, I ought to know about that, oughtn't I? Now then, for how many? There's you and Mr. Woodley, should he return and the young gentleman, ditto—and the lady, which is four, unless there are others of whom I'm not as yet aware of?"

"No—just us. And you, of course."

Freddy waggled his hands in front of him. "No, not for me, Sir Lewis. Coffee doesn't care for me and I don't care for it, so we're even, aren't we? No, I'll snatch a cup of tea in the kitchen—which is in which particular direction, might I ask?"

Lewis pointed at the door on the far left of the room. "Through there. This is most awfully kind."

"Oh, no, Sir Lewis. No, it's my privilege."

"Well, through there and then you sort of dog leg round to the right."

"I shall find it, Sir Lewis, never fear. I've got a nose like a bloodhound where the arrangements are concerned." Freddy trotted across the room and opened the door. Then he turned and gave a little wave and said, "If I'm not back in half an hour, send a search party." He waved again and slipped out and the door closed behind him.

"How obliging," murmured Lewis.

"Isn't he?" said Olga. The feeling of unease was coming back, stronger than before and she wished that the little Freddy man had stayed and not deserted her, because as long as he was at her side, Sir Lewis seemed to be more interested in him than in her. But now she was alone with him and facing a conversation for which she felt utterly unprepared, particularly since it had seemed, from his reaction to her name, that he really had no idea who she was and didn't appear to remember her letter either.

Lewis touched her on the elbow and Olga jumped. "Would you like to sit down?" he said, gesturing towards the well. Olga smiled and nodded and they stepped down into the sunken area and sat in two, deep armchairs on either side of a white marble coffee table.

"So," said Lewis, sitting back and steepling his fingers just under his chin. "So—how do you like Saint Marta's?"

"Well, we only got in last night, so I haven't seen too much of it but it looks lovely. I walked up from the hotel—the Regency—"

"Oh, that's nice," said Lewis.

"Mm, very."

"I've never actually stayed there myself but that's where we tell everybody to go when we can't stand them staying with us any longer and throw them out." Lewis grinned to show it was a joke and Olga smiled back. She was a nice looking woman, he thought. Quite well dressed, almost no jewelry and only a touch of makeup. Sensible sneakers on her feet and a small but sensible handbag on a shoulder strap. Not a huge amount of money there but enough to be comfortable. Her voice was her best feature; very low and musical, with an accent that indicated a thoroughly sensible education at a good boarding school, somewhere in the West Country perhaps. Where the hell had he heard the name? Olga Whitehall. Not a name from the past, he was sure. Names from the past he remembered. No—he'd heard it recently, he was sure of that but where and when and in what context he hadn't, for now anyway, the faintest idea. Of course, the trick under these circumstances was to keep chipping away until the answer dawned—and then, of course, you had to be careful to conceal the flash of recognition and the consequent flood of relief at finding out who it was, exactly, that you'd been talking to.

"Well, it was a lovely walk," said Olga. "I got rather hot though—all uphill."

"Well, from the Regency, it is—all uphill."

"You'd think I'd be used to it, living in Hampstead."

Hampstead. Hampstead-presumably-in-London. Another bell, but still no help.

"Good old Hampstead," said Lewis, in a faraway voice.

"Do you know it?"

"No. Well, I knew the Heath, of course. Haven't been there for years."

"I suppose not."

There was a pause while Lewis and Olga thought of what they were going to say next. Olga, in desperation, fell back on the weather.

"Lovely to get away from all that rain."

"That's one of the reasons we came here. Couldn't stand the rain, any of us." Lewis glanced over to the distant door. "Do you think your friend can manage?"

"My friend? Oh—he's not my friend. I don't know him at all. We met coming up the drive."

Lewis sat up, sliding forward on the seat of the deep armchair until he was perched on the edge of the cushion.

"I thought you were together?"

"No."

"Oh. I must confess, I haven't the faintest idea who he is. I suppose he might be a friend of Michael's."

"He's not, I know."

"I think I've met him but where or when, I can't say. How embarrassing."

Lewis relapsed back into the armchair and stared at the ceiling and Olga gathered her courage together and said, "Well, you haven't the faintest idea who I am, either, have you?"

Lewis lowered his gaze and looked at Olga through lidded eyes. The corners of his mouth twitched.

"Well, to be perfectly honest, no, I don't. At first I thought you were both fans—autograph hounds—and, to be even honester, I still think *he* is. You're not, I'm fairly sure of that and I'm also fairly sure I've heard your name mentioned recently but, beyond that, you're absolutely right, forgive me—I haven't the faintest idea who you are, although I have a horrid suspicion that I ought to."

"I wrote to you."

"Yes, well—we get a lot of letters from strangers. They go in the bin, I'm afraid. The fact is, when you're as old as we are, you've met everybody you could ever want to meet and see little point in getting to know anybody new—but I daresay that's where I've heard your name. What exactly was your letter about?"

It was odd, Olga thought, how relaxed she felt suddenly, as though Lewis coming clean with her had broken down the barriers of pretense between them. She opened her bag and took out Giselle's letter in its envelope and silently handed it to Lewis. He glanced down at the envelope and Olga saw his start of recognition at the handwriting.

"You knew Giselle?"

"The first line explains things."

Lewis took the letter out and unfolded it. Olga watched his eyes move over the words and then he became very still, as though turned to stone and even his eyes stopped moving and there was a long silence, broken at last by the sound of footsteps outside the French windows and a querulous voice saying, "It's too early to be meeting people, for Chrissake. Why can't they piss off and come back later? At Christmas or something?"

Michael came through the door, half supporting and half dragging Orson. He said, "It won't take a minute and then you can go back. Besides, I'm following orders."

Michael saw Lewis and Olga in the armchairs and called across the room.

"I've got him."

Lewis didn't look up and Olga saw that his eyes were moving again, flicking to and fro across the spidery lines with an ease that betrayed his familiarity with the handwriting. Michael and Orson came slowly across the room.

Orson said, "Whose orders? Lewis's? The hell him, that's what I say. Who's the boss around here, that's what I'd like to know? Don't push, boy—what am I, a stalled car? Pull if you like, I don't mind that but I won't be pushed."

When they came near, Olga got up. Orson said, "Hello. Who are you?" Then he turned to Michael and said, "Where's the other one? Didn't you say there were two?"

"He's making coffee, I think," said Olga, stepping forward. She held out her hand. "I'm Olga Whitehall."

"Hello, Olga Whitehall," said Orson, cheerfully.

His face was red and fat and his broken nose was bulbous and pitted. When he took off his hat, Olga saw that he was almost completely bald, apart from a narrow fringe of white hair over his ears. White stubble speckled his lower face. His clothes—an old flannel shirt and an even older pair of gray flannel trousers—were smeared with mud and there was an accumulation of the stuff on the soles of his boots; Olga saw that he'd left a trail of footprints that stretched back to the French windows.

Orson shook Michael's hand off his arm and sank down into Olga's armchair. "You don't mind, do you?" he said, looking up at her with a friendly smile. "Done in, that's what I am. Who's making coffee?"

"Well, we're not sure," said Olga.

"His name is Freddy," said Lewis, without looking up from the letter. He finished a page and turned to the next one.

"Where's Bella?" said Orson, scratching vigorously at his knee.

"Bella has gone," said Lewis. "Perhaps you'd like to tell us why?"

"Gone? Where?"

"Away from here and, I suspect for good, which are the only elements that should concern us, Ossie. What did you do to Bella?"

"I didn't do anything to Bella. I wouldn't touch Bella with a forty foot pole unless there was a cliff nearby." Orson grinned up at Olga like a street urchin. Then he patted the arm of his chair and said, "Perch on this, dear. You look so stiff, standing there."

"Leave her alone, Ossie," said Lewis coldly. "Tell us about Bella."

Orson sighed. "She did something unforgivable to a favorite pair of pants so I had words with her."

"Words? Which ones, exactly?"

"Oh, I don't know—*fat* was one and *black* was another and *useless* came in somewhere but the clincher, I think, was probably *elephant seal*. Yes, that would have done it, I imagine."

Lewis glanced up from the letter in his lap. Olga saw a flash of interest—almost academic, she thought—in his eyes.

"Elephant seal?"

"Yup."

Lewis nodded pensively. "Very good, Ossie, although fat, I think, is redundant when talking of elephant seals. I don't know if black is as well?" Lewis looked enquiringly at Michael and Michael said, "Why are you looking at me?" and Lewis shrugged and said, "I thought you might know what color they are."

"Brown, I think," said Michael.

"And are they useless?" asked Lewis.

"At laundry, probably they suck."

Lewis glared at Orson. "There you are—another redundancy. If you *had* to insult her, why didn't you simply tell her she was immoderately steatopygous, and leave it at that?"

"Immoderately what?"

"That she had a big bottom, Ossie. You could have insulted her without her knowledge and thus we might have held onto her services. Besides—fat and useless? That's a serious case of the pot and the kettle.

What are *you* if not fat and useless—and with a heart as black as the Pit? Old bastard. So—what have you to say for yourself?"

"Has she really gone?"

"So it would seem."

"Well, rah rah rah and three cheers for me—*that's* what I say."

Lewis snorted. "I don't think you'll be quite so pleased with yourself when your bed isn't made and your lunch isn't cooked and your underwear remains unwashed. We are now without any staff at all and it's going to be impossible to get anybody. Well done, Ossie. Here, read this." He leaned forward and pushed the letter at Orson.

"What's this?"

"A letter, you old fool. Read it."

Orson fished a pair or wire-rimmed spectacles from the breast pocket of his shirt and balanced them on the end of his nose. Then he peered at the pages.

"It's Giselle," he said. He looked up at Lewis and Lewis nodded. Orson looked back at the letter and Olga saw him begin to read. Then he did a perfect but exaggerated double take. He brought the letter closer to his eyes and read the opening sentence again; then he looked up at Olga, his eyebrows raised as high as they would go.

"What *can* she mean?"

"I rather think she means that this person is Gloa," said Lewis quietly.

"Gloa?" spluttered Orson. "*Gloa*? Nonsense, Lewis. She can't be."

"Why can't she be?"

"Well—because—because—well—she's far to old, for Chrissake."

"A paragon of chivalry," said Lewis to the ceiling.

Orson looked up at Olga. "You're not Gloa, are you? You can't be. I mean, maybe Giselle thought you were but you're not, are you? I mean, apart from being too old, well—you look nothing like her, do you?"

Lewis said, "Ossie, stop it. She's not too old and how the hell would you know what she looks like now? She was a baby. Babies look like babies and rarely, if ever, look like what they become as adults." He turned to Olga. "You look very nice, whoever you are."

"Thank you," said Olga in a small voice. "I think I'm who she says I am. Would she lie about a thing like this?"

"Oh, yes. She lied about everything, incessantly. But this time, perhaps not." Lewis rose to his feet and put out his hand.

"How do you do. I think you're very probably who she says you are too. And how lovely to see you again and, this time, I actually mean it."

Olga took his hand. It was warm and dry and the pressure he exerted was just enough to tell her that everything was all right, at least with him. He let her hand go and stepped back and put his head on one side and looked her up and down. "I think you've turned out very well. Don't you think so, Ossie?"

Orson waved irritably, his eyes devouring the letter.

"I'm kinda lost here," said Michael.

Lewis positioned himself next to Olga. "It's quite simple, Michael. Giselle had a baby. It was adopted. It grew up and turned into this. All clear now?"

Michael gaped. "You're Giselle Palliser's daughter?"

"According to her, yes, I am."

Orson let the letter drop to his knees. "Well, I'm damned," he muttered. "It's a full deathbed confession. Extraordinary. Why would she want to do such a thing?"

"Why indeed?" said Lewis. "And then again, why not?"

"Bizarre," said Orson. "Probably had some idea of stirring up trouble again. Just like her. Not that we aren't pleased to see you, of course," he added hurriedly, looking up at Olga. "On the contrary, it's turning out to be one of the pleasanter days of my life if you don't count my pants."

"Oh, do let's not," said Lewis.

Orson reached out and grabbed Olga's hand. "Gloa," he said softly and the pressure of his mud-flaked fingers told Olga that everything was fine as far as he was concerned too.

Chapter 6

The kitchen wasn't hard to find. Once through the door, he was in a passage in which all the doors were closed, except one which was a bedroom; Freddy peeked into the room and noticed that the doors to the wardrobe were open wide and a forlorn collection of empty wire hangers hung from the rail inside. The room smelled strongly of patchouli. Bella's room. Bella's ex room.

He turned a corner and there was light at the end of the passage and Freddy made for it—and here was the kitchen, a nice, bright, airy sort of place, with everything neat and ordered, although the cupboards were straight out of the fifties and so were the countertops. Of course, he was used to that; Mum had refused to update anything in Dollis Hill and, anyway, there was never enough money to make changes to what was a perfectly good kitchen. "As long as it's clean," she'd said, "I don't mind making do." And it had been clean, scrupulously so and her standards had rubbed off on Freddy and hygiene had always been very important to him, particularly when it came to serving food. The hotel kitchens were all stainless steel, which was a bit cold and clinical but undeniably hygienic and Freddy had always taken pride in doing room service because he could be fairly sure that everything the guest put in his mouth hadn't been anywhere it shouldn't.

There was a big pine table in the middle of the kitchen, which was even older than the sink. On the table was a note, torn from a lined notepad and held down by a cheap glass salt cellar. The note said:

'You bloody rude man. I quit. Yours, Bella Post.'

A sensitive flower. She should try working at the Park Place—some of the guests seemed to make a hobby of their rudeness. Well, if you couldn't take the heat, you should get out of the kitchen, which was what Bella appeared to have done. He wondered what had happened? Then he wondered if there were any other servants about the place, or if Bella had been alone here. He stood very still, listening; there was a comfortable silence, the sort Freddy liked. He preferred doing things on his own, without the distractions of people and their conversations. Of course, he loved a good chat as much as the next person but if he was *doing* something, then he was much better being on his own, which was probably the main reason that he had grown tired of the tours and the pantos—all that muscular teamwork had got him down.

Freddy opened the cupboards one by one. He found coffee and sugar and there was milk in the aged refrigerator, which was one of the dangerous sort with latches that little kids were always killing themselves in. An ancient percolator stood on the countertop. The makings were there—now, all he had to find were the servings and Bob was his uncle, thank you very much. He certainly wasn't going to use that chipped white china pot that was next to the percolator, or the really nasty plastic tray that it stood on; surely they had some better stuff than this? He'd have a bit of a poke about and, if anybody asked him what he was doing, he could always say that Sir Lewis had asked him to help out. There might be a mop somewhere, too.

"How old are you, in fact?" asked Orson.

Lewis pressed the first two fingers of his right hand to his forehead. "Ossie, please," he muttered. Then he took the fingers away from his head and made a small gesture in the air which Olga took to indicate some sort of apology for his friend. Then he shook his head and said, "We could work it out, of course, which would be more polite than an outright question. Let me see—" he counted on his fingers for a few moments and then looked up and smiled at her. "Forty eight," he announced triumphantly.

"Fifty, actually," said Olga.

"Well, yes, I know," said Lewis. "I said forty eight to be chivalrous. If you don't *want* any help, I shan't give you any. Fifty it is."

"I was born in 1939. That made me fifty in February," said Olga.

"It *was* February, wasn't it?" said Orson, staring at Olga intently. "Good God, it's amazing. Absolutely extraordinary."

"Oh, really Ossie," said Lewis, irritation in his voice. "What's so amazing and extraordinary? She grew up, that's all."

"But she grew up so much."

There was a silence. Lewis and Orson stared steadily at Olga, as though trying to imprint her image on their retinas and their gazes were so expressionless that Olga feared for a moment that the disparity between what she was now and what she had been fifty years ago was so great and so disappointing to them that perhaps coming here and presenting herself to them had been a bad idea. Then Orson leaned forward and smiled at her and waggled his eyebrows up and down like Groucho Marx.

"Well, I think you are terrific improvement. You were disgusting when we knew you before. An ear-splitting noise at one end and no sense of responsibility at the other. You ruined one of Lewis' shirts, you know."

"Pale blue silk from Sulka's," Lewis murmured.

"You had this revolting habit—"

"Ossie, must we go through all this?" said Lewis.

"Why not? You had this disgusting habit of throwing up all over everybody—but from a hell of a distance. Like an artillery barrage, it was. Across a decent-sized room, you understand—boom!—and some innocent person fifteen feet away would have to duck."

"I can't do that any more," said Olga.

"Good," said Orson, settling back in the chair. "It wasn't at all endearing. Also, I have to say, you were not pretty. You looked like a lamprey. *Much* better now. Positively human, now. In fact, thoroughly easy on the eye. Not, of course, a patch on your mother, who was one of the most striking women on either side of the Mississippi—but you're quite nice-looking."

"Thank you."

Orson waggled his eyebrows some more and then said, in a voice of excruciating coyness, "Do you have a boyfriend?"

"Ossie," Lewis moaned. "She's fifty years old, for God's sake."

"Well, I don't actually," Olga said, smiling. "Not at the moment. I'm divorced."

"Divorced?" said Orson, in an outraged voice. "Divorced? Why? What was wrong with the poor guy?"

"Nothing really," said Olga. "We just didn't have very much in common."

Lewis shuffled forward in his chair and touched Olga's wrist. "You don't have to put up with this, you know," he said. "I wouldn't for a moment, so I don't see why you have to."

"It's all right," said Olga. "I don't mind. It's to be expected and besides, if I answer all yours, then I'm hoping, when it's my turn, that you'll answer all of mine."

"Don't count on it," said Lewis.

"How long were you married to him?" said Orson, waving irritably at Lewis.

"Nine years."

"*Nine years*? Good God, woman, it took you nine years to find out you had nothing in common? I would have thought that, after nine years of mingling your bodies and minds, you'd have managed to find *something* in common—unless of course you did no mingling at all, of either, in which case I can't see the marriage lasting nine minutes, let alone nine years. Explain, please."

Olga realized that she was enjoying this. It had been a long time since anybody had taken such an interest in her affairs. "Well, you see, we both terribly young. Far too young, really. We didn't know anything about each other. We *didn't* have anything in common. I went to rugby matches with him and froze and Henry came to theaters with me and fell asleep—and then, after nine years of trying to make it work, I said I couldn't stand rugby and Henry said he loathed plays—of course, there were other things we hated too—and then we had this huge fight and said lots of things we probably ought to have regretted saying, except that we found that neither of us did. Regret saying them, I mean. So we got divorced and now we're quite good friends. Henry married again. To somebody called Serena, who's very nice."

"We're not too interested in him, you know, and even less in his new wife," said Orson. "I don't mean to be rude—"

"Yes, you do," said Lewis.

"—but there is only so much new information you can absorb at our age, so it's best to leave out all irrelevant stuff. I am in the process of forgetting both Henry and Serena's names even as we speak and in five minutes it shall be as if you never mentioned them. There—poof! Gone. What did this poor man do, that he should be dumped so unceremoniously?"

"He's an accountant."

"An accountant? Giselle's daughter married an *accountant*? Jesus Christ, it's all too much. Michael, get me a drink, would you.?"

"Michael, don't," said Lewis.

Orson twisted in his chair and glared. "Lewis, mind your own business for once in your goddam life. Michael, I should like a large bourbon, on the rocks. You know where it is." He looked at Olga and said, "Would you like something?"

"No thank you."

"Lewis?"

"It's a little early for me, Ossie."

"Well, it's a little early for me, too but this is a morning stuffed with thunderbolts and I could use a little help fending them off." He glanced up at Michael, who was hovering by his chair. "Well, go on then," he said, making shooing gestures. Michael crossed to the other side of the room and opened a cupboard and Olga heard the sound of glass on glass. Orson turned back to her and said, "An accountant, for Chrissake. Well, no wonder you ditched him."

"Don't you like accountants?"

"They are dandy in their proper place and time, which is in their office and only once a year—"

Lewis suddenly stood up, uncoiling himself from the deep armchair with serpentine grace. "This is tedious. Would you like to see the house?" he said.

"Oh—very much," said Olga.

Orson said, "Wait a bit—are you leaving me all of a sudden?"

"You can come too, if you like," said Lewis.

Orson settled back into his chair with a sigh. "No. I've seen it. Besides, if you're so desperate to talk about me then I suppose I ought to let you. Michael and I will sit and sip and talk about you, only we shall probably be rather more charitable. Off you go."

Lewis led the way to the stairs and Olga followed him. Orson watched as they climbed to the gallery. At the top, Lewis opened a door and stood aside to let her pass and they disappeared from Orson's view. He swiveled in his chair and a stab of pain shot through his pelvis. Michael was walking across the floor towards him, with a glass in his hand and Orson made frantic pushing movements at him with both hands.

"Back! Back!" he hissed, "and fill it up! Quick, before they come down. I need a decent drink, for Chrissake, not just a smear in the bottom of the glass."

Michael looked down at the whisky. "It's hardly a smear."

"It's a smear, kid. Take my word for it."

Michael went back to the cupboard and splashed more whisky into the tumbler. He brought it to Orson and gave it to him and Orson swallowed half of it and smacked his lips and said "Aah," appreciatively.

"Thank you. I needed that. Lewis is getting restrictive about it. What a morning. What do you suppose she wants?"

Michael settled into the chair where Olga had sat.

"I don't know. Perhaps she doesn't want anything. I like her."

"So do I but it's a bombshell, nevertheless. I mean, it's been fifty years. Well, forty nine and a half. I'd almost forgotten about her and then Lewis says, 'This is Gloa' and I'm blown into the next county. And what do you mean 'perhaps she doesn't want anything'—of course she wants something, otherwise she wouldn't have come all this way." Orson flapped the pages of the letter at Michael. "Here—you read it. Perhaps you can find a clue."

Michael took the sheets of paper and read them slowly. Twice he tilted the letter towards Orson and pointed to a word and raised his eyebrows and Orson craned forward and deciphered the word for him. Michael finished reading. He frowned and said, "Well, it's hardly anything as subtle as a clue. More like a flashing neon sign."

"What do you mean?"

"I mean it's obvious what she wants, since there's no mention of it in the letter—a glaring omission, if you ask me."

"What?"

"I expect she'd like to know who her father is, Orson. And I expect you and Lewis will be able to tell her, won't you?"

Lewis and Olga were in Giselle's room.

"It's a lovely room," said Olga, peering through the shuttered gloom. There were shadows everywhere but she could see that the room was softly feminine in a dated sort of way. There were swatches of gauze over the bedhead and more draped around the posts at each corner of the bed. A mound of pastel pillows was heaped at the head end. A dressing table was by the window; there were silver-backed brushes arranged neatly on its glass top and a pretty tilting oval mirror stood on small clawed feet next to them. Two glass atomizers, with fine mesh casing round their bodies, were placed on one side of the mirror and a silver photograph frame with three young laughing faces was on the other.

Lewis said, "She wasn't really as tidy as this, you understand. Usually, everything was all over the place."

He lapsed into silence, remembering when they'd first come here and looked over the place. The owner had moved out and had taken all the furniture with him and they had run through the empty rooms, leaving the estate agent far behind. They'd opened all the cupboards and looked out of all the windows and turned on all the faucets and then turned them off again and, when they got to this room, Giselle had said, "This is mine."

Lewis said, "We haven't bought it yet," and Giselle said, "We will and, when we do, this is mine."

"It's dark," said Orson. "It faces the wrong way."

"For you but not for me," said Giselle. "I'm like rhubarb. I do better in the dark."

Olga couldn't make out the color of the carpet but it was thick and soft under her feet.

"She died in here," said Lewis. "And lived, too, of course. For hours on end. We often wondered what she did in here all that time, apart from painting her toenails."

Olga glanced at Lewis. His face was in profile and shadowed and she wondered if he realized the amount of information his last remarks had contained—that Giselle shared her bedroom with nobody, at least nobody on a permanent basis—unless, of course, this room had only been hers in later life—

"Was this always her room?" said Olga, staring hard at the carpet. A sort of yellowish-gray, perhaps?

"Oh, yes. Always. She liked it dark. She never opened the shutters and only put the light on when she wanted to read. And, being practically illiterate, she did precious little of that."

"She was illiterate?"

"You've read her letter. Come on."

Lewis turned abruptly and left the room and Olga followed. He led her down a tiled passage, pointing out the doors as they passed them.

"That's my bedroom, you don't want to see that and that's Orson's and you *certainly* don't want to see that and that's a bathroom, which we never use because all the rooms except Sodom have their own."

"Sodom?"

"Yes. Pretentious but after all this time we're stuck with it. There are three guest rooms—here we are."

Lewis opened a door and they looked into a bright room with flowered wallpaper. He said, "This is Sodom, there's Gomorrah over there, and Zeboiim's opposite. It's Orson's fault. He called them that when we were first here and we thought it funny, so the names stuck. Now, of course, it's quite silly but there you are."

Lewis showed her the other two rooms and demonstrated the workings of their bathrooms, vigorously flushing both lavatories. Then he brought her back to the corridor and said, "Which would you like? I recommend Zeboiim, because it wasn't quite as wicked a city as Sodom or Gomorrah—and because it's the furthest from Orson's room, which can get noisy at the oddest times."

"Which one would I like? I'm sorry, I don't understand."

"Well, you've got to stay here now. I mean, you've seen me in my dressing gown, haven't you? Now all you need to complete the picture is to see Orson in his underwear and you'll be a real member of the family, won't you?"

Olga began to make demurring sounds and Lewis waved them away dismissively. "No, no. I insist. If Orson was here, he'd insist, too. Really—we can't have Giselle's daughter staying in an hotel, even if it is the Regency. Please say yes and then we can get young Michael to organize the move."

Olga blushed. "I'd love to but—well—there's not just me."

"You came with somebody?"

Olga nodded.

"I thought you said you didn't have a boyfriend?"

"I don't. It's my daughter. Amanda."

"Your *daughter*?"

"Yes."

"How old is she?"

"Thirty last month."

There was a pause and then Lewis began to laugh. It started quietly, a huffing sound at the back of his throat and grew until he was bent double and gasping for breath. His hand reached out and grabbed Olga's and, through the laughter, she heard him say "Sorry, sorry," several times. Then he slowly straightened and let go her hand and wiped his eyes with the tips of his fingers.

"Sorry," he said again. "It was the idea of Giselle as a grandmother. Of a *thirty* year old, for God's sake. She'd have been so cross. Where is this daughter of yours?"

"At the hotel. Being discreet."

Lewis' eyes narrowed and he tilted his head to one side and said, "How much did Giselle know, do you suppose? About you, I mean? And how did she find out, come to that?"

"I think she knew quite a lot," said Olga, slowly, "I think she even used a private detective."

"No!" Lewis' eyes were wide. "What makes you think that?"

"Well, about a six months ago a fat little man rang my doorbell. He had some sort of census form on a clipboard and he was asking all sorts of census-like questions. He said they were covering the neighborhood but he seemed rather odd and, in the end, I stopped answering him and shut the door in his face. Then I asked some of the neighbors if he'd been round to them at all and they all said he hadn't, so obviously he wasn't on government business. Then I got the letter, which was a tremendous shock. I wondered if she'd known about me all the time, or just recently and I decided it was just recently, because of the little man, you see. And, if it *was* the little man, then she'd have known quite a lot about me. Where I lived, obviously, my marital state, Amanda, what I did for a living—"

"What do you do for a living?"

"I write children's' books. And illustrate them, too."

"What sort of children's' books?"

"For the very young. I've got this squirrel called Skippy."

Lewis took Olga's arm and they began to retrace their steps along the passage. Lewis said, "You know, about six months ago, amidst the misery of her illness, she suddenly got dreadfully irritable. Instead of behaving gracefully, like Camille, she kept snapping our heads off and asking us if we thought she looked old enough to be a grandmother? Priceless. Let's tell Orson, it'll cheer him up no end."

Freddy looked at his watch. He'd been gone ever such a time and he wondered if they'd forgotten about the coffee and, indeed, about him, too. Mind you, when things got busy at the Park Place, coffee in the room could take easily as long as this, so a few more minutes wouldn't make much difference. It would be worth it and he was nearly done anyway. Honestly, the things they'd got, lovely things, stuffed higgledy-piggledy into dirty cupboards, the silver all dreadfully tarnished of course but, at least they'd got some silver polish and a good collection of old rags and he'd be done any minute now and it was looking lovely, even if he did say so himself. He just hoped it would be noticed, that was all. And, if they *didn't* notice, then he'd ruddy well point it out to them.

"Are you implying," said Orson, "that she might think it's one of us?"

"I think that's a conclusion I'd have reached if I was her," said Michael.

"Oh. How awkward—to have come all this way—she'll be so disappointed—"

"What?"

Orson shook his head. "No, no. I shan't speak behind her back. She has the right to know before you do. Now, get rid of this glass, would you, before they come back. I'm not supposed to booze in secret."

Michael took the tumbler and put it back in the cupboard and, a moment later, Lewis and Olga appeared at the top of the stairs.

"Ossie!" Lewis called, "Ossie—Giselle was a granny! Gloa's got a grown up daughter, easily old enough to be a mother herself, which means Giselle could have been a great granny, too! Priceless!"

Olga said, "*Gloa*?" but Lewis didn't hear her. He seized Olga's hand and dragged her down the stairs. Orson, in a subdued voice, said, "Hold your horses, Lewis—"

Lewis waved his free hand excitedly. "I shall hold nothing—the daughter's called Amanda and she's here! Well, at the Regency. We must get her up here at once. Michael, take the car and get her." Lewis turned to Olga. "What does she look like?"

"She's tall. By the pool, I think. Look for a yellow bikini."

"Why did you leave her behind?"

"Well, we thought it best that I was alone with you for a bit."

Lewis grimaced. "How very ominous. I don't care for that 'alone' at all. What do we need to be alone for?"

"Lewis—" Orson said again and then the door on the far side of the room opened and Freddy appeared, a big silver tray supported on one palm at the level of his ears.

"Room service," he called gaily and started across the floor. Orson stared at him and then looked at Lewis.

"Who the hell is this?"

And suddenly Lewis knew who it was. The cadence of the voice hadn't changed at all. Nor had the flashily expert handling of the heavy tray and that odd little gliding walk that zigzagged around the furniture, the slim body leaning into the curves, like a slaloming skier. These idiosyncrasies had been repeated by the little waiter several times without the trace of variation for however many days he'd stayed—

which London hotel was it? And how long for? The affair had been nothing more than a ridiculous little one night thing, quite meaningless, with no strings attached, surely? And yet here he was, the diminutive waiter with the button eyes and the pointed nose, older now but otherwise startlingly the same. What the hell was the hotel?—oh yes, The Park Place—just off Grosvenor Square.

"This is Freddy," said Lewis. "An old friend. Freddy—this is Mr. Orson Woodley."

Freddy reached the group and in a swift, professional move, he brought the tray down from beside his ear and put it on a low table between the chairs. Then he bowed to Orson and pressed both his hands together under his chin.

"Mr. Woodley, sir—what an honor. And a pleasure, if I might be so bold."

Orson was staring at the tray. There was a gleaming silver coffee pot on it, with a matching milk jug and a matching sugar bowl with a pair of silver tongs at its side. Four delicate bone china cups and saucers were arranged to one side and a lace mat was spread under everything. A fine plume of steam was coming out of the spout of the pot.

"What's all this stuff?" said Orson.

Freddy started to pour out the coffee. "I hope you don't mind, Mr. Woodley—Sir Lewis? I took the liberty—grasped it with both hands, actually—and went rummaging. Found these lovely things buried in cupboard, in a terrible state they were, which explains the tardiness of the refreshments, since they needed a thorough going over. Such lovely pieces, it seemed a shame they weren't being seen. I got the distinct feeling that your Bella didn't even know you had them. All cobwebby, they were. How do you take it, madam?"

"Black, please," said Olga. She raised her eyebrows at Lewis and he shrugged his shoulders and said, "Freddy, this is very good of you but surely you're on holiday? You don't have to be a waiter here, you know."

"He's a waiter?" said Orson.

"A very good one," murmured Lewis. "One of the best I've ever met."

Freddy wriggled. "You're too kind, Sir Lewis."

For a while back there, he hadn't been at all sure that Sir Lewis remembered him and he had dreaded having to explain and had even thought that it would probably be best if he just slipped away before explaining became necessary—but now that Sir Lewis had made it ever so clear that he *did* remember him and had even paid him ever such a nice compliment, Freddy felt quite comfortable doing what he was doing slipping, as he was, into the familiar routines of serving other people and making a little performance out of it.

"There you are, madam, nice and black. And for you, Sir Lewis?"

"Black for me too."

"Ooh, snap. Mr. Woodley, sir?"

"Black."

"And you, young sir?"

"White please."

"Righty ho. All black except for you—"

Freddy's hand jumped to his mouth and he pressed his fingers against his lips and stared wide-eyed at Michael. "Ooh, dear-I'm ever so sorry, sir. What a slip."

Michael laughed. Freddy said, "It's just that it's hardly noticeable at all, with you, sir. I mean, you're not what I would call black at all. Not really. I mean, you're a lovely color, actually, more sort of honey with coppery overtones, if you know what I mean?"

"Who is this man?" said Orson, testily.

"I'll tell you later," said Lewis.

"No, tell me now."

Lewis sighed. "His name is Freddy. Freddy—?" He looked enquiringly at Freddy and Freddy said, "Millsap, Mr. Woodley, sir. Freddy Millsap."

"Freddy Millsap," said Lewis. "Freddy was a waiter at the Park Place Hotel."

"Still am, Sir Lewis."

"And still is. I met Freddy many years ago when I was staying there. I cannot for the life of me remember *why* I was staying there."

"They were doing a program on you, Sir Lewis. The BBC."

"That's right. The BBC was doing a program on me and Freddy looked after me extremely well and now he's very kindly dropped in to say hello right in the middle of his holidays. Isn't that right, Freddy?"

"Right as rain, Sir Lewis."

"You didn't tell me you'd invited him," said Orson. "Otherwise I'd have been more polite."

"No you wouldn't," said Lewis. "Anyway, the visit is impromptu. A quick pop in and a quick pop out, I think."

"Just to pay my respects, as it were," said Freddy, nodding vigorously. "I don't mean to impose."

Orson said, "This coffee is very good. Actually tastes of something." He peered at the coffee pot again. "I think," he said slowly, "that Douglas and Maisie gave us this set. I haven't seen it for years. It's Georgian, I think."

"You're spot on, Mr. Woodley, sir," said Freddy. "But then you would be, wouldn't you, having the artistic eye, as it were. Yes, it's very Georgian. As Georgian as Georgian can be." He produced a clean handkerchief from his trouser pocket, leaned forward and deftly wiped away a drip of coffee from the spout.

There was a pause and then Lewis shook himself and said, "Well, off you go then, Michael and fetch this daughter back here."

"She might not want to come with me," said Michael, putting his coffee cup down on the table. "You know—being accosted by a complete stranger?"

Olga smiled. "You're not really a stranger. We saw you on the plane."

Orson said, "Of course, once she discovers you're an agent, she might want to change her mind." He turned to Olga. "Michael works for Anatole Utteridge, otherwise known as 'Tolly' by his friends and enemies. Tolly is Lewis' New York agent, a wicked, unprincipled dwarf.

You must never have anything to do with him. Michael is all right, I suppose, although why an intelligent young man would want to be an agent is beyond comprehension. Particularly one that works for Tolly Utteridge." He darted a glance at Michael. "Why are you here anyway?" he said slyly.

Lewis said, "Stop it, Ossie. We know why he's here."

"Oh, so we do."

"A fool's errand. I shan't budge from here, no matter how much of the British taxpayers' money Finlay is prepared to throw our way."

"They're putting out the red carpet," said Michael.

"So I should hope," said Orson. "When is this do, anyway?"

"In three days."

"Jesus—you've left it a bit late, haven't you?"

Michael smiled. "Tolly thought it ought to be as last minute as possible. That way, you wouldn't have much time to think about it."

"Stupid old jerk."

Michael turned to Lewis. "They want you really badly."

"Bollocks. It's only Finlay that really wants me and he doesn't really want me because we hate each other. He only wants the publicity I'll churn up for him and his theater. And he's probably got that wrong too. Nobody knows who I am anymore and those who do couldn't care less."

"Ooh, you'd be surprised, Sir Lewis," said Freddy. Everybody turned to look at him and he lowered his eyes and stared at the floor and said, very quickly, "I mean, the last time they did one of your plays it was packed and I had to sit in the gallery and it was wonderful, everybody said so and in the Daily Mail they said you were the most influential playwright of the Twentieth Century and I was ever so pleased when I read that and I said, 'Eat your heart out, Harold Pinter,' but not to his face of course."

"How kind," said Lewis.

Orson sniffed. "Not very kind to Harold Pinter."

Lewis said, "The daughter, Michael."

Michael said, "OK," and walked quickly to the front door. Olga called after him. "She might not be wearing the yellow one, actually. She brought rather a selection—it could be any of them. Ask for her—Amanda Whitehall."

"I'll find her," said Michael. The door closed behind him.

Lewis said, "Well, this is fun. Does she look anything like you?"

"Not a bit," said Olga. "She's rather beautiful."

"I think you're very handsome," said Orson, in a comforting voice.

"Very," said Lewis.

It was, Olga thought, extraordinarily difficult, this business of communication. Why couldn't they all simply say what they meant right at the very beginning? Instead, they must first wade through these courtly exchanges—and all in the name of manners. Surely they could see how awkward this was for her and, if they could, surely they would drop their manners and come to her rescue? Perhaps they could see the awkwardness of it all and were cravenly avoiding the moment. The last thing she wanted to do was embarrass anybody, which was, of course, such an English reluctance—

"Oh lord," said Lewis and, for a moment, Olga thought he was going to tackle the paternity question. Then he said, "I've just had a thought, Ossie. All these people in the house and no lunch. Not to mention no tea and no dinner either. What are we to do?"

"Go out," said Orson. "Restaurants."

"If I might make a small interjection?" said Freddy, putting one hand in the air, like an eager schoolboy.

Lewis said, "Interject away."

Freddy wriggled with pleasure. "Well, Sir Lewis, I'd be ever so pleased to help out if you'd permit me. I could see what I could do, if you know what I mean. There's provisions in the fridge, I saw them and I could rustle something up in a jiffy."

"How extraordinarily kind of you," said Lewis.

"Not really, Sir Lewis. It's what I like to do. Busy hands make for a light heart."

"Do they?" said Orson, raising his right eyebrow high on his forehead. "I must remember that."

"Ooh, I'm at my best when I'm busy," said Freddy. "And helping others is always so rewarding, that's what I always say."

"Do you?" said Orson. "I think it's a pain in the ass but there you are."

Freddy picked up the tray. "All finished with the coffee? Then I'll just remove the evidence, shall I? And there'll be a light luncheon at one o'clock, if that's convenient?"

Freddy hoisted the tray to ear level and tacked his way across the room and disappeared through the far door.

"I don't understand," said Orson, beetling his brows together so that two deep furrows appeared between his eyes. "I don't understand anything this morning. Who the hell is this little man and why is he here? Is he working for us, or is he a guest? How do you know him, Lewis—or is that a question best left unanswered?"

"He's a fan, Ossie," said Lewis, patiently. "He was a fan back when I met him and he's a fan today but, unlike most fans, he seems to be useful. The coffee was wonderful and he polishes silver, too. Don't look gift horses in the mouth."

"He could be a Trojan gift horse, for all you know."

"No, Ossie."

"He might shoot us all," said Orson, gloomily. "Fans do, you know."

Chapter 7

Behind her sunglasses and her closed eyelids there was a dark red glow but the shadow of something appearing suddenly between her and the sun darkened the glow almost to black. Amanda slitted open her eyes and squinted up at the silhouette that loomed over her.

The silhouette said, "Are you Amanda Whitehall?"

"Yes."

"Oh, good. Thanks for wearing the yellow. I appreciate it. The yellow was good. A good choice. Of course, I haven't seen the others but the yellow is great."

He had a soft American accent but that was all she could tell about him, since he was nothing but a black shape against the harsh blue-white of the sky. She waved him to one side and he moved obediently and sat down on the lounger next to her. She closed her eyes against the sudden glare and said, "We shouldn't be doing this, you know. So bad for us."

"What is?"

"This sunbathing."

"I'm not. I've got all my clothes on."

Amanda rolled onto her side and peered at the man. He was wearing a light tan suit, with a white tee-shirt under the jacket. His face was brown and his teeth were very white and she recognized him and said, "You're the man from the plane."

"So I've been told. You have to come with me."

"Fine," said Amanda, swinging herself upright. "Where are we going?"

"Don't you want to know who I am?"

"Nah. Let's go."

The man laughed and put out his hand. "I'm Michael Corbo. I just met your mom. I've been sent to get you."

"Oh," said Amanda. "Now that's really disappointing. I thought I was being picked up—and on my first day, too."

"Sorry."

"So you should be. Give me five minutes."

She wrapped a beach towel round her and got up and walked across the hot concrete towards the hotel lobby and, while she couldn't be certain without turning round and confirming it with her eyes, she was quite sure that the man was looking at her the whole way. He was quite right. The yellow was the best.

Lewis and Orson had started to complete each other's sentences, which was something they did when they were enjoying themselves. Orson wasn't enjoying himself quite as much as Lewis. He knew that Michael was right and that this woman had come to settle the identity of her other parent but he could see that, however impatient she might be, her manners were good enough to quell her eagerness and allow them the latitude of telling her all sorts of things about them without actually revealing the Big Secret—at least, not yet. Oddly, Lewis, with all his acuity, appeared blind to the obviousness of the woman's quest and was babbling away at her like a lunatic.

"Adopted, yes. Well, you know that. I do hope you're not seething with resentment. I've heard they do, sometimes. Seethe a bit. Adoptees, I mean. Are you seething at all?"

"Not a bit."

"Oh good. It was Giselle. She couldn't stand the nappies. In fact, we did most of that, didn't we Ossie?"

"If you mean the diapers, I did most of them. I don't know about you—"

"Fifty fifty, let's say. I'm afraid she wasn't cut out to be a mother."

"None of us was," said Orson.

"We had so much fun, you see," said Lewis. "So much fun. Well, we were young and things were going well—"

"When *were* these things that were going so well?" said Orson.

"In London."

"Oh, in *London*. You're going back a bit, aren't you? Ages before she was born." Orson turned to Olga and put his hand on her arm. "Things *were* going well. For him, you understand."

"And not so bad for you either," said Lewis. "He started selling pictures to all sorts of people—"

"And he was having a rip-roaring success with his first play in London. Fêted by everybody, a little literary lion, he was—"

"Giselle was with me then, of course—"

"We'd been back and forth a bit, you understand—"

"To-ing and fro-ing, a bit—"

"Indecisive creature, she was—"

"And this first theatrical success of his coincided with a short period during which Giselle happened to be with him in a stinking awful apartment, I might add—"

"If you can call any apartment in Cadogan Square stinking awful—"

"There were goddam mouse droppings everywhere, Lewis."

"Giselle was fond of the little chaps and fed them with Garibaldi biscuits—"

Olga held up both her hands and Lewis and Orson stopped talking at once. "I'm sorry," Olga said, "but when was this, exactly?"

"Exactly?" said Orson. He shrugged. "No idea, *exactly*. In the mid thirties. A bit before you. We're leading up to it, you see."

"If you don't mind?" said Lewis.

"No. No, I don't mind. It's very interesting."

"Well, it would be if Ossie would stop interrupting all the time—"

"You leave things out, Lewis—"

"Some things are best left out. Mouse droppings. Irrelevant. Anyway, there we were, Giselle and me, in London and then he turns up, in a bright yellow overcoat—"

"Oh, that's *profoundly* relevant, that is—"

"On the one weekend I happened to be away in the country and, yes, it is relevant, actually, because Giselle loved his yellow coat almost to the point of idiocy and Ossie knew that quite well."

"I knew it well enough to hope it would help," said Orson.

He'd watched the outside of the flats all morning. Earlier, he'd telephoned from a box on the corner of Cadogan Square and Lewis had answered and Orson had stayed silent while Lewis shouted, "Hello? Hello?" into the mouthpiece. Then Lewis had said, "Somebody's playing silly buggers," and Orson heard Giselle in the background say, "Silly buggers," and then Lewis had put the receiver down. Orson left the phone box and walked up the street and looked up at their window, willing Giselle but not Lewis to come to it and look down and see him. When she didn't, he opened the iron gate into the small communal gardens and found a bench with a good view of their window and the front door of the flats. He sat down on it and waited.

Two hours later, Lewis came out of the front door with a small suitcase in his hand. He put the case into the passenger seat of a shiny little black two-seater and then got into the driver's side and drove off. Orson got up and walked slowly out of the garden, across the road and into the flats. He didn't take the lift; the small guilt he was feeling was enough to persuade him to pay an equally small penance, so he walked up the stairs that surrounded the lift shaft, tramping round and round the well until he reached their floor. He walked down the passage, looking at the numbers on the doors and, when he came to theirs, he stopped and waited until his breathing settled back to normal. Then he knocked and there was a pause and then the door opened and Giselle was there.

She was wearing a sort of wrap, made of smoke gray satin and her hair was very curly and blonde—and much shorter, he noticed. A London style, probably.

"Hello," he said. "It's me."

"So it is," said Giselle. "I thought you were in Paris."

"I was. Now, I'm here."

"So you are."

They spent the rest of the day in bed and Giselle cried several times. "I'm such a bitch," she moaned. "How could I do this to poor darling Lewis?"

Orson said, "On the other hand, how could you not?"

When he woke up the next morning, the sun was streaming through the window, Giselle was gone from his side and Lewis was standing at the end of the bed, looking at him with a strange expression on his face.

"Oh. Hi." said Orson. "Where's Giselle?"

"You may well ask," said Lewis.

"I *am* asking."

"Well, I rather think she's gone, if you must know. Why don't you have a bath and get dressed and then come into the kitchen and have some coffee and we'll discuss the matter."

Orson did as he was told and then, with his hair tousled and damp, sat down at the kitchen table and allowed Lewis to serve him coffee.

"Gone where?"

"You've really done it this time, you know. I mean, it's bad enough for a chap to come home and find his best friend in his bed—but when the best friend manages not only to seduce the chap's girl but also to drive her away in despair, then all a chap can say is you're a rotten cad."

Orson put his cup down carefully. "Is that the sort of crap you write in your plays? Because if it is, maybe you ought to try another line of work. Giselle was fed up with you, anyway. She said you were getting too goddam big for your boots and needed taking down a peg or two."

"She said that, did she?"

"Yup."

"Those exact metaphors?"

"Yup."

"They were her clichés, not yours?"

They stared at each other across the table, belligerence flaring in their eyes. Orson said, "Do you want to fight?"

"No," said Lewis. "No, you'd win."

"Goddam right, I'd win."

"Besides, it won't get her back, will it?"

Lewis reached into his coat pocket and took out a crumpled sheet of blue writing paper. "This was pinned on the door," he said. He handed it across the table and Orson read the scrawled, spidery writing slowly.

Darlings, I'm awfull a complete bitch sorry sorry sorry gasp sorry I'm going away and please don't try and find me and if you do please don't speak to me I'm not worth it realy I'm not I love you both and that's the trouble and we just can't go on like this realy we can't so goodbye I've gone.

At the foot of the page Giselle had drawn twenty little x's and a crude, vaguely female face with tears on the cheeks and a downturned mouth.

"Where do you suppose she's gone?" said Orson.

"I've no idea."

"What do you think we ought to do?"

"Wait for her to come back, I think."

"Do you think she will?"

"She's sure to. You'll see."

They waited for a week but Giselle didn't come back and didn't write or telephone either, which was odd because Giselle loved writing short, badly spelt letters almost as much as she loved talking at length on the telephone—and of all the people in the world that Giselle loved writing her letters to and chatting on the telephone with, Lewis and Orson were her two favorites and, when she was with one of them, she would spend happy hours writing to or talking with the other, which could be irritating to the one she happened to be living with at the time. Now she wasn't with either of them it seemed—and wasn't intending to be in any kind of contact as well, which turned out to be painful for both of them.

"What shall we do now?" asked Orson, at the end of the miserable week.

"We *were* going on a cruise," said Lewis. "Giselle and I. Round the Mediterranean on the Appleton's yacht. We were supposed to leave tomorrow."

"Who are the Appletons?"

"People with a yacht. Do you want to come?"

"Won't the Appletons mind?"

"I don't think so. It's me they want. They won't care who I bring."

"All right."

They took the boat train to Paris and then the Golden Arrow to Nice. The Appletons—Dicky and Margery—met them at the station in Nice and whisked them off to the harbor and onto the biggest, whitest boat that Orson had ever seen. Dicky and Margery seemed eager to please and quite happy with the substitution of Orson for Giselle, just so long as Orson didn't cut into the time they'd allotted to their admiration of Lewis, whom they seemed to regard as a worthy successor to Shakespeare. They were much older than Lewis and Orson, devoted to the Arts, the Theater in particular, with enough money to sink several yachts the size of their enormous one, which was called *Melpomene*.

There were other guests on board *Melpomene*. A famous Hungarian ballet dancer called Misha, who wore a silk bandanna on his forehead and deep purple polish on his fingernails; a recently published novelist from America called Alicia Belt, who was blind and very young and who had lived all her sheltered life in a small town in rural Wisconsin but still wrote books filled with torrid love affairs, littered with enough references to pubic hair to make the novels best sellers and Alicia notorious. Alicia had her fiancé with her; he was awkward, with a bad haircut and a bovine face, his oversized hands thrusting out from too-short sleeves. His name was Bill and nobody spoke to him. There were three others on the boat, all very young; two boys and a girl; they were related in some way to the Appletons, who treated them with fond indulgence. They had slight Cockney accents and laughed constantly at some private joke and neither Lewis nor Orson ever learned any of their names.

"So sorry that darling Gigi couldn't come," cooed Margery. They were standing on the open after-deck at six o'clock, having cocktails served to them by two white-coated servants.

"Gigi?" said Orson.

"Gigi has left me," said Lewis, narrowing his eyes dramatically and staring out across the harbor.

"Oh, *Gigi*," said Orson. "Yeah—me too." He drained his martini in one gulp and grabbed another that was passing by on a silver tray. "Left us both. Darling Gigi."

"My dear—*left* you?" said Margery, looking sympathetically at Lewis and ignoring Orson.

"Left me flat."

"As a pancake," said Orson. "There we were, all three of us, perfectly happy and then suddenly off she goes without so much as a by your leave. Extraordinary. What had we done, I ask myself?"

"I ask myself that, too," said Lewis, getting into the swing. "Constantly. What did we do to deserve this? She wanted for nothing—"

"We lavished her with baubles," said Orson, grandly. "Dripping with them, she was."

"And yet," sighed Lewis, shaking his head sadly. "Off she popped. So fickle. Fickle, fickle, fickle."

Margery decided that she was almost certainly being teased so she smiled distantly and went off to talk to Alicia Belt, who was fun to be with because Margery didn't have to try to be pretty with her—which was preferable to being teased by a couple of young men, no matter how attractive and clever they were.

Misha sidled up to Lewis and Orson.

"I hear everyting," he said, rolling his eyes under lids of iridescent green makeup.

"Well, you're very naughty," said Lewis. "You should put your fingers in your ears."

Misha took Lewis and Orson by their arms and walked them to the rail. "I understand everyting. We know dese tings in my country. It happen dere all the time. Very sad. You know what you should do?" he said, looking pertly at each of them. "You should forget de woman, throw her from your heads and be togeder for all the time."

"Who?" said Orson. "Be together with who for all the time?"

"With *him*," said Misha, squeezing first Orson's arm and then Lewis'. "You with him and him with you. It's good. No?"

"If you mean what I think you mean," said Orson, "then no, it's not good at all." He patted Misha kindly on the top of his head. "Not up my street. Of course, I can't speak for Lewis."

"No, you can't, can you?" said Lewis.

They looked carefully at one another. Nothing of this matter had been mentioned for some time and it was, as Orson later said to Lewis, a moment of truth. Then Orson broke the eye-lock and glanced down at Misha and then back to Lewis, smiling faintly now and his look said: *If you want to play with this, then go ahead.* Lewis raised his eyebrows, sending back: *Are you sure you don't mind?* and Orson's eyes returned an unequivocal green light, so the next day, when the yacht stopped in a deserted bay some way down the coast on the way to Italy, Lewis and Misha went off for a swim together. Orson sat under the shade of the canvas awning stretched over the after-deck and sketched lazily on a pad of cartridge paper. One of the crew, a short, brown man in a striped jersey was polishing the brass windlass and Orson drew him in a few, quick strokes.

"That's frightfully good," said Dicky Appleton, peering over his shoulder. "I didn't know you were an artist."

"Yes," said Orson. "Well, I try to be."

"This is marvelous. Absolutely marvelous. Can I buy it?"

Orson tore the sheet from the pad and pushed it at Dicky. "It's yours."

"How much do you want for it?"

"Nothing. I'm singing for my supper."

Dicky laughed and his face creased in a hundred wrinkles. "My dear fellow, that's very nice of you and I shall accept it. But after this, you must charge, you know. Otherwise people won't think your stuff is any good."

"I usually charge."

"How much?"

"Well, it depends."

Dicky held his drawing at arms length and squinted at it. "I'd put this round about the five hundred mark," he said and Orson's eyebrows shot to the top of his forehead, because he'd never dared ask more than fifty for a pencil sketch and the top price for one of his oils had been a hundred and twenty five and the man who had been prepared to pay that was soon after declared insane and taken away in a van.

"Five hundred? Really?"

Dicky lowered the drawing and looked at Orson ruminatively. "Do you have somebody looking after you? Helping you with your work, I mean?"

"No. No, I don't. Should I have?"

"There's a chap I know. I get some stuff from him. He looks after a few artists. If he takes you on—and I have a feeling he will—then you won't ever be giving anything away again. We'll all have to pay through the nose, including me. Oh, well—at least I can say I got this for nothing."

Later, that evening, when Lewis and Misha returned (Lewis sporting a small, fatuous grin, Orson noticed) Dicky brought out the sketch and everybody admired it. To Orson's surprise, Dicky didn't say that he'd got it for nothing. Instead, he said, "An absolute bargain at five hundred, I don't mind telling you," and he winked at Orson. And such was Dicky Appleton's reputation—as an art collector with a good eye—that Misha immediately demanded that Orson do something for him too—

perhaps a sketch of Lewis, standing by the capstan?—and Alicia Belt said she'd like one too, of anything, really but preferably of the yacht in the harbor? Orson wondered what she would do with it, since she wouldn't be able to see it and Alicia, sensing his hesitation, said that she wanted the picture as a memento of a glorious, glorious vacation, an explanation that Orson felt left everything to be desired. Margery chimed in and said she'd just adore one of Dicky at the helm, with his pipe and his jaunty yachting cap. Then she took a check book and a gold pen from her handbag and said, "And since it's my yacht and I want mine first, I shall pay in advance." Misha ran to his cabin and came back with a wad of cash and waved it under Orson's nose and shouted, "Me first! Me first!" and everybody laughed. Alicia Belt whispered to fiancé Bill and he nodded and lumbered off to their cabin and came back with Alicia's traveler's checks and she wrote her name in the proper place with Bill guiding her hand.

"I don't mind when I get mine," she said, extending the check in Orson's direction, "if you'll just promise to be famous."

Lewis watched Orson accept, with fumbling embarrassment, his advance fees and later he strolled to Orson's cabin and flopped down on the foot of the bed.

"Well, well. Fifteen hundred quid. Not a bad day's work. Money for old rope, if you ask me."

There was a trace of spite in Lewis' voice and a little, drawly, sing-song cadence that Orson recognized as belonging to Misha. He's jealous, thought Orson—not only of the money but of the sudden switch of attention from him to me.

He said, "Did you have a nice day?"

"Very. We swam. Hither and yon."

"Just swam?"

Lewis sighed heavily. "You don't *really* want to know, do you?"

"Not the details, no. But I do want to know if you *liked* whatever you did besides the swimming."

"Why?"

"I'd like to know that you're happy. One of us ought to be, at least."

"We frolicked among some rocks. It was uncomfortable but enormous fun. We shall probably do it again tomorrow. All right?"

"Perfectly."

"You mean you approve?"

"If it makes you happy, absolutely."

"Thank you."

That was the start of their two years together and the memory was as fresh in Orson's mind as if it had happened a week ago.

Lewis was saying, "Playing at mothers and fathers palled after a while. I'm afraid Giselle just didn't seem to possess a maternal bone in her body, so we discussed it—"

"At length," said Orson, who hadn't spoken for some time.

"At length, yes. Well, we don't want you to think you were just any old piece of flotsam—"

"Or jetsam."

"—to be cast aside easily. No, it was discussed and, for once, quite seriously. We weren't serious very often, you know. Everything was funny, then. I mean, a passing cloud could reduce the three of us to hysteria. We were, I'm sorry to say, ridiculously silly."

"It was fun," said Orson.

"Oh, great fun. One endless party. A bit of work every now and again—a little play from me, a little picture from him—and then back to the revels. We had—problems looking after you and Giselle couldn't stand doing it herself, so one day we all sat down and discussed it and agreed that adoption was the only course."

"So that's what we did. How did it work out for you?"

"Fine," said Olga, meaning it. "It was a very comfortable childhood."

"Wouldn't have been with us," said Orson. "Goddam uncomfortable with us."

"And it was settled, too," said Olga. "Ordered and rather quiet. My mother—well, you know—I was very fond of her."

"Good," said Lewis.

"I had a father, too," said Olga.

"And were you fond of him as well?"

"Yes. Very. He was a bomber pilot during the war and then went, very successfully, into advertising."

"Dead, are they?" said Orson.

Olga nodded. "Within three weeks of each other. Five years ago."

"How sad," said Lewis, sadly.

There was a long, sad pause. Then Orson said, brightly, "I like your name. Olga. Very clever, that."

"I hate it. Why is it clever?"

"Well, it's an anagram, you see, of your real name," said Orson. "I mean, the name we gave you, although of course you weren't baptized or anything, so you're not stuck with it and, in fact, I think you ought to hang on to Olga, which is altogether more practical, since it is, at least, a recognizable name, which Gloa isn't."

"Gloa?" said Olga, slowly, testing each letter as it emerged from her mouth.

"That's what we called you. Gloa. It was Giselle's idea."

"I thought it was idiotic at the time," said Lewis. "And I think it's even more idiotic now."

"Gloa?" said Olga again, looking at Lewis and Orson in turn.

Orson traced letters in the air with his forefinger. "G for Giselle, L for Lewis and O for me. Thus Glo. The A on the end was for being the first. Thus Gloa."

"So logically, according to Giselle, at least," said Lewis, "if she was ever to have another baby—which she said she would only over her dead body, which would have been a feat in itself—if she was ever to have another, it would have to be called Glob. As I said, it was idiotic but we thought it amusing at the time. Sorry."

Olga laughed and Orson said, "What a nice laugh you have," and Olga said, "Thank you," and then there was another long silence.

Lewis stared at her, as surreptitiously as he could. It was odd, he thought—here was this adult stranger, with a complete, rounded personality all her own, with her own memories of a lifetime which they could never share, and with a face and a body that was so far removed from his memory of her—all he could bring to mind was a blurred image of a toothless, squalling thing, devoid of any of the charm that made you want to stroke a kitten or pat a puppy—that it was almost impossible to connect this mature and intelligent woman with the noisy nuisance they had so cheerfully given away. And then he wondered why the woman was here at all, given that the connection between them had been stretched so very thin by the intervening half a century that there couldn't be anything she could possibly want that they could possibly give her, other than some sort of anchor, perhaps, for her origins, some sort of identity that some adopted people seemed to crave—

"Oh," he said, suddenly understanding. "Oh, my God. How very slow of me."

"Got it, have you?" said Orson, as though talking to a small child.

Lewis snorted. "You're not going to pretend you've been on top of things all this time?"

"Certainly I have. It's been amusing waiting for your penny to drop, I must say. Like watching paint dry, it's taken so long."

Lewis turned to face Olga. "Giselle makes no mention, in her letter, of your actual father, does she? And that's what you'd like to know about, isn't it?" His voice was kind.

"I'm sorry if it's awkward," said Olga, lowering her eyes. "But you're right. That is one of the things I'd like to know. Well, wouldn't you?"

"There's other things?" said Orson, nervously. "What other things?"

"Oh, you know," said Olga, spreading her fingers wide and waving them gently in the air, so that they looked like swaying sea anemones. "Your lives together—things like that."

"You're American, you know," said Lewis, suddenly. Olga looked quickly at Orson and Lewis shook his head and said, "No, no. Don't jump to conclusions. You're only American by the location of your birth. You were born in New York. At some hospital or other, I forget the name of it but it was hideously expensive—and I'm afraid your father didn't pay a penny of it. I'm afraid your father was a mean son of a bitch."

"Lewis," said Orson. There was a note of warning in his voice.

"Well, Good God, Ossie—there's no point pussy-footing about the thing. He behaved quite extraordinarily badly throughout and the woman has the right to know."

"Even so," said Orson, quietly. "Even so."

"I'm sorry," said Olga, looking in bewilderment from Lewis to Orson and back again. "I'm sorry but—but are you saying it wasn't either of you?"

"Yes, that's exactly what we're saying," said Orson. "A terrible disappointment, I should imagine. You've come all this way for nothing. Well, not for nothing, of course. It's lovely to see you again and all that and we shall most definitely be keeping in touch from now on but, you see, there really is no actual blood attachment here at all. You must look elsewhere for that."

"Where?"

"Well, now, that's a problem," said Orson. "Do we have the right to spill the beans on the guy? What will you do with the information? We have to think of these things, you see."

The front door was hurled open and Michael marched in. "Here she is!" he announced, stepping to one side and letting Amanda walk past him. Amanda strode confidently into the room and then stopped, confused momentarily by the size of the space and the many levels of the floor. Then she saw Olga sitting in a big armchair, between two more big armchairs that contained two old men—one thin, with a shock of white hair, the other fat and red-faced, with almost no hair at all. Amanda stepped forward.

"Hello," she said, sticking her hand out to Lewis. "I'm Amanda Whitehall." Then she turned her head a little towards Olga and said, without taking her eyes from Lewis, "Which one is it?"

"Oh, Good God," said Lewis faintly. "Oh, Good God Almighty." His right hand stayed in his lap.

"What?" said Amanda.

"Jesus," muttered Orson. "Jesus Christ on a bicycle. It's amazing. Absolutely goddam amazing."

"What is?" said Amanda, with a trace of asperity in her voice. The two old men were staring at her as if she was a ghost and Lewis' eyes were brimming with tears. "What's the matter?" she said.

Lewis gulped. "Ossie—" he began and Orson held up both his hands and said, "No, shut up, shut up. You don't need to say another word, Lewis and, goddammit, if you're going to cry, go away and do it somewhere else."

Lewis swallowed hard and swiped at his eyes with the back of his hand. Michael stepped forward and said, "I should have warned you. I'm sorry."

"Nonsense," said Orson. "No time, was there? She barrels in here, all the confidence in the world, you couldn't get a word in, could you?"

"Would somebody tell me what's going on?" said Amanda. "I seem to be having the most awful effect on everybody. Warned them about what?"

"You look a bit like her," said Michael.

"Like who?"

"A bit like her?" Orson exploded. "A *bit*? She's the spitting image, for Chrissake."

Lewis drew a long, shuddering breath and then let it out in a sigh. He got out of his chair, with surprising grace, Amanda thought and took her hand in his and shook it gravely. "The thing is, you see," he said, staring into her face with eyes gleaming with tears, "the thing is, you look very like Giselle. Your grandmother, you know. Quite extraordinarily like her and it's a bit of a shock, to be honest. We didn't think we'd see her again."

"But I've seen photographs of her," said Amanda, still holding Lewis' hand. "I don't look like her at all."

"Well, no, you wouldn't. Not in the photographs. She always posed dreadfully in the photographs. She put on this face with the cameras because she thought it made her look more glamorous. We called it her Dietrich face, although really she looked more like Betty Boop when she did it. But, in repose, she really was just like you."

"Except for the hair," said Orson, coming to stand beside them. He peered at Amanda, looking her up and down. "Except for the hair and the makeup and the clothes and she certainly would never have been caught dead in those shoes—and the height. You're much taller than she was, we never saw eye to eye with her but we do with you."

"Is this a good thing in your books?" said Amanda. "Looking like her, I mean."

"Fine by me," said Orson. "As long as you don't mind us staring."

"I think it's wonderful," said Lewis.

"Oh, Christ—look at him," said Orson. "He's going to cry again."

"Coming from you, Orson," said Lewis, stiffly, "that's a joke."

Chapter 8

Freddy served them lunch and, in the excitement of eating it and look-ing at Amanda, Lewis and Orson seemed to have forgotten all about the paternity question.

The lunch Freddy had put together was very good. He'd scoured the kitchen and the pantries and found tins of tuna fish and jars of mayonnaise and bottles of pickled things. The old refrigerator had yielded a salami, a jar of olives, two kinds of lettuce and a cucumber and Freddy had done this and that to everything he'd found and put it all out on some pretty china he'd discovered in a cupboard—a whole set of dusty, grimy porcelain, with a few chipped pieces but mostly in good condition. He'd scrubbed them clean and then he'd stacked everything on an old trolley and wheeled it in through the door to the living room at exactly one o'clock and everybody seemed so pleased to see him—almost relieved, he thought—that Freddy glowed in their pleasure and allowed them to persuade him into sitting down with them at the refectory table and digging in, just as if he was a guest—which, if you looked at it one way, he supposed he was.

There were a couple of bottles of white wine, too and Orson had three glasses, quickly. He stared at Amanda and let Lewis do most of the talking. Lewis asked Olga about her books.

"A squirrel, you say?"

"Skippy."

"Doing squirrely things, I suppose?"

"No. Doing domestic human things, I'm afraid. Going shopping. Having his hair cut. He leads an uneventful life. I write for the very young, you understand."

"Are there pictures?"

"Yes. I do them too."

"Really? Orson, do you hear that?"

"Huh?"

"Oh, do tear your eyes away for a moment and listen. She does the pictures as well. Art and Literature combined. What about that, eh?"

"All right," Amanda said. "Enough of this. Why won't you tell us?"

Lewis put one finger to his lips. "We will, we will. But pas devant les domestiques," and he nodded furtively in Freddy's direction.

"He isn't a domestique, Lewis," said Orson. "I'm not sure what he is but he isn't a domestique."

"I hope I'm a friend, Mr. Woodley, sir." said Freddy, aware that they were talking about him, even if he didn't know what a domestique was, exactly.

"Possibly. In time. Meanwhile, Lewis, why don't we spill the beans? We have no business protecting anybody, particularly him, so let's not. Besides, there are obligations here, I think."

Lewis shrugged. "All right." He looked at Olga and said, "Well, don't say I didn't warn you. Your father was a man—is a man, I should say—called Finlay Ferguson. Actually, now Lord Finlay Ferguson. Perhaps you've heard of him?"

Freddy gasped. He'd certainly heard of him and surely the ladies had too? He looked at Olga and then at Amanda and saw, by the stillness in their faces, that they had, of course, heard of Lord Ferguson. It would have been difficult not to have heard of him. Lord Ferguson was on the telly practically every day, being a guest on art panel shows or popping up in news bites and giving his views on, well, practically anything that came to mind. Lord Ferguson seemed to know a lot about a lot of things, Freddy thought. Add to that the trick of expressing himself in a voice famous for the roundness of its vowels and the rolling of its R's—

and notwithstanding the tendency to call everybody in earshot by the sort of endearments barmaids use to favored customers—it was no wonder Lord Ferguson was in such media demand.

"You mean the man who runs the National Theatre?" said Olga, in a voice that was almost a whisper.

"The very same," said Lewis. "I'm terribly sorry."

"What are you sorry for?" asked Amanda.

"I'm sorry for the fact that your grandfather is such an unmitigated smear of dried cat's vomit. That's what I'm sorry for."

Freddy gasped again and, when everybody looked at him, he put his hand over his mouth. Nobody had ever called Finlay Ferguson names, at least not in his hearing. Surely Finlay Ferguson was the most respected of men? Well, he was a lord, wasn't he? And before that he'd been a sir—you didn't get to be a sir and then a lord and go on the telly all the time if you were a smear of dried cat's vomit, surely?

Lewis saw Freddy's dismay. "He's not a friend of yours, is he?" he said and Freddy, his hand still pressed to his lips, shook his head. He'd never met Lord Ferguson but, if Sir Lewis said he was a smear of dried cat's vomit, then that's what Lord Ferguson was and that's how he would think of him from now on.

"Of course, I suppose he does have some friends," said Lewis, "although I don't know who they are and I imagine they keep pretty quiet about it."

"He is rather awful," said Amanda. "Do you dislike him because of what he is now or what he was when you knew him before?"

"How did you know we knew him before?" said Lewis.

"Your opinion of him has a sort of precision. It implies you know him personally, rather than in the general way that the rest of us know him. We see him on television and read him in the papers. Our opinions of him are based on what he's said and done, rather than who he is, which I think is what yours are based on."

"She doesn't *talk* like her at all, does she?" said Orson. He patted Amanda's hand. "Your grandmother could only manage very short sentences but she could pack a lot of them into half a minute. She had a mind like a butterfly. Flitter, flitter. Yours is more like a hornet. Zoom, bang."

"Actually," said Lewis, "my opinion of Finlay is based entirely on what he did. Personally, we rather liked him. When he was young he was very charming. Now, I daresay, he really is the pompous idiot that everybody thinks he is but back then, apart from one or two bizarre ideas about the direction the theatre ought to be taking, he was good company. Very good company indeed."

Finlay had been an actor, a juvenile leading man, before he became a director. Lewis and Giselle had seen him in a couple of shows during occasional trips to London. Finlay had been quite bad in both of them and Lewis and Giselle had laughed about him. So, when Lewis' play, *View Hollow*, was accepted by the impresario Daniel Harsent and when Daniel Harsent had suggested that they get young Finlay Ferguson to direct it, Lewis had said, "But he's terrible. I've seen him. He can't do it at all."

"Do what?" said Daniel.

"Act. He's hopeless."

"I quite agree. He's dreadful. But we're not asking him to act, are we? We're asking him to direct and he's very good at that. Very good indeed. We'll be lucky to get him. You've been in Paris too long, Lewis. You ought to keep up with things. Finlay Ferguson is a busy little chap these days."

Finlay came into Daniel's office the next day and talked to Lewis and Daniel about the play and what he thought they ought to do with it and everything Finlay said, Lewis found himself agreeing with. Later they all went out to lunch and Lewis found himself liking Finlay very much. He was attractive, in a short, willowy way—quite different from Orson, who was tall and strongly built, like a prizefighter. Finlay had long, tapering fingers and a long, thin face. His hair was brilliantined flat to his skull and he had a slim moustache and he looked a little like an English Valentino. His suit was pale gray and his waistcoat had four pockets, which Lewis thought was stylish.

"We might try and get Beryl Cambridge for Laura," said Finlay.

Beryl Cambridge was exactly the actress that Lewis had in mind when he wrote the part of Laura, so now he smiled happily and said, "Absolutely. Beryl Cambridge. And who for Rupert?"

"I thought Neville Starkey."

"So did I. How marvelous."

Daniel Harsent felt a glow of satisfaction. It wasn't often that the playwright and the director agreed so conveniently.

Rehearsals started soon after, with Muriel Gaspeard instead of Beryl Cambridge, who had declined the part of Laura, saying she didn't understand it and couldn't in fact, see the point of her at all.

"What a donkey," said Finlay.

"Imbecile," said Daniel.

"Complete ass," said Lewis. "Muriel Gaspeard will be so much better."

Muriel Gaspeard was very good and her scenes with Neville Starkey had a humid eroticism about them that was puzzling, since they were playing husband and wife.

"I think they're having an affair," said Finlay, sitting with Lewis at the back of the stalls. "I mean, just look at them."

They laughed companionably for a moment and then Lewis said, suddenly and without thought, "Would you like to come to dinner?"

"Love to. When?"

"Tonight." That, too, was said suddenly and without thought and Lewis wondered for a moment what Giselle would say. He'd never brought anybody home before. She wouldn't cook, that was certain. They'd have to go out somewhere.

"Lovely."

"27 Cadogan Place. Flat 18. Pop round about seven. Bring somebody, if you like."

"There isn't anybody at the moment, ducky—except my mother and I can't bring her. I'll come on my own, if that's all right?"

"Of course. We'll go out somewhere."

Any idea (and it was only ever a small suspicion) that Lewis might have had about Finlay being queer was dispelled that evening. Finlay took one look at Giselle and was obviously smitten. He watched her closely all evening—they had cocktails at the flat and then went to the Savoy—and he laughed very hard at all her jokes and agreed enthusiastically with all her opinions and complimented her on everything about her appearance, until Giselle was almost writhing with the pleasure of being so entirely approved of and by such an up-and-comer like Finlay Ferguson.

After dinner they took a taxi to Ebury Street and dropped Finlay off at his block of flats. Finlay got out and then turned back to them, holding the door of the taxi open. He leaned in and said, "Now, angel, you're quite sure you're not an actress?"

"Quite," said Giselle. "I'd die, simply die up there."

"Well, it's a tragic shame," said Finlay, staring at Giselle's knees. "You'd have been so marvelous as Laura. He must have written in for you, surely?"

"No—he wrote it for Beryl Cambridge," said Giselle seriously. "It was always for Beryl Cambridge. Or Muriel Thingy, too. But not for me. No point writing it for me. I can't act. I can't do anything."

"But he must have had you in mind. There's so much of you there."

Lewis decided he hated sitting in the back of a taxi while a man made love to his girl through the open door of the passenger compartment. He said, "There's practically nothing of her there at all and I *never* had her in mind. It was Beryl Cambridge or Muriel Gaspeard or anybody, actually. Anybody but Giselle. Goodnight, Finlay. See you tomorrow."

He leaned forward and pulled the door closed and Finlay gave a cheery little wave and Giselle gave a cheery little wave back and Lewis said, to the taxi driver, "27 Cadogan Place, please," in a cross voice.

"What's the matter?" said Giselle.

"He was all over you. The whole evening. Remarkably aggravating."

"Don't be so pompous. Anyway, I liked him. He's very sweet."

"He's *sticky* with sweetness. Like toffee. Pretty funny—him thinking you might be an actress."

"A hoot. Ho ho ho."

They didn't speak for the rest of the night.

Finlay must have understood how thin the ice had become because, when they met later at a party for the cast on the stage of the Haymarket Theatre a week before the first night, he behaved quite differently towards Giselle and was almost brusque with her. He said, "Oh, hello. Drinks are over there." Then he walked away and joined Muriel and Neville in a corner.

Lewis felt a flash of irritation at Finlay's abruptness. It was obviously done for his benefit, which meant that Finlay was probably even more infatuated than he'd imagined. It was Giselle's fault. She encouraged that sort of thing all the time.

"If we must have a party," said Lewis, testily, "why can't we have it somewhere comfortable? Whoever thought that you could have a party on a stage must be barking mad. Look at all those ropes. Too depressing. What are you staring at?"

"Muriel. She's quite plain in real life, isn't she?"

"As opposed to in artificial life, you mean?" said Lewis.

"I mean, as opposed to on the stage. Why are you being horrid?"

"I'm not."

"Yes, you are. You're all stiff and clipped and sneery. All I'm saying is, lots of actresses are quite plain *off* the stage but ravishing on. Muriel Gaspeard's almost ugly, really—but when she's acting, she's quite lovely."

"Whereas you, of course, are an absolute vision when you're yourself and a hideous harridan when you're pretending to be somebody else. Interesting."

"You're a beast. I'm going to talk to somebody else until you're friendly again."

Giselle marched across the room and sat down next to Finlay. Giselle saw that Lewis was looking at her and she stuck her tongue out at him and crossed her eyes in a squint and then slipped her arm through Finlay's and turned to him and began an animated conversation. Lewis wandered off and found Daniel Harsent. They spent a dull evening talking about the play and how marvelous everybody was going to be and Lewis regretted being nasty to Giselle. Later, on the way home, he tried to make love to her in the back of the taxi.

"I don't want to," said Giselle. "I'm upset."

Lewis sat back and stared out of the window. "Are you going to be upset for long?"

"I don't know."

She was upset for the rest of the week. They were polite to each other and slept in the same bed but they didn't go out together and didn't laugh together at all. Lewis spent all his days and some of his nights at the theater and was busy enough so that he hardly noticed the coldness between them.

Then the first night came and Giselle bought a new dress and looked beautiful and smiled at him on the way to the theater and squeezed his hand encouragingly. Lewis was very nervous. They sat together in the stalls and Giselle leaned her head on Lewis' shoulder until the curtain went up and then she sat up and listened intently. The set got a round of applause and so did Muriel Gaspeard when she ran on through the French windows in her slip. Giselle laughed at all the funny parts and dabbed the corners of her eyes at the sad parts and, when the curtain fell on the final act, she applauded and cheered as loudly as anyone. Later, at the party, she stayed very close to him, clutching his arm and beaming with pride when people came up to congratulate him.

When they got home, drunk and excited, a watery sun was climbing up from the rooftops. They fell into bed and made fast, passionate love. Then they fell asleep until the telephone rang. It was Finlay.

"The best, Lewis—the absolutely *best* notices I've ever seen. For everybody. You, me, the play, the set, the actors—you name it, it's all wonderful. The box office is buzzing, the punters are agog and we're a hit, duckies, a palpable hit."

Lewis became an overnight sensation. He was interviewed by all the papers and photographed endlessly. Everybody wanted to talk to him, to have him to their parties—to sit at his feet and practically *worship* him, it seemed to Giselle. She trailed round after him for a while but listening to him trot out the same bons mots day after day, hearing the same mildly exaggerated stories being passed off as the truth and watching Lewis become more and more pleased with himself, made Giselle decide quite quickly that she liked him much better when he wasn't quite so successful.

They spent some of their time with the cast of *View Hollow* and they were fun to be with. Muriel and Neville got married early in the play's long run and Giselle became close to both of them. Finlay Ferguson was always there too and, the more Giselle saw of him, the more she liked him. He certainly liked her and was much nicer to her than horrid old Lewis, who was becoming impossible. She and Lewis rowed a lot and, when Lewis said he was going off for the weekend, Giselle felt a small flood of relief. It would be lovely to be alone for a few days. She might ring up Finlay and get him to take her out. There'd be no harm in that. In fact, there'd be no harm in looking as nice as possible for him—so she washed her hair and was fluffing it out with her fingers when there was a knock on the front door

Orson was on her doorstep and she forgot all about Finlay Ferguson for the next twelve hours.

"When she left us," said Lewis, "she went straight to Finlay. Apparently he'd been pestering her with his infatuation for some time and Giselle was always a great opportunist. Any old port in the storm, as it were. I don't think she ever loved him but he certainly adored her."

Orson grunted. "She couldn't be alone, you see. Hopeless alone. Had to be with somebody. Finlay was available and more than willing—"

"And, most important of all, he wasn't either of us—"

"So off she went. Moved into his flat in Ebury Street—"

"Finlay couldn't decide whether he was delirious with joy or embarrassed beyond belief. He avoided us at first and then later—"

"When we got back from the Appleton cruise—"

"He kept ringing up and apologizing. We told him he had nothing to do with it, that he was a mere pawn in Giselle's life and that, sooner or later, she'd be back with us again—"

"It was round about that time that we sorted everything out—our relationship with her and with each other—"

"Of course, Giselle didn't join in these discussions, since she wasn't there—"

Olga held up her hands and said, "Could you stop for a second? Sorry but there's something odd about all this."

"Of course there is," said Orson. "The whole thing was bizarre."

"No—I mean all this about Finlay Ferguson. There's no mention of him in the book and surely, if Giselle lived with him, there would have been?"

"The book? What book?" said Orson.

"There is only the one, Orson," said Lewis. "That ghastly *Jeunesse Dorée*. You haven't been reading that, have you?"

Olga and Amanda exchanged glances. Amanda said, "That's the one."

Freddy felt cheated. He didn't know there was a book. If he'd known there was a book, he would have bought it and read up on them all. Fancy there being a book. When he got home, he'd be sure to get it out of the library. They had quite a good library at Dollis Hill. He'd have to ask them to write the title down for him.

Orson said, "If you want to know about us, then for Chrissake, don't read that book."

"Apart from the pretentiousness of the title," said Lewis, "it's riddled with inaccuracies and half truths and several outright lies. Then there are the omissions—"

"Glaring omissions—"

"One of which is the whole question of what Giselle was doing during the two years we were busy being famous and successful and sad. She was with Finlay Ferguson the whole time and the reason the bloody book doesn't mention this fact is because it was written—if you can call that writing—"

"It was written by that godawful little shit, Oliver Louche, who just happened to be married to Finlay Ferguson's ugly niece—"

"Finlay got to him, we think and clamped down on that bit and Oliver Louche left it out, just to please the great man, would you believe? Mind you," said Lewis, smiling slyly, "Giselle was pleased too. The last thing she wanted was to have that unflattering period of her history in print."

"When was this, exactly?" aid Olga.

"Exactly?" Lewis sighed. "Don't ask us to do the sums. All I can tell you is that the second year of her living with him was fifty years ago and the only reason I know that is because you're here to remind us."

Michael had been quiet, watching Amanda's changing emotions slip over her face, like fast-moving clouds. He looked away from her, transferring his gaze to Orson and Lewis. He said, "Tolly wouldn't tell me why you didn't like Finlay. I get it now. I can see why you don't want to have anything to do with him."

"Oh?" said Lewis, raising one eyebrow. "And what's your take on this, Michael?"

"Well—he stole your girl—"

"Hah!" said Orson, explosively. "Crap. He did no such thing. He couldn't if he tried. We simply made her life so difficult that she ran away from us. Finlay just happened to be there, poor bastard. One ought really to sympathize with him—she didn't make his life particularly happy for the two years they were together—"

"Utterly miserable, if Giselle was to be believed—"

"I mean, I don't think he was too depressed when she walked out on him and came back to us. Probably glad to see the back of her."

Michael shook his head. "So why the animosity now?"

Orson pointed at Olga. "It was about her, of course. About a month after Giselle came back to us, she found herself pregnant. There'd only been Finlay in those two years, so there was no question about it, he was the father—but he refused to acknowledge the baby. Said it was nothing to do with him, it wasn't his and he wouldn't be blackmailed into paying a red cent for its upkeep—"

"Could we, do you think, substitute 'she' for 'it'?" said Lewis. "It is, after all, sitting here in front of us."

"I say 'it' because that's how Finlay referred to you," said Orson, smiling sympathetically at Olga. "He was adamant about the whole thing but refused to come up with an alternative father for you. I suppose it was some vengeful way of getting back at us for damaging his pride. Giselle was livid. She swore blind it was him and, of course, it was. His flat rejection of both you and the responsibility you brought with you made all of us rather angry. He wouldn't even pay for your birth. We had to cough up for that. Goddam fortune, it was."

"It was our pleasure," said Lewis, quickly. "Really, Ossie, I wish you'd stop putting your foot in it."

"Oh, of course we didn't mind. We were rich. Different if we'd been poor. Anyway, he didn't come and see you, or Giselle for that matter. So, when she'd recovered, we stayed in New York for a bit and then decided to come down here for a vacation."

"We liked it so much, we bought this house."

"And we've been here ever since."

There was a silence for a few moments and then Olga said, "I'm dreadfully sorry." She stared, frowning, at her plate.

"What are you sorry for?" said Orson.

"For barging in on you like this. I mean, I only did it because I thought one of you was—well—you know—"

"Your father?" offered Lewis, gently.

"Yes. I had the idea that being so closely related gave me some rights of passage. Some sort of entrée which couldn't be refused. As though I was owed something, if you see what I mean?"

"We see," said Lewis.

"And now I find that you don't owe me a thing, do you? If anything, I owe you, don't I?"

"A new shirt would be nice," said Lewis.

"You've been awfully kind. Thank you so much." Olga got up awkwardly.

"Where are you going?" said Orson. "We haven't finished our lunch yet."

"We ought to get back to the hotel. I'm sure you've had enough of us."

"Stop!" shouted Orson and Olga jumped at the violence in his voice. "Stop," he said again, more quietly this time. He pointed to her chair. "Sit down. You can't go anywhere. You must stay here now. We can't have you rushing off just because we're not your father. We're still involved. You're Giselle's daughter, for Chrissake and this creature here is Giselle's granddaughter and what do you suppose the old girl would say if we let you disappear again?"

"The old girl let her disappear without any qualms before," said Amanda.

"You shut up, creature," said Orson. "I'm not talking to you. No, no. You're both staying here. Olga shall have Zeboiim and the creature shall have Gomorrah and Michael shall be in Sodom, which hasn't got a bathroom but Michael won't mind that because he's a gentleman. And being a gentleman, he also won't mind taking you to your hotel and helping you pack everything up and bring you back here, will he?"

Michael said that he wouldn't mind at all. Olga tried to protest but Orson overwhelmed her objections and Amanda said, "Come on, it'll be fine. They want us."

Quietly—and unnoticed—Freddy began to clear the things from the dining table and, by the time Michael brought the car from the garage to the front door and loaded Olga and Amanda into the back seat, he had disappeared with the trolley into the kitchen.

Orson and Lewis stood in the front door and waved until the car drove out of sight. Then Orson said, "I'm tired. Going to have a nap," and he limped away up the stairs. Lewis wandered back through the house and went out onto the terrace. He lay on a lounger in the shade and stared up at the fronds of the big palm tree.

Getting Giselle back from Finlay had been such fun, he remembered. Mostly because it was easy but also because they'd all laughed so much—and with the callousness of youth. How cruel they'd been.

Their cruelty was born from recklessness and their recklessness was born from spending two years in each other's company and vying with each other in causing scenes. They were defiant years. They lived in the flat at Cadogan Square. They went everywhere together—to parties and first nights and gallery openings, always arm-in-arm, Orson in one of his big black hats, Lewis impeccable in tailored suits (the waistcoats had four pockets)—becoming a couple famous for the closeness of their friendship, to the point of scandal and, sometimes, well beyond. The fact that nothing sexual was going on between them (and that the rest of the world thought that there was) was a source of endless amusement to them and they played up to their reputation shamelessly. The more they played, the more notorious they became; and, with notoriety, came great success too. Dicky Appleton's friend took Orson into his patronage and Orson's paintings and drawings began to sell as fast as he could execute them; Lewis joined the prestigious Tolly Utteridge Agency and wrote three more plays and two musicals and they were all hits. It was, they later agreed, a desperate, giddy, golden time. They radiated a febrile happiness and were miserable as hell.

The newspapers loved them both and wrote stories about them at least once a week and Lewis and Orson each privately hoped that Giselle was reading the stories and understanding how wonderfully happy they both were without her. In fact, Giselle rarely read anything about them because she and Finlay were in New York, where the stories of Lewis and Orson's escapades were of less interest. Finlay was in New York because the American producers of *View Hollow* had asked that he recreate the show on Broadway, with Muriel Gaspeard and Neville Starkey reprising their roles. Finlay accepted and he and Giselle sailed over within a week.

View Hollow was as big a hit on Broadway as it had been in the West End and Finlay was in vogue. He was asked to direct several other plays, so he and Giselle took a duplex on Fifty Seventh Street and began to bask in some of the same kind of glory—albeit the American version—that Lewis and Orson were enjoying in London.

A month before the end of the two years, Lewis said to Orson, "Have you actually been to bed with anybody in the last twenty three months?"

They were having a late breakfast in the kitchen and Orson was wearing his paint spattered dressing gown from the Paris days. Orson put down his coffee cup and stared at the ceiling.

"Do you know, I haven't. I haven't been to bed with anybody."

"Don't you think that's remarkable?"

"Goddam peculiar, if you ask me. Oh, wait. There was that one from the gallery—that odd girl—"

"The one who thinks you're Seurat reborn?"

"Yes—but I don't count her. I mean, we never even lay down. We never sat down either, come to think of it."

"Not knee-tremblers in some alley?"

"Not always in an alley, no."

"I haven't either, you know."

"No? What about Misha?"

"I haven't seen Misha in ages. He got a bit funny."

"You don't think he was a bit funny to begin with?"

"Oh, hilarious, yes."

They drank some more coffee in companionable silence, each wondering if the other was thinking along the same sort of lines. Lewis broke first.

"I think it's time, don't you?"

"I think so, yes. It's been quite long enough."

"Too long, really. We shouldn't have let her get away with it in the first place."

"Too goddam true."

Lewis thought for a moment and then said, "We might pop over to New York and see how the show's doing. See old Muriel and old Neville. See how their marriage is getting along. Give them helpful advice if it isn't. That sort of thing."

"And, along the way, we might drop in on young Finlay. See his apartment."

"His books."

"His pictures."

"His little friend."

"Mm."

Lewis and Orson booked a first class cabin on the S.S. Berengaria. Half way across the Atlantic—and sitting huddled under tartan rugs high on the promenade deck—Orson said, "How are we going to arrange this, exactly?"

"Arrange what?"

"Well, the situation. I mean, we can't both have her, you know. Of course, if you've entirely made up your mind to be a queer, then there's no problem."

"Well, I haven't. At least, I don't think I have."

"Maybe a decision could be reached before we pass Ellis Island?"

"I wish it was that easy, Ossie."

Orson shifted under his blanket. "Perhaps you're nothing any more? Neither one nor the other? I mean, if you haven't been with anybody in two years?"

"I don't think so. I've missed it, you see."

Orson cleared his throat. "The thing is, if we're going to live together—all three of us—well, we can't *both* have her in that way, can we?"

"Well, not at the same time, I don't think. Unless we stick to the other way."

"What other way is that? Jesus, you don't mean—"

"The platonic way, Ossie."

"Oh, the *platonic* way. Don't be dumb, Lewis."

They sat and watched the ocean slide past. Then Lewis said, "What I think we ought to do is have a pact. I think we ought to agree that neither of us has anything to do with her in *that* way until we decide on a number of things."

"What sort of things?"

"Where we're all going to live, for one."

"We *are* all going to live together, then?"

"Oh yes. I think so. Don't you?"

"Oh, sure."

"You agree to the pact?"

"I certainly do. The pact is a must."

They stayed at the Algonquin Hotel. On their second night, they went to see *View Hollow*. They sat in house seats in the stalls and, by the interval, Lewis was fidgeting. They went to the bar and had drinks and Lewis said, "What is Muriel doing, I'd like to know?"

"Seems all right to me. Neville seems kind of dull, though."

Lewis shook his head. "He's just bored—but Muriel is demented. All that girlish laughter and lifting one leg every time she kisses him. Honestly, I'd like to wring her neck."

"Shouldn't Finlay be doing something about this? He's the director."

"Yes, he should—but he isn't. Obviously too busy to bother."

Orson swallowed some gin. "What do you think we ought to do about it?"

"Well, we shall have to go and see him. Put him right, I think." Lewis downed the rest of his drink and smiled balefully. "Now is as good a time as any. I don't know about you but I've seen enough of this travesty."

"Yeah, well—I never cared much for it in the first place."

They took a taxi to 57th Street. The apartment building was very tall and Lewis and Orson stood on the sidewalk and craned their heads backwards and stared up at the dark façade.

"How very high it is," said Lewis. "Very high indeed."

"And they're on the very tippytop," said Orson. "Among the clouds."

"With the angels."

A maid answered the door and, when she seemed unsure about letting them in, Orson said, "It's all right, honey lamb, we're expected," and he swept past her with Lewis tucked in behind and riding his slipstream. There was a babble of voices down the end of a passage and Orson headed for the sound. They came into an open area, half living room, half dining room. There were six people in the dining area, all in evening dress, sitting round a table and all six heads turned as Orson and Lewis burst in. Orson stopped so suddenly that Lewis bumped into him.

"Hello," said Orson. "What have we got here?"

Giselle was at the head of the table and she said, "Oh God," and buried her face in her hands. Finlay was at the other end of the table and he got up hurriedly from his chair and came towards Orson and Lewis. He still carried his napkin and Orson saw that his face was red.

Finlay said, "Good Lord. Hello, ducks. How simply marvelous. Where—um—where have you sprung from?"

"We've been to the play," said Lewis, darkly.

"Have you? Marvelous." Finlay looked at his watch. "But, surely it hasn't finished yet, has it?"

"It has for us," said Lewis. "May we please have a drink?"

"And something to eat," said Orson. He stared wolfishly at the table.

Finlay introduced them to the guests. Lewis was pleased that Finlay managed it awkwardly, with lots of little embarrassed laughs and stammers and with more effusiveness than was necessary. Giselle kept her eyes lowered and said nothing.

The guests were two American couples. Lewis gathered they had something to do with Finlay's latest theatrical project. One of the men was a producer and the other was a lawyer. Their wives looked like sisters and Lewis forgot all their names as soon as Finlay announced them and, when both couples began to enthuse about *View Hollow*, Lewis said, "Ah, but have you seen it recently?"—and he glared at Finlay from under his eyebrows.

There was no room at the table, so Orson and Lewis sat in the living area, on a sofa and the maid brought them plates of food and glasses of wine and they ate from their laps. They had their backs to the dining area and they could hear the conversation resume round the table. It sounded satisfactorily stilted and artificial.

When they'd finished their food, they both turned round and stared over the back of the sofa. Finlay was nearest to them, facing the other way and they could see past his shoulder clear down the length of the table to where Giselle was sitting. They hunkered down, so that only their eyes and the tops of their heads could be seen and they stared, unblinking at Giselle. She frowned at them fiercely and shook her head but they went on staring, their eyes so wide that they looked a little mad. Giselle's mouth twitched at the corners.

"Got her," whispered Lewis.

When the maid brought in the coffee, everybody left the table and joined Lewis and Orson in the living room. Lewis and Orson became affable and expansive, steering the conversation their way until they had silenced everybody else. Lewis started telling them a sad story about a golden retriever he'd once had that had been run over in St. John's

Wood by a number seventy four bus and Orson punctuated the tragedy
with a strange, braying laugh.

"And then," said Lewis, in a low, quivering voice, "and then, those soft
brown eyes clouded over and, with his last ounce of strength, he placed
his right paw trustingly in my hand, sighed deeply and, I may say, even
contentedly—and then went quietly sleep."

"Haw, haw, haw," said Orson.

"How awful sad," said one of the wives, her eyes filled with tears.

"Yes. But that isn't the end of the story," said Lewis.

"Yes it is," said Giselle.

"No—you see, he visited me that night."

"No!" said the wife, her hand to her mouth.

Lewis nodded gravely. "I woke up—it was well past midnight—and
he was there. Sitting on the end of the bed. Spectrally and without
weight—but it was him. There was a nobility about him, a sort of
radiance that filled the room."

"Haw, haw, haw."

"And then—then he spoke to me."

"He spoke to you?" gasped the wife.

"Well, not in words," said Lewis, kindly. "Dogs can't speak, you see.
No, he spoke to me on the astral plane. His thoughts projected into my
consciousness, so that I understood him with extraordinary clarity.
Would you like to know what he said to me?"

"No, we wouldn't," said Giselle.

"He said to me—'Master, banish sorrow and never weep for me, for
I am in a better place.' Isn't that beautiful?"

"Haw, haw, haw."

"I didn't know you had a dog," said Finlay.

"Oh yes," said Lewis. "His name was Bimky."

"Binky?" said Finlay.

"No. *Bimky*—with an M. One wouldn't call a dog *Binky*, surely?"

The other wife began, "We have a labrador—"

"Bimky could do tricks," said Lewis. "He could sit and lie down and roll over and play dead and fetch and carry and I was teaching him to ride a motorcycle when the accident occurred. Pillion, of course. Without an opposing thumb, he couldn't get the hang of the clutch. In time, perhaps, he might have mastered it. But time was the one element he didn't have. Time and a working thumb. Sometimes God can be so cruel."

"Our labrador is great with kids—"

"Bimky was too. I miss him so much. Please, let's not talk of dogs any more."

"Haw, haw, haw."

Giselle put her coffee cup down on the low table in front of her and, for the second time that evening, she buried her face in her hands—but now her shoulders were heaving up and down and muffled, choking sounds were coming from between her fingers. The wife with the labrador put her arm round Giselle's shoulders and gave them a squeeze.

"I know, honey," she said. "They all go sometime, though. Our labrador—"

"I knew a man who went to Labrador," said Orson. "He came back though. Said he didn't like the place at all. Hellish dark and nowhere to sit, he said."

"If we must talk about dogs," said Lewis, brightening up, "isn't it interesting that they are all, without exception, named after places? The Alsatian, the Dalmatian, the French Poodle, the Boston Terrier—"

"The Pekinese," said Orson, helpfully.

"The Chihuahua—"

"Don't forget the Dachshund."

"Yes, him too. Named after a charming town in Westphalia. Orson and I were there only last year."

The lawyer leaned forward. "Surely dachshund means badger hound? I read that somewhere—*dachs* means badger in German."

"Certainly," said Orson, coldly. "Badger hound is correct. Which happens to be the name of a town in Westphalia. Nothing funny about that. I myself am from Buffalo and Lewis was born in a small village in the North of England called Ramsbottom Green."

"You have to go now," said Giselle, raising her head and glaring at Lewis and Orson. "You absolutely have to go this minute, or I shall scream."

"I shouldn't like that," said Lewis. "Would you, Orson?"

"Not in the least," said Orson. "It might bring on my neuralgia."

"It was lovely seeing you both," said Finlay, getting up.

"And it was lovely seeing you," said Lewis. "Lovely seeing all of you. And if anybody here would like to see more of Orson and me, we are staying at the Algonquin Hotel."

"Room 402, to be precise," said Orson. "And now, Lewis, we must go. Goodbye."

They shook hands with everybody except Giselle, whom they ignored. Then they let Finlay escort them to the front door.

"What lovely friends," murmured Lewis. "You're so lucky."

He patted Finlay gently on the cheek and then he took Orson's arm and walked out into the corridor. Finlay called out, "Cheerio, then," and they waved and Finlay closed the door.

Lewis turned to Orson. "How long, do you think?"

Orson looked at his watch. "A couple of hours, I imagine. Can you wait that long?"

"Oh, yes. We've waited two years, after all. Two hours more won't make much difference."

They took a taxi back to the Algonquin and sat in their room and waited and, three hours later, Giselle knocked on the door. Orson opened the door and said, "You're late."

Giselle said, "And you're pigs. Both of you. For God's sake, give me a drink." She was shaking and tears were running down her face. Orson and Lewis didn't know whether the shaking and the tears were from laughter or grief. Later, they decided, it had been a bit of both.

Chapter 9

The house was awfully quiet. Freddy had popped his head out of the door that separated the domestic quarters from the rest of the house and nobody seemed to be around. He wondered what he ought to do. He'd finished all the clearing up of the lunch. He'd washed everything by hand—they didn't have a dishwasher but then, neither did he back at Dollis Hill—and put it all away. He'd even cleaned out the drawers where the things went and that had been a bit of a chore and no mistake. Still, it was lovely when it was done, although he didn't believe anybody would ever actually notice. Somehow, he couldn't imagine either Sir Lewis or Mr. Woodley bothering themselves with whether the kitchen drawers were clean.

The domestic quarters were quite big. There was the kitchen of course and the pantry, where Bella seemed to have dumped all the really nice things they had. There were dusty vases stuck up on high shelves in there and lots of mismatched china, some of it quite lovely, too. Then there was a kind of scullery next to the kitchen, with a washing machine and a dryer and a marvelous old porcelain sink for scrubbing vegetables and, beyond that there was a little room with brooms and mops—the mops were of a very inferior quality—and buckets and dusters and aerosols of cleaning things and a battered old Hoover.

"You've seen better days, dear," said Freddy to the Hoover. "Due for retirement, you are."

He wandered back along the dark corridor to the bedroom, which still smelt strongly of patchouli. It was a nice room, with a little window that looked off to the side of the house. Freddy peered through it and saw three palm trees and a patch of blue far below.

"Oh I do like to be beside the seaside, oh I do like to be beside the sea—" He couldn't remember any more. It was funny that—how you could always remember the first bits but never what came after.

Quite suddenly, he felt tired. It had been a long day in terms of excitement. Back at the Park Place he could keep going all day and half the night and, quite often, he'd had to; but things never got very exciting at the Park Place and, if they did, you rather wished they hadn't, so excitement was something he wasn't used to and this day had certainly taken its toll. The bed looked comfy. There was a fat eiderdown covering it and two fat pillows as well. A bit of a kip wouldn't come amiss. A bit of a loll in the arms of Morpheus, a bit of a trip to the Land of Nod.

Freddy lay down. It was ever so soft, this bed. Poor old Bella didn't know what she was missing. Well, she did—of course she did—she'd been sleeping here, hadn't she? It still smelt of the patchouli scent. But she wasn't going to sleep here any more and that was her loss and Freddy's gain.

Freddy closed his eyes. Half an hour and he'd be as right as rain.

When Michael came back from the Regency Hotel, with Olga and Amanda and their three suitcases, they found Lewis asleep on his lounger on the terrace and no sign of Orson anywhere.

"He's probably asleep too," said Michael. "He usually is about this time of day."

"I'm a little tired myself," Olga said and Michael was instantly solicitous. He carried their suitcases up the stairs and Olga and Amanda followed him. They tiptoed past Orson's door and heard the sound of snoring. Michael made sure they were settled in their rooms and then asked Amanda if she'd like to go swimming and Amanda replied that she thought perhaps she would—and quite soon, she and Michael went off to the beach together. As they left, with whispered good-byes at Olga's door, Amanda's wrap fell open and Olga saw that she was wearing the yellow bikini again.

The Zeboiim room was pretty. It was at the end of the passage and had windows in two walls, one overlooking the terrace and the other the beach far below. For a few moments, Olga watched as Michael and Amanda threaded their way along the path that led steeply downwards. When they disappeared from sight, she looked straight down and saw Lewis stretched out on the lounger. He was shaded by a big tree of some sort and a straw hat was over his face. Olga felt her tiredness grow, so she lay down on the bed and was soon asleep.

Amanda decided that Michael's body was even more beautiful than his face. He looked chiseled, as if carved from some warm, brown marble. All Americans were like that, she thought. They took so much more interest in their physiques than the British; of course, sometimes the results were ludicrous and their bodies looked like socks with bowling balls stuffed inside but Michael had known when to stop. She wished they could get out of the water and sit on the beach so that she could look at him a bit more.

"I'm cold," she lied.

They walked up the beach and sat under a palm tree and Amanda stared openly at Michael, looking him up and down.

"You are fucking *gorgeous*," she said.

"So are you."

Amanda let a decent interval pass to allow the compliments breathing room. Then she said, "Are you available at the moment?"

"Yup."

"Well, well. How about that? So am I."

There was another silence between them for a few moments and then Michael said, "That's cool."

"Yes, it is. But—"

"Oh, there's a but, is there?"

"Yes. But—we won't do anything about it for a while."

"Is that right?"

"Yes. I don't believe in holiday romances. It's like buying a bottle of that really nice wine you've been drinking every evening in the taverna on Mikonos and then taking it home and finding out that, back in Fulham, it's turned into cat's piss."

"You think I could be cat's piss?"

"There's always that possibility."

"OK." Michael said, cheerfully. Then he lay back on the sand and closed his eyes and Amanda stared at him again and thought if this is cat's piss then I'm a monkey's uncle.

Freddy woke with a start, not understanding for a few seconds where he was. Then he remembered and looked at his watch. Ooh, lord—he'd been asleep for hours and whatever would everybody think? He swung his legs off the bed and scurried out of the room and along the corridor to the door. He opened it a crack and peeked out into the living room. Nobody was there. He listened for a moment; the house was quiet and he wondered where everybody had got to? It was a bit of a puzzle what to do, really. Should he go or should he stay—if he went, he really ought to say goodbye and how could he say goodbye if there was nobody to say goodbye to? Equally, if he stayed, then he really ought to make himself useful and how could you be useful if there was nobody around to be useful to? A bit of a dilemma, really. He closed the door and thought for a moment, deciding at last that he would stay—if only to find the opportunity to say his thank yous. Meanwhile, surely there was something he could be busy with? He went back to the kitchen and looked around. The windows could do with a wash. There was more muck than glass and enough dead flies lying at the bottoms of the frames to feed a swamp full of frogs. Well, he'd make short work of them.

Some sort of instinctive, internal clock must have chimed at the same moment for everybody, because at five o'clock that evening, there was a general movement in the house and, within twenty minutes, they were all gathered in the living room.

"Settled in all right?" said Orson. He had changed into a pair of baggy blue Basque fisherman's trousers and a patched and darned denim shirt, untucked, that flowed over his stomach.

"Would anybody like a drink?" said Lewis.

Freddy, his ear pressed to the panel of the door, heard his cue. He pushed open the door with his trolley and then wheeled it—almost at a run—towards the knot of people standing in the well.

"A little alcoholic refreshment," he called gaily. "And there's soft for those who don't indulge."

"You're very good," said Orson. "How do you time things so cleverly?"

"I was listening at the door, Mr. Woodley, sir. It always pays, I find."

He served everybody and then stood attentively beside the trolley and pretended not to listen to the conversation and, so polished was his talent for behaving exactly as a good servant should that, quite soon, everybody began to treat him like one, which was fine as far as Freddy was concerned because, while he'd been behind the door waiting for something to happen, an idea had germinated in his head and he was toying with the thought of letting it sprout.

It was the same idea that had occurred to him when he'd got so fed up with trying to get dancing jobs all those years ago and, that time, he'd ended up at the Park Place Hotel—and, while the Park Place Hotel was lovely and he liked working there, perhaps it was time for a move. Pastures new.

So Freddy dropped all pretense of being on the same footing as the others and called everybody Sir or Madam or Miss and was painfully deferential and, within minutes, the old trick had worked and everybody stopped noticing him and the conversation swirled about him but never quite came into contact unless it was to ask him for something, which Orson did the most, since he seemed to have elected himself chief host for the evening.

Freddy's only worry was dinner; there wasn't any food in the house, they'd finished it all at lunch and he hoped nobody was expecting him to produce something out of thin air—but then Lewis said that they would all go out to dinner at a restaurant down the road, so that particular worry was out of the way and Freddy sighed with relief and collected all the glasses and quietly wheeled his trolley out through the door before anybody had to deal with the embarrassing question about whether or not to ask Freddy to come to the restaurant with them.

They were getting into the car when Olga said, "What about the little man?"

Amanda said, "Oh, yes, we can't leave him behind."

"Yes we can," said Lewis.

"But he might steal everything," said Orson.

"He won't," said Lewis, with an air of such quiet confidence that nobody felt the need to take it any further.

Freddy heard the car drive away and he smiled to himself. Now he could have a good poke about the place, see what was what and get a general picture of the set up. Then, if he liked what he saw—and so far everything had been right up his street—then he'd know that his idea had merit and he could move on to the next phase of the operation. It was rather exciting, all this information gathering. Like a James Bond film. Sort of.

The restaurant turned out to be a small room with four tables. There were two framed photographs on the wall. One was of Lewis and the other was of Orson, both taken when they were much younger and posed in the photographic style of the early fifties. The owner of the restaurant, a small, gray-haired woman with a strong French accent, greeted Lewis and Orson like favorite nephews and served them all with the only dish the restaurant seemed to offer, which was a herb omelet. Orson ate all of his and most of Amanda's.

Michael was talking to Lewis. "I don't suppose there's any point pushing you with this, is there?"

"Pushing me with what?"

"With this idea of going over for your musical revival. It's a big deal and they're making a terrific splash with it and I know they'd all consider it a blast if you came."

"A blast being a good thing?"

"But I guess with the whole Finlay Ferguson business, you won't even consider it."

Lewis put his fork down and patted his mouth with a paper napkin.

"Well, you know, I just might, young Michael. How important is it to *you* that I go?"

"Tolly thinks if anybody could pull it off, I could. It would be kinda neat if I did."

"Neat, eh? For whom, neat? For Tolly, and his reputation with the lord? For Tolly, to get one up on his London colleague, who failed so miserably with me? For the horrible lord, and his reputation in the Theater? For you, and your reputation with Tolly and the horrible lord—and perhaps to show London how things are done?"

"All of that."

"Oh, my—put like that, how can I refuse?"

That, thought Michael, had been too easy. Lewis had turned them down before, flatly and with no room for argument. There was almost certainly a condition to be attached.

"The thing is," said Lewis, very quietly, "I wonder if we can persuade those two to come with us?" He jerked his chin towards Olga and Amanda, who were busy at the other end of the table, talking to Orson. "It would mean breaking their holiday, of course. But then, afterward, we could all come back here again, couldn't we?"

"But I've only got three tickets—for you, Orson and me."

"You're being uncharacteristically slow, Michael. Of course it would mean getting two more tickets. There and back. I'll tell you what—if you can persuade them—and Finlay, of course—then I'll do it. I leave it to you. I'm sure you'll have no difficulty persuading the girl so I suggest you start there."

"Let me get this straight. You want Lord Ferguson to pay their fares?"

"Of course I do. I suggest you get your London office to organize it. What's his name?"

"Julian."

"Julian. Give him something to do. All we'll need are two more round trip tickets, first class of course. Simplicity itself."

Later, when they got back to the house, Michael drew Amanda aside and told her what Lewis wanted.

"Will you be there?" asked Amanda.

"Every second. I'm like a permanent fixture on this."

"Why do you think he wants us to go to this do?"

"I have no idea."

"Yes, you do. You've got a very good idea because I have the same one. I think he wants to see Finlay Ferguson's face when he introduces us to him."

"I guess you're right. Does that mean you won't come?"

"Hell no—of course I'll come. I want to see his face too.'

"How about your mother?"

"Leave her to me."

When Olga went upstairs to bed, Amanda followed her into her room. They sat on the end of the bed together and Amanda said, "What do you think?"

"About what?"

"About today."

Olga shook her head. "I don't know. I'm a bit numb, if you want the truth. It's been a series of shocks, hasn't it?"

"What do you think about the Finlay Ferguson business?"

"Well, that's the biggest shock of all. That awful man."

"We don't know he's so awful. Personally, I mean. He's just awful on television. He might be lovely in real life."

"He wasn't lovely to Giselle, was he?"

"She wasn't lovely to him, either. Do you want to meet him?"

Olga was silent for so long that Amanda stopped staring at her shoes and turned sideways to look at her mother. Then Olga took a deep breath and let it out in a sigh. She said, "I don't know. Perhaps. Or not. I don't get the impression he'd be very interested, do you?"

"Maybe he ought to be *made* to be interested."

"Maybe. Why? Do you think I ought to meet him?"

Amanda told her what Michael had said and, at the end of it Olga, whose eyes had become very round, said in a disbelieving whisper, "Lewis wouldn't do that, surely?"

"I think he would."

"Well, if he's going to do that, then forget it. I couldn't possibly cope with that."

Amanda patted Olga's knee. "I don't see why," she said. "You coped this morning beautifully. All on your own, too."

"I think you only get that sort of courage once in your lifetime," Olga said. "I don't think I could muster it again."

"At least think about it. And then, we can all come back here afterwards and have a proper holiday. I'm rather taken with these two old buggers."

"I thought you were rather taken with the young bugger?"

"Him too."

Amanda left Zeboiim with Olga's promise that she would, indeed, think about it. When she got to her room, Amanda found, on her pillow, a small spray of purple bougainvillea and a foil-wrapped chocolate biscuit.

Chapter 10

Freddy had found the chocolate biscuits in a cupboard in the pantry. The packet looked a bit old but it was unopened and the one that Freddy tasted was fine, so he ate three more and then wrapped up five of them in aluminum foil. Then he went out into the garden with a pair of kitchen scissors and clipped some bougainvillea, five little sprays in all and then came back inside and went round all the bedrooms and left his contributions on the pillows. There was one room that he missed out, because it was obvious that nobody was actually sleeping there, although there were clothes in the wardrobe. He looked through the dresses, fingering the materials. There was some lovely stuff here. It must have been Miss Palliser's room, Freddy decided and they'd left it just as it was, which was ever so sad, really. Miss Palliser had had lovely taste, that was obvious.

Downstairs, on the piano, were lots of photographs in silver frames and Freddy looked at them for a long time. Some of them were yellow with age. The people in the photographs were mostly ever so famous. There was one signed by the Duke and Duchess of Windsor—the Duke looking depressed as always and who could blame the silly old dear? Then there was one with Sir Lewis and Mr. Woodley, looking young in bathing suits with tops to them, standing in shallow water on some beach, with Giselle Palliser cuddled between them. Pablo Picasso's grinning chimpanzee face was clamped between her knees. All four were looking into the camera lens and smiling away, as happy as larks they must have been. There was one with all of them round a restaurant table with Ronald Colman and Hedy Lamarr, and a real old studio portrait of Neville Starkey and Muriel Gaspeard, both with cigarettes held stiffly in straight fingers, the smoke curling up dramatically round their heavily made up faces. There was a newer looking photo of Lewis and Orson and Giselle, in fantastically feathered masks that half concealed their faces; they were gathered, like three alien birds of prey, round the diminutive form of a beaming Truman Capote—and there were lots of other pictures, too, with people Freddy didn't recognize, although that didn't stop their glamour simply tap dancing out of the frames at him.

He looked at his watch. It was getting on and there were still things to be done. There was no telling what time they'd all be back. He didn't want to be caught idling here, wandering about the place like some sort of intruder. That wouldn't make a good impression at all. He hurried now, trotting to the laundry room with the little bit of washing that seemed necessary and, when the wash cycle was over, he put the stuff in the dryer and switched *that* on and, when that was finished, he folded the things and put them on the end of Mr. Woodley's bed where he'd be sure to find them.

He looked at his watch again. Definitely time for his marching orders. He picked up the telephone and called the Vacation Inn and, when the operator answered, Freddy asked for a taxi to collect him from Gladstones—and he asked in just the right sort of polite but imperious way that he'd seen and heard so many others do, that a most deferential Hall Porter found himself promising a taxi at Gladstones within twenty minutes. Freddy said 'thank you' in his grandest voice. Then he put the receiver down and went quickly round the living room, smoothing cushions and straightening magazines and generally making the place look tidy. He tried various combinations of lighting until he found one that gave the right sort of impression—money-saving and burglar-repelling but welcoming all the same. Then he took a last look round, slipped out of the front door and pulled it shut behind him. He began to walk down the dark drive and, quite soon, heard the sound of one of the island taxis laboring up the hairpin bends. He waved it down and got in and the driver, who didn't look at all like a pirate this time, turned the taxi round and drove back down the hill.

Miss Wilkes arrived, ever punctual, on the doorstep of her office at nine o'clock the next morning and found a small man, with a pinched face and an ingratiating manner, waiting for her outside on the pavement.

Miss Wilkes nodded politely to him and the man nodded back, looking at her sideways. He seemed a little nervous, she thought.

"Are you the employment agency?" asked the man and Miss Wilkes thought she caught a hint of North Country—perhaps Yorkshire, she couldn't be sure but it was nice to hear an accent from home. Before she could answer, the man said, "I mean, are you the only one on Saint Marta's? Because I asked and they thought you were. The only one, I mean."

Miss Wilkes thought that he sounded eager that she should be the only one and, since she was, she said, gaily, "Oh, yes. The only one. Well, there's not a great deal of call for two, you see."

She led him into the office and sat him down and then took out a Personal Information sheet from the drawer.

"Frederick Millsap," said the man, before she had time to ask and they shook hands across Miss Wilkes' desk. "I'd like to be on your books," he said, taking off his straw hat and putting it on his knees.

"Well, I'm sure that can be managed, Mr. Millsap. What do you do?"

"What do I not do? I do everything. Everything. I cook, I clean, I wash, I buttle, I valet. Everything. Polish silver, drive a car, hum a tune, dance a jig—um—everything."

Miss Wilkes sat up a little straighter and looked at Freddy with dawning respect. She hadn't come across this sort of wide range of skills—and an obvious enthusiasm to put them to use—in a long time.

This Mr. Millsap could turn out to be her prize client. Or, of course, he could turn out to be completely mad and a danger to all he came into contact with. Either way, he was brightening what had promised to be a dull day. She asked him his qualifications and was impressed when he reeled them off.

"But, why do you want to work over here, Mr. Millsap? I mean, if you have a job at the Park Place—a lovely hotel, I believe—why would you want to leave it?"

Freddy took a deep breath. Here was the risky part—the part that he had no control over. "Well," he said, forcing himself to look Miss Wilkes directly in her eyes—"Well, I wouldn't want to leave at all, in the normal course of events. But it has come to my notice, Miss Wilkes, that there are certain parties on Saint Marta's that might have need of my services, so to speak—and, well, I'm here to offer them. But only, you understand, to those certain parties. I'm not interested in working for anybody else. I'm picky, you see."

Miss Wilkes sighed. Nothing was ever perfect and, if one thought for a minute that it was, then, in another minute, one would find one was wrong. The little man—a bit of a mother's boy if Miss Wilkes hadn't lost her judgement—wanted to pick his employer and that meant he was a snob and would only work for the very best and probably the richest of employers, at a fee that nobody on Saint Marta's could pay, except perhaps Sir Lewis Messenger and Orson Woodley, who were certainly the richest people on the island but also the absolutely worst employers Miss Wilkes had ever come across, which probably was going to cut them out of the picture entirely.

Freddy saw the disappointment flood Miss Wilkes' face, so he said, quickly and with a kind of naked directness that surprised him, "You know that their Miss Bella's gone, don't you?"

"What?" said Miss Wilkes, taken off guard. "Who?"

"Sir Lewis and Mr. Woodley. Their Bella. The big, bla—the big lady. She's gone and doesn't work there any more."

"Really?" said Miss Wilkes. While hardly surprising, the news seemed a little odd to be coming from this man, a complete stranger to the island as far as Miss Wilkes knew, which was quite far, in fact, since Miss Wilkes made it her business to know as much as she could about everything.

"Really," said Freddy. "She upped and left yesterday morning and now they haven't got anybody."

"Really?" said Miss Wilkes again, more faintly this time because it seemed to her that, while the news of Bella's departure, if true, was a disaster, there was also a possibility that this little man was steering himself towards a position at Gladstones and, if that was the case, then Miss Wilkes would proclaim this day a national holiday and break out the flags, because over all the years she had run her agency, she had also run through all the local domestic servants who were prepared to work there. Bella had been the last of them and was, Miss Wilkes admitted to herself, of rather low grade material—but Bella had lasted for several months longer than anybody else and Miss Wilkes had dared to hope that she wouldn't be hearing from Gladstones in the near future.

"I was up there yesterday," said Freddy, importantly. "I happened to be passing and, having some personal connection with Sir Lewis—many years ago now but sufficient to warrant a quick yoohoo, as it were—I popped my head round the door and quite swiftly determined that all was not well on the domestic front. I believe Mr. Woodley, in a tizzy at the time, uttered a few unkind words to Bella and she took umbrage and left them flat, not to mention high and dry."

"Oh dear," said Miss Wilkes.

"Oh dear is right, Miss Wilkes. Those two can't be left on their own for a minute. Helpless, they are, like newborn kittens."

Anything less like newborn kittens than Sir Lewis Messenger and Orson Woodley, Miss Wilkes couldn't imagine but the possibility that this little man—who was certainly aware of at least one of the problems of working at Gladstones—actually *wanted* employment there, gave her heart a lift. She nodded, suppressing the desire to shout hallelujah, and said, "Well, they're not the easiest of employers, you know."

"Hoo—I should coco," said Freddy. He winked and tapped the side of his nose with his forefinger and Miss Wilkes wondered what he meant.

"Mr. Woodley can be a little—ah—abrasive at times," she said.

"Like a nail file?" said Freddy and, when Miss Wilkes raised her eyebrows and tilted her head to one side and put on a winsome smile— a smile that said a nail file wasn't the half of it—Freddy nodded slowly and said in his most serious voice, "Miss Wilkes, nail files I can cope with. Sticks and stones may break my bones but words just roll off my back like water off a rhino's hide. Anyway, I've got Mr. Woodley's number, I have. He's a teensy bit of a bully, is our Mr. Woodley, when he's not being a cuddly teddy bear and, if you know that, then he can't hurt you. Besides, I can give as good as I get, Miss Wilkes. Don't you worry about me."

There was one more point to be raised here, thought Miss Wilkes and it was a sensitive one. She cleared her throat.

"Well, Mr. Millsap, I must say this is all very interesting and, if everything works out then I'm sure it will—well—work *out*, ha ha, very well. But I have to put to you the thought that, while you may be quite keen to work for Sir Lewis and Mr. Woodley, how can you be quite so certain that Sir Lewis and Mr. Woodley will be equally keen to employ you?" Miss Wilkes face became a little pink and she wondered if perhaps she had put it too bluntly but Freddy smiled confidently and said, "I think I can safely assure you, Miss Wilkes, that Sir Lewis will certainly welcome the opportunity to take me on board, as it were. I can't be so sure about Mr. Woodley but, after all, Miss Wilkes, who else is there? I ask you—who else is there?"

"What about a work permit?" said Miss Wilkes, wondering why, when faced with what appeared to be some sort of paragon, she was finding it necessary to bring up these small difficulties.

"I don't have one, Miss Wilkes but, for the moment, that won't matter."

"It won't?" said Miss Wilkes, meekly.

"No, Miss Wilkes—because, you see, I'd like to offer my services on a trial basis, as it were, free of charge. For let's say, a week."

"Oh my goodness," said Miss Wilkes, clutching the base of her neck.

"If they want to keep me on after that—and they will—then I'm quite sure Sir Lewis and Mr. Woodley will be able to obtain all the necessary paperwork, on my behalf, as it were. Would that, do you think, be agreeable?"

Not only was it agreeable, thought Miss Wilkes, it was unheard of in her experience. For a moment she was too flustered to speak. Then she gathered herself together and gave Freddy one of her pretty smiles. "Well, we shall just have to see, won't we, Mr. Millsap?"

Miss Wilkes bent her head away from the paragon and asked her questions with her eyes averted, filling out the rest of the form in her small, neat handwriting and, when she was finished she shook Freddy's hand and said, in her business voice, "We shall be in touch, Mr. Millsap."

Freddy looked quickly at his watch. He could hang about, waiting for the phone call that he was sure would come but he didn't think Miss Wilkes would like that, so he smiled his thanks and put his hat back on his head and sidled out of the door and into the hot street outside. When he got back to the Vacation Inn—it was a short walk through the town—Freddy went straight to his room and started to pack.

They were all in the kitchen, except Lewis, who had gone to telephone.

"I am pessimistic," he had said, pausing in the doorway. "Deeply pessimistic. I hold out no hope at all."

All they could find to eat in the kitchen was a packet of Rice Krispies. Amanda found some cracked china bowls in a cupboard and a carton of milk in the refrigerator and they sat round the pine table, crunching audibly. After a while, Lewis came back in, looking cheerful.

"A miracle. Miss Wilkes has found us somebody. Only thing is—it's a man."

"What is?" said Orson.

"What Miss Wilkes is sending us. A man."

Orson looked bewildered and Lewis said, "As opposed to a woman, Ossie. We usually have a woman but now we're to have a man, you see."

"I don't want a man," said Orson. "I want that little person who was here yesterday. He put a flower on my pillow and a chocolate cookie next to it. At least, I think it was him." He darted a look at Amanda. "It wasn't you, was it?"

"No. I got them, too."

"Hell of a nice touch, that. Sort of thing you get in hotels. And this morning, my pants are themselves again. Look."

Orson swung sideways in his chair and stuck his legs out in front of him. The worn corduroy draped softly over his knees. "I don't know how he managed it, or when, come to that but I thought I'd never be able to wear them again and here I am, wearing them."

"Oh, the thrill," said Lewis.

"Why can't we have *him*?" said Orson.

"Ossie, don't be silly. We'll take what we can get and what we can get is coming at eleven from Miss Wilkes and all I ask is that you let me do the interviewing because if you do the interviewing, we're snookered."

After the scratch breakfast, Amanda and Michael went down to the beach for a swim. Orson went back to his begonia bed and Olga and Lewis went for a stroll on the terrace.

"Are you going to come?" asked Lewis, leaning on the stone balustrade that curved round the outer perimeter of the terrace. "To London with us?"

"I'm not sure."

"We shall have fun."

"The thing is—"

"What?"

"The thing is, I'm a little nervous about what you're going to do. About Finlay Ferguson."

"Your daddy," said Lewis, grinning like a wolf.

"There, you see? That's what I'm afraid of. You're not going to do that, are you?"

Lewis turned and looked at Olga over his shoulder. "My dear, of course not. All I shall do is make sure you meet him, that's all. The rest is up to you. I just want to be there. See his little face."

Freddy turned up at five minutes before eleven o'clock and rang the doorbell and Lewis opened the door. They stared at each other for a moment—Freddy nervous, his head ducked down and Lewis quizzical, his head thrown back and his gaze sliding down his long nose like a ski jumper—and then Lewis smiled wryly and said, "How funny. I had an idea it might be you. Do come in."

Lewis took Freddy into the kitchen and sat him down at the pine table. Freddy wriggled in his chair. "I'm ever so serious about this, Sir Lewis. It would be the absolute zenith of my career, it really would. The pinnacle, as it were and I can promise you I won't disappoint. Is it something you could live with, Sir Lewis?"

"Well, that depends, Freddy. I think I could, I *think* I could—so long as there weren't any expectations on your part that what happened many, many years ago might ever be repeated, or any idea entertained by you to use the encounter to any sort of advantage, or any belief in your mind that I might have any sort of sentimental attachment towards you. You understand?"

Freddy's face changed and, what was remarkable about the metamorphosis, Lewis thought, was how Freddy's pinched, weaselly little features became somehow dignified and noble. He still looked like Freddy Millsap but he didn't look funny or camp any more; in fact, for a brief moment, Lewis thought he looked a little like a bust of Julius Caesar he'd once seen in the British Museum.

Freddy said, quietly and simply, "I'm not that sort of person, Sir Lewis."

"I'm sure you're not."

"I'm just a great admirer, of both you and Mr. Woodley and nothing would give me greater pleasure than to serve you both. It's what I do, you see."

"I understand."

Freddy dropped his mask of nobility and flashed Lewis a smile. "And Sir Lewis, if you don't like the arrangement after a week, you've only to say so. You can throw me out on my shell-like, no questions asked, no offense taken *and* no money changing hands—and I hope that's amenable on all sides?"

It was, Lewis thought, probably too good to be true. He said, "Can you drive?" and Freddy said that he could, so long as the car wasn't too big or new, because that made him nervous. Lewis took some money out of his pocket and pushed it across the table.

"I wonder if you could organize some food, Freddy? Take the car and go to the shops and stock us up? Could you do that?"

Freddy looked uncertainly at Lewis, his head cocked to one side. "Does that mean you're taking me on, Sir Lewis?"

"Well, I rather think it might, Freddy. If only for your work on Mr. Woodley's trousers, for which we're all profoundly grateful."

The car turned out to be an old Mercedes, with leather upholstery. It was an automatic as well and not too big and Freddy felt grand, sitting in the driver's seat.

Freddy served them a Greek salad for lunch, and they had it out on the terrace. Orson said, "Ah—so you got him, did you, Lewis?" when he saw Freddy setting the table under the old olive tree.

"The other way around, Ossie," said Lewis and Freddy made a funny face and rolled his eyes at the sky. Orson said, "Good, good. Terrific. Is he coming with us? Are you coming with us?"

Freddy looked at Lewis and Lewis said, "No, Ossie, he's not. He's only just got here. Ridiculous to make him go anywhere. No, he can stay and look after things. It'll be only a few days."

"I think he should come," said Orson. "How can we get used to him—and him to us, come to that—if we're not all together? He can look after us."

"We're going to be in an hotel, Ossie. There'll be hordes of people clambering over each other to look after us."

Orson's mouth set in a stubborn line. "I think he should come. I might need him for my pants. I *want* him to come."

Lewis groaned audibly and then caught Freddy's eye and Freddy said, "I'm yours to command, Sir Lewis—Mr. Woodley, sir. Whatever you say. I'm a gypsy at heart."

"I say he comes," said Orson and he pushed a forkful of salad into his mouth so that he wouldn't have to argue the point any more. Lewis, avoiding Olga's eyes, said to Michael, "One more ticket, Michael, if possible," and Michael put down his knife and fork and went off to the small room at the side of the house where Lewis did his writing and telephoned Julian in London.

"There's to be an entourage," he said.

"What do you mean?" Julian's voice sounded querulous and panicky.

"I mean, it's not just Lewis and Orson and me coming. Now it's also three more—two women and Orson's new valet—"

"Wait a minute, wait a minute. How many people in all?"

"Six."

"Six? Oh, good heavens—Lord Ferguson isn't going to like this."

"Do your best, Julian."

"Look—is this Tolly's idea?"

"No, Julian."

"Because, if it is, then Lord Ferguson will put his foot down, I can tell you that for a start. The National Theatre isn't made of money, you know."

"It isn't Tolly's idea, Julian—and the National Theatre is made of money. I shall be waiting by the phone. Call me back as soon as you can."

Fifteen minutes later, Julian called back. "Well, Lord Ferguson is very excited at the thought of Lewis and Orson coming over and is very pleased that our agency has been able to win the day, as it were—and he was prepared to agree to everything but we've hit a problem, I'm afraid. There are no more seats, first class or otherwise, to be had. Everything's full."

"What about a charter?"

"Lord Ferguson is keen, Michael but not that keen. Besides, there would be questions asked by the Board of Governors. No—no charter."

"I don't think they'll come, then."

"Don't do this to me, Michael. I know you're Tolly's man but remember, we're all one agency and what's good for London won't hurt New York."

Lunch was finished when Michael rejoined them. Freddy was serving coffee. Michael sat down next to Lewis and, in a low voice, explained about the tickets.

"There are no more tickets," said Lewis, loudly. "We can't have any more than three. If Olga's to come with us, somebody will have to drop out."

"I don't have to go," said Michael.

"Yes, you do. I need you. There are things to be done."

Olga reddened and stared at the floor and said, "Look, I've been thinking and I really would rather not do this."

"Well, of course, I can't insist you come," said Lewis.

"Well, I want to go," said Amanda.

"I suppose you'll do at a pinch," said Lewis. "We need at least one representative of the Whitehall family and if your mother is adamant–"

"I think I am," said Olga.

There was a silence and then Orson cleared his throat and said, "To be honest, Lewis, I'd just as soon not go. The thought of that plane ride—and God knows I've seen the show before, several times and I don't see much point in seeing it again. I'd rather stay here too, if you don't mind."

"But you said you wanted to go," said Lewis.

"No I didn't. I said, *if* I was going, that I wanted him to come." Orson waved a hand in Freddy's direction. "I never wanted to go at all. So there you are—it's all worked out perfectly well—those who want to go can go and those who don't, needn't. You and the creature and Michael fly off and be glamorous in London and Gloa and me and Whatsisname shall stay behind and do nothing at all. Now, having organized you all, I'm pooped. I'm going to bed."

If Freddy felt any disappointment, he was careful to conceal it; and really, if he thought about it, what did he need to go back for? And where would he stay? Not at Dollis Hill, that was for sure. He couldn't very well be a valet and not stay with his employers and that would have meant being in an hotel and how embarrassing for everybody if the hotel had been the Park Place. On the other hand, staying on at Gladstones and having Mr. Woodley all to himself would mean he could work his magic on him, so that by the time Sir Lewis came back, he'd have Mr. Woodley eating out of his hand and he was well on the way to that already, thanks to an old pair of trousers that ought, by rights, to have been thrown out twenty years ago—and thanks also to a half full plastic bottle of fabric softener that he'd found right at the back of the cupboard in the laundry room.

Chapter 11

Lewis stepped into the center of the terrace, dressed in a dark gray suit with a matching waistcoat. The waistcoat had four pockets. His shirt was white and his tie was dark blue, with small embroidered sea horses all over it. He carried a black Homburg hat in his right hand and an overcoat draped over his left arm and he was sweating—partly from the suit and partly because he had left his packing to the last minute and, with the taxi expected within two hours, he was panicking.

Orson said, "You look like an Armenian carpet salesman."

Lewis began to explain about his anxiety, so Orson hurried away in the direction of the begonia bed. Lewis stood fretfully in the full sunshine and began to cry, "Help—oh, help," in a plaintive and reedy voice. Freddy and Olga reached him at the same moment.

"Oh, thank God," said Lewis, sinking into a lounger and putting his right hand across his eyes. "Santa's little elves are here. I can't find a case, you see. I've got all the shirts and ties and socks and things out but without a case I'm up the creek. I think they're in a cupboard somewhere. I'm not up to finding one, I'm afraid."

Freddy clicked his tongue. "Haven't you even started packing yet, Sir L?"

"No, I haven't. Well, I've piled things on the bed but that's as far as I got. Actually, it's as far as I've ever got. Do please take over, will you?"

Freddy knew where the cases were because he'd spent all his spare time finding out things like that. He and Olga went to a small room near the kitchen which was filled with old luggage. They pulled out a suitcase that looked less battered than the rest and took it to Lewis' bedroom. The bedroom had a small balcony that overlooked the terrace and, during the packing, Olga and Freddy opened the double windows and started coming out onto the balcony, holding a suit or a shirt or selections of ties and Lewis would either nod his approval or shake his head—and then Olga and Freddy would go back into the bedroom and either pack article of clothing in the suitcase or put it back in its drawer.

Freddy did the packing. It was obvious that he was much better at it than Olga—but he left the final choice of ties and socks to Olga and didn't seem to resent her help at all.

"Are we sure it's just three of everything, madam?" he asked.

"That's how long they're there for. Three days."

"Then let's do four of everything, shall we? In case of accidents?"

There was an old shoe box on the bed, obviously placed there by Lewis, for it was squeezed carefully between a pile of handkerchiefs and a fold-up umbrella. The box was bound with Scotch tape—yards of it wrapped round and round the box so that the lid was immovable. More Scotch tape was bound lengthwise round the box, forming an hermetic seal between it and the lid. Olga picked it up. It was heavier than she'd expected. She shook it and there was a rustling sound from inside. She looked enquiringly at Freddy and Freddy peered closely at the box and gave it a little tap and said, "Well, it's not shoes, is it?"

"Do you think we're supposed to pack it?"

"Better ask, madam. When in doubt, spit it out, that's what I always say."

Olga went out onto the balcony. Below her, Orson was limping slowly back onto the terrace, carrying a small wooden basket and Olga waited and watched while he approached Lewis lounger. Orson thrust the basket under Lewis' nose and said, "Look what I found in the begonias."

"What?" said Lewis, his eyes closed.

"Cigarette butts, Lewis. Hundreds of them. She just dropped them out of the window, I suppose and later, when we weren't looking, she went and buried them in the flowerbed."

"And you've only just found them? You've been digging in that bed for weeks."

"They were right at the back."

Orson looked away from Lewis and caught sight of Olga, standing on the balcony. Freddy was peering over her shoulder.

"Hello," he called. "Having fun?"

Olga held up the shoe box. "Do you want this packed? It was on the bed but we're not sure what's in it."

Orson peered upwards and Lewis said, his eyes still closed, "What is it?"

"A shoebox. An old one but we don't think it's got any shoes in it." Olga shook the box vigorously and there was the sound of dry rustling.

"Definitely not shoes," said Freddy.

Lewis sat up with a jerk and grabbed Orson's free hand and Orson sank down onto the lounger next to him. They both stared up at Olga with a look of despair. Olga shook the box again and Lewis winced and looked away. Orson said, "Oh, now look—please don't do that."

"I'm so sorry," said Olga. "Have I broken something?"

"No, no. It was broken ages ago. Only, please don't shake it any more. In fact, please put it down somewhere, would you?"

Orson pulled out a crumpled handkerchief from his trouser pocket and swiped at his eyes and Lewis said, under his breath, "Oh, for God's sake, Orson, no need for that."

Olga said, "What is it? Have I done something terrible?"

"No, you haven't done anything terrible at all," said Lewis. "It's just Giselle, you see."

"Giselle?"

"Yes. Your mother, you know."

"What about her?"

"She's in the box," said Orson.

It was, Olga later told Amanda, all she could do to not let the box fall from her suddenly nerveless fingers but the oddly cinematic image that came to her in that split second—of the shoebox flipping over the balcony, turning end over end as it fell in inevitable slow-motion and then exploding in a cloud of dust when it impacted the marble floor of the terrace—was enough to make her tighten, rather than loosen, her hold on it. She stared down at it in fascinated horror, feeling its weight and the slight shifting of its contents every time she tilted it this way or that.

"You mean—these are her—?"

"Her ashes, yes," said Lewis. "They were in an urn, you understand—"

"A revolting thing," said Orson. "We wouldn't give it house room—"

"So we took her out of that—poured her out, actually—and put her in a shoe box instead—"

"Because she always loved shoes, you see."

"Almost to the point of lunacy."

"So we thought she'd like that. Being in a shoe box."

There was a silence and then Orson said, "She liked hats too but a hat box would have been too big."

"Not to mention too absurd," said Lewis.

"Too big to go in a suitcase," said Orson. "And it wouldn't do to have her as a piece of carry-on luggage, would it?"

Olga took a breath. "You mean, you want to take it—her—with you? In the suitcase?"

Lewis scratched at an eyebrow with the little finger of his right hand. "I don't want to, no. Horribly macabre, the whole thing—traipsing about the place with a box full of bone fragments. But it's what she wanted, you see."

"What—to travel after death?"

"No, no," said Lewis, smiling slightly. "No—she wasn't that whimsical. No, it was that she specified in her will precisely where she wanted her ashes to be scattered—in England, oddly enough, since she never really cared much for the place—"

"It's a practical joke, Lewis," said Orson.

"I know that, Ossie but that doesn't make her request any less binding, does it?"

Orson curled his lip. "I think it makes it completely unbinding, playing dumb games from beyond the grave. I wouldn't do it, I can tell you that for nothing. I'd drop her over the cliff, that's what I'd do."

"No, well, you're not going to *have* to do it, are you?" said Lewis, tersely. "It'll be me and Michael and the girl, won't it? And we shall all probably go to prison for it but it can't be helped, it has to be done."

"Prison?" said Olga. She wanted to put the box down, get it out of her hands and not think about what was inside but the balcony was small and there was nowhere to put it and, anyway, Freddy was right behind her, staring with round eyes down at the box and she thought he'd probably scream if she turned round quickly and tried to give it to him.

Orson said, "She was quite specific as to the location, you see. An impossibly awkward spot, which is, of course, why she picked it."

"To make it difficult for us, you see," said Lewis. "Mischief-making to the end and beyond."

"Where did she want—to be—um—scattered?"

Lewis looked at Orson and Orson looked back at Lewis and then they both turned their heads and looked up at Olga on the balcony.

"On the floor of the food hall in Fortnum and Mason's," said Lewis.

"Crumbs," said Freddy in Olga's ear.

"Why?" said Olga, before her voice failed her entirely.

"Well, as I said, it's a practical joke," said Orson. "From beyond—"

"It's also, I think, some sort of retribution," said Lewis. "Giselle could hold a grudge forever. We were in Fortnum's years ago, before the war and she stole a pot of Beluga caviar and she got caught. They were very nice about it and just made her put it back but she was furious with Orson and me because we ran away to the Burlington Arcade and bought shirts, instead of helping her."

"We should have helped her," said Orson, staring down at the little collection of cigarette ends. Some still had traces of lipstick under the dust.

"I don't know how we're going to manage it," said Lewis.

"Perhaps you could do that thing they did in Colditz," said Orson. "You know, the prisoner of war camp, when they dug the escape tunnel and had to get rid of the dirt. They had these cloth bags inside their pants and they wandered about the compound, letting a bit of the dirt out at a time. They did it with string, somehow."

"That was a lovely film," said Freddy. "John Mills was in that."

"There won't be any string involved," said Lewis. "Far too complicated. No, I shall give the responsibility to Michael, who is young and resourceful and who will find a way."

"And the creature can help too," said Orson.

Amanda had managed to put everything she would need for the three days into her carry-on bag. She was stuffing the last of her makeup into a side pocket when Michael knocked gently and put his head round the door.

"Ready?" he said.

Amanda turned and looked at him. He was holding a small leather bag in both hands and the bag was hanging in front of his groin, like a shield and Amanda felt a sudden flash of irritation. All this defensive restraint was getting on her nerves.

They had spent all their time together, mostly swimming and sunning on the beach. They had gone with Freddy into the little town and explored the shops and helped with buying some of the food, although Freddy made it obvious that he would have preferred them not to and, all that time they had done nothing more than hold hands and Amanda was getting tired of it. Setting limits in the early days of a relationship was an acceptable custom but surely this man understood that those limits could be overstepped with ease and, indeed, ought to be?

"Where do you stay when you're in London?" Amanda asked, sitting on the edge of the bed.

"The agency keeps a small apartment in Fulham. It's for visiting clients, mostly. I get to use it, too."

"Is it nice?"

"It's OK."

"Can I see it?"

"Sure."

"When?"

"Tomorrow."

"When tomorrow?"

"We could have dinner—"

"I'd like to spend the night."

"OK."

Amanda gave an exasperated growl. "You're making this really difficult," she said. "Why?"

Michael stepped into the room and leaned back against the door until it closed. He said, "Because I don't rush these things, that's why. I'm from old Baptist stock. They're kinda slow with this stuff. And then there's the black/white thing, too."

"You're joking."

"No. You don't know anything about it, otherwise you'd know I wasn't. It's something you've got to think about."

"Well, it doesn't mean a thing to me."

Michael smiled. "Good."

He put his bag down on the floor and crossed the short space between them. He bent over and put his face very close to Amanda's and then stopped, as though some internal circuit breaker had been tripped, suddenly immobilizing him. Amanda stared up into his eyes, expecting to see some kind of doubt or insecurity there, some passing anxiety that had caused the halt in his progress towards her mouth; but all she saw was a smiling confidence and, in the tilt of one of his eyebrows, a wry expectation that she might consider taking some of the responsibility for closing the gap that still lay between them.

Michael's mouth was in front and a little above her and, to reach it, Amanda straightened her spine and elongated her neck, which brought her mouth to within an inch of his. Still, Michael made no move to her. Amanda said, "Oh," impatiently and reached both hands round behind his neck and pulled him down onto her face.

Most of the men that Amanda had kissed had lips that were harder and thinner than Michael's and kissing his was a revelation. It was, she thought, like kissing a girl. His mouth was relaxed against hers, neither giving nor receiving. Amanda pushed her tongue between his lips and forced his teeth apart. Michael opened his mouth.

"If we stay like this too long," he mumbled into her, "any minute now, my back will go out."

Amanda pulled away, letting go of Michael's neck. He straightened and put one hand on the small of his back and winced. Amanda said, "You are the most fucking awful man I've ever met. Go away."

"I'm sorry."

He looked so stricken. Amanda said, "I didn't mean it. You're actually the *second* most fucking awful man I've ever met. The thing is, I like fucking awful men. My problem, you see. What do you say to that?"

"I say—well, I say that I'm crazy about you and that I want you badly and I hope that's going to happen real soon—but, it's not going to happen here and now because—" Michael took a glance at his watch— "because the taxi is due within the next fifteen minutes and I'd like to take longer than that, if it's OK with you?"

"You're crazy about me?"

"Yes."

"And you want me badly?"

"Yes."

"Right. Well, I suppose that'll have to do for the time being. All right, go away. I have to pack my curlers and I'd really rather you didn't see them."

Michael went to the doorway. Then he turned and said, "Can I just ask you something?"

"Quickly."

"How do you feel about me?"

Amanda's eyes narrowed. She said, "If you really have to ask that, then I shall change my estimation of you. You are the most fucking awful man I've ever met. Just go away."

The taxi arrived, as Lewis knew it would, three quarters of an hour late, which was why he had ordered it to the house four hours before their plane took off. Plenty of time, Amanda thought resentfully, for something to have happened between her and Michael—although, she couldn't help but admire his restraint. She'd always been impatient, particularly where sex was concerned and that had got her into trouble in the past; it was rather wonderful, she decided, that this new man was protecting her from her own impetuosity by refusing to play with her until he felt the time was right—men like this were, in Amanda's experience, rare.

The taxi horn blared its arrival and Amanda heard Lewis calling frantically from the terrace, "It's here! Oh God—it's here! Come along! Quickly—or we'll miss the plane!"

Michael was waiting for her on the landing at the stop of the staircase. He took her case from her hand.

"*Forty five minutes*," Amanda hissed as they went down the steps.

"I like to sleep afterwards," said Michael. "Not sit bolt upright on a plane for five hours."

"Oh do come *on*," cried Lewis, hurrying in from the terrace. He looked up at them, fretfully. "Have you got everything? Tickets? Passports? We won't have time to come back if you've forgotten anything, you know."

Orson limped in through the French windows. Olga followed closely behind.

"That's why I hate travelling with him," said Orson. "Panic, panic, panic."

Michael said, "We've got it all, Lewis and there's plenty of time."

"That's what you say," said Lewis gloomily, heading for the front door.

Freddy poked his head round the door that led to the kitchen.

"Off are we, Sir L? Well, might I wish you all a bon voyage? And might I beg the privilege of taking a few commemorative snaps? I've got my Kodak Instamatic handy and it won't take a sec. If you'd all be so kind and gather round the door—that's it, Sir L, you in the front and Mr. Woodley—Mr. Woodley, sir, if you wouldn't mind—yes, you next to him—and the young sir and Miss Amanda and madam, too—if you could squash in there somehow?"

"We haven't really got time for this, Freddy", said Lewis, looking at his watch.

"Yes, you have," said Orson.

Freddy fiddled with the camera and Lewis said, "Well, if we must, we must. Only quickly, please, Freddy."

Freddy raised the camera to his eye and pressed the button.

"Did it work? The flash thing? Did it go off?"

"Yes," said Lewis, loudly, although it hadn't. "All right, everybody, now do let's go."

When the sound of the taxi had faded away down the drive, Orson turned to Olga.

"Well—here we are. All alone. I hope you can find something to do. I putter about, you understand, looking after the garden. Not much of a host, I'm afraid."

"I've got a couple of books I want to read. Don't worry about me."

"And don't you worry about me, either, sir" said Freddy. "I've got my hands full, I don't mind telling you, what with all the cleaning and everything. I shall be a whirlwind over the next few days. When Sir L gets back, he won't recognize the place."

"Just so long as I can," said Orson, walking slowly towards the French windows.

"Dinner will be in half an hour, sir—madam. A lovely bit of fish, with asparagus tips and baked potatoes—and a fruit salad for dessert. I found some lovely mangos at the market."

"Spiffing," said Orson and he disappeared into the dusk.

The next morning, Olga was woken by a pounding on her bedroom door. She said, "Come in," and Orson burst into the room.

"I know it's only seven o'clock and I'm sorry but I've had the greatest idea," he said. "It came to me in the middle of the night. Drove all thoughts of gardening out of my head. What we're going to do, you and I, is we're going to our bank in town and we're going to open Giselle's safe deposit box and we're going to bring all her stuff she hid away from us back here and we're going to look at it and, if there's anything you want, then you shall have it. What do you think of that?"

Olga was still rubbing the sleep from her eyes. She said, without thinking, "Well, what's in it?"

"I have no idea but the fact that it's there is exciting enough, isn't it? Her lawyer had the key and now I've got it. Lewis and I never got round to having a look. We were too busy being sad—but now's the time to do it. I suspect most of her jewelry is there and you'll like that, won't you?"

"I couldn't take her jewelry—"

"Why not? It's no use to either of us. We don't want it."

"You could sell it."

"What for? We've got plenty of money. No, no. It ought to be yours."

Orson reached into his pocket. "For starters, here's her ruby ring. It was the only thing she wore when she got old. Catch."

Olga caught. The ring was old, yellow gold and the stone was a smooth, convex oval of deep red.

"It's lovely. But, I really couldn't—"

"Oh, stop with all that crap, please. Who else should have it, I'd like to know? Except perhaps the creature, who isn't here at the moment. If you want to give it all to her, that's fine—but I wouldn't if I were you. She's not old enough to deserve it. Oh, do please say yes. It'll be fun."

"Well, I'd love to see it—"

"That's a yes. Definitely a yes. Well, get up, get up. I can smell coffee brewing, I think. That little man is extraordinary, even if he does flap around a bit, like a bird with a broken wing. He must have been listening again. Well, I don't mind. I'm not doing anything filthy these day, so he can listen all he wants."

After breakfast, Freddy drove them in to town. He followed Orson's directions to the bank and parked neatly at the kerb.

"I shall wait here while you do your business, sir, madam," he said.

When the bank official slid the box out of its slot and brought it to the table, Orson became excited. It was, he pointed out, much wider and deeper than the usual long, narrow steel carton that most people used.

"There must be a lot of stuff. Lucky you," he said.

He opened the lid. Much of the space was taken up by six, leather-bound books. There was no titling on the covers. Orson pulled out the top book and opened it.

"Oh, my God—they're her diaries. I'd forgotten all about them. She used to keep a journal in the old days—I have no idea when she stopped but it must be years ago—and I remember her scribbling away like crazy in her bedroom. She'd never let Lewis or me read any of it. Now she can't stop us, poor old thing. What date is the last entry?"

He opened each book at the last page, settling at last on one. "Here we are—November 1968. Nothing after that. She must have got bored with it at last. Oh, this will be fun for you. You can forget your other books, now. This will be much more interesting and, if you find out anything really scurrilous about us, I want you to tell us all about it."

"I don't know if I ought to," said Olga. "I mean, they're private, surely?"

Orson tapped the pile of books with his forefinger. "What is the point of writing diaries if nobody else ever reads them?" he said. "Diaries are *supposed* to be read by somebody else, especially when you're dead. Aren't you interested?"

"Yes, I am. Very."

"There you are, then. Your reading matter over the next few days—if you can make out her handwriting, of course. Now, what else is there?"

The rest was jewelry and there were some wonderful pieces. Orson pawed through them. "Oh look—here's the brooch we gave her just after the war! And here's that awful watch that never worked—now, where's that necklace?"

"What necklace?"

"The best piece, as far as I can remember. It always irritated us, that necklace. Partly because Finlay gave it to her but mostly because it was so much better than anything we'd ever gotten her. How odd—it's not here. Perhaps it's in one of her boxes at home. Remind me to look for it—it's a ten carat emerald pendant which I know you'll like."

Olga wondered exactly how rich they must have been, to spend so much on Giselle. They must, she decided, have been very rich indeed.

"I can't possibly take all this," she said, holding up a bracelet that dribbled with diamonds.

"Oh, why the hell not? You don't have to wear them. You can sell them if you like. Give them to a cat's home. I don't care and neither will Lewis. Let's just clear out this box and go home. I hate banks, don't you?"

One the way home, Orson said, "I wonder how they're all doing? In England? I'm glad I didn't go—although I think I might have enjoyed at least one part of it."

Chapter 12

"This is the part Ossie would be enjoying the most," muttered Lewis as they pushed open the doors into Fortnum & Mason's. "If only for the element of embarrassment. Ossie always liked embarrassing people. I could take it or leave it but Ossie reveled in it." He tapped Michael on the arm. "What would you like me to sing?"

"I've always like *Nora*."

"Everybody likes *Nora*. I'm rather sick of it, myself. It's not very good, you know. But have it your own way. *Nora* it shall be."

They had arrived at Heathrow very early in the morning of the previous day and Lewis had gone straight to the Savoy, insisting that Michael and Amanda come with him, to make sure that everything was all right.

"You might as well earn some of that ten percent I pay the agency."

He was very tired. He'd only managed a few, short dozes on the flight, even with the pill that Dr Beale had given him. Michael and Amanda, sitting together across the aisle from him, had talked in undertones the whole way and the strain on his ears—trying to hear what they were saying to each other—had been exhausting. The film they had shown had been incomprehensible and he'd tried to read but there was something wrong with his reading light, which had made him nervous; if his reading light didn't work, what was the probability of other, more vital parts of the airplane also being faulty? If he said something about it to one of the waitresses, she'd be sure to fiddle with it and Lewis didn't want anybody, other than a qualified aeronautical engineer, to fiddle with any non-functioning elements of an airborne plane, no matter how unrelated they might be to the smooth running of that other machinery so essential to keeping them aloft—so he'd given up and closed his eyes and thought about other things all the way across the Atlantic.

The Seersucker Suite wasn't his best show but it was all right, he supposed. Quite what the National Theatre was going to do with it, was anybody's guess. He hadn't heard of any of the cast, although Michael had assured him that every one was a star. The only person involved in the project whose name he knew was Finlay Ferguson, who had descended from his lofty perch and elected to direct the thing himself. Well, Finlay, for all his other shortcomings, had always been a good director. Oh well—let them all do their worst. Which was probably going to be exactly what they *would* do.

What could those two be talking about? Themselves, probably. That was what everybody did, of course—talk about themselves. What was it that Rebecca West had said about conversations—'a series of interrupted monologues', or something like that. He never could read her stuff.

This book on his lap though—not bad, if only his bloody lamp worked. All about brave Russian submariners and brave American submariners trying to torpedo each other. Exciting—until night had arrived in his oval window and they'd turned out all the overhead lights and he'd found his reading lamp didn't work.

He dozed again, for twenty minutes. When he woke up, Michael and Amanda were still muttering to each other and his sodding light still didn't work.

The room at the Savoy was better than he'd expected and he sent Michael and Amanda away, with instructions to leave him alone for the next twenty four hours, at which time he *might*—he would make no promises—just might be up to seeing them again.

"You must have so much to talk about," he said acidly, closing the door on them.

"I don't know about you," said Amanda, gazing steadily at Michael, "but I think I've done enough talking."

"So what do you want to do?"

"I want to go home and have a bath and look at my post and wonder where you're going to take me for dinner."

They went down to the lobby and got into a waiting taxi. On the way to Holland Park, Amanda said, "Now, remember, don't go to sleep. If you do, your internal clock will be shot to hell. The trick is to stay awake until nighttime."

"Got it," said Michael, who knew rather more than Amanda about coping the effects of jet lag. "Do you know Francini's, in the Fulham Road? We could go there. I'll pick you up at seven."

Amanda kissed him lightly on the lips and got out of the taxi. "I'll be waiting," she said.

When Michael reached the agency flat, his first instinct was to stretch out on the bed and close his eyes. His neck was stiff from turning his head to talk to Amanda on the plane and his lower back twinged with sharp little pains every time he bent to pick something up; but he resisted the temptation to sleep and took a stinging shower instead and then called Julian.

"We're here, Julian."

"Oh, splendid. Lord Ferguson will be pleased. Bring me up to date—who, exactly, is here?"

"Lewis, me and a young and very pretty woman called Amanda Whitehall."

"Oh. Not quite what Lord Ferguson envisaged—he was hoping for Orson Woodley as well—but Sir Lewis is what it's all about, isn't it?"

"So Lewis thinks, anyway."

"Now, there's quite a lot of newspapers and magazines who are frightfully keen to get an interview with him, so I was wondering how he would feel about an impromptu news conference this afternoon? Say around three o'clock."

"Say whatever time you like, Julian, but Lewis won't be there. We have strict instructions not to bother him until tomorrow morning and, even then, he's said he won't do any press at all. A regal wave to the cameras is all they can expect."

"Oh dear. Lord Ferguson won't like that."

"There are several thing Lord Ferguson probably isn't going to like, Julian."

"Oh dear—Sir Lewis isn't going to make a scene, is he?"

"Why would he do that, Julian?"

"I have no idea. I'm under a lot of pressure and odd things keep spewing out of my mouth. He is coming to the opening night, isn't he?"

"Yes."

"And the party afterwards?"

"He wants to know if the party's on the stage?"

"Why?"

"He says he won't come if it is."

"Oh God. No. It's in the foyer. There'll be a string quartet playing some of Lewis' songs, which he'll like, surely? Everybody who is anybody will be there—a glittering evening, I promise."

"We shall need a car from the Savoy."

"Oh. Right."

"And three tickets to the play."

"You really don't have to tell me that, Michael."

"And somewhere to sit at the party. Lewis is insistent on that. He says he won't stand for standing about any more."

"Somewhere to sit, right. Oh God."

Michael finished making the arrangements and put the telephone down. Julian had seemed more flustered than usual, if that was possible.

Altogether overawed by the great Lord Finlay Ferguson—but then, the British had always been unduly impressed by titles, hadn't they? No wonder Tolly thought so little of his London branch.

He stared longingly at the bed—but no, Amanda was right. Better to stick it out until bedtime. He switched on the television and found a cricket match. He'd never understood the game but, if he really concentrated this time, perhaps the rules would, miraculously, reveal themselves? And, at the same time, perhaps the riddle that was Amanda Whitehall would also let go its secret?

He managed to stay awake until it was time to pick up Amanda. She came down when he pressed her bell.

"You look awful. Are you all right?"

"I'm tired. Aren't you?"

"Not really."

The reason Amanda wasn't tired was because she had slept for four hours—most of the afternoon, in fact. She decided she wouldn't tell Michael—obviously he'd taken her admonition to heart, because there were dark circles under his eyes.

They had dinner at Francini's. Michael didn't talk much. Then they took a taxi back to Holland Park.

"Are you going to come in?" said Amanda.

"Would you like me to?"

"All right, let's get one thing clear, shall we?" said Amanda briskly. "I want to fuck you, OK? I've wanted to fuck you ever since I saw you. Question is—do you want to fuck me?"

"Yes."

"Then come in and stop fucking about."

She took his hand and pulled him up the two flights to her flat. She opened the door—one-handed, still clutching tight to his with her free one, as though suspecting that releasing it might give him the chance to run away—and then drew him inside.

"The bedroom's down there," she said, waving towards a door at the end of a short corridor. "I'm going to the bathroom. Take your clothes off and get into bed. I won't be a minute."

Michael stood, looking down at the bed. He felt shaky and weak and his eyes didn't seem to be working very well. He undressed and crawled between the sheets and put one arm over his face to cut out the light. When Amanda padded, naked into the bedroom ten minutes later, Michael was asleep.

"Oh great," she muttered, slipping under the covers and draping her long legs over his longer ones. "That's the last time I give anybody advice."

She slid her hands over his body, feeling the hard planes of his chest. She moved them down to his groin and seized him, squeezing hard. He was limp, so she opened her fist and began to stroke him gently with the tips of her fingers. Michael moaned and turned away, pulling himself from her grasp. Amanda sighed and turned her back to him, pressing her buttocks against his.

"Fucking awful man," she whispered into the darkness.

When Michael woke, morning light was streaming through the window and Amanda, fully dressed, was sitting at her dressing table, brushing her hair.

"Hi," he said.

"Good morning," said Amanda, briskly. "Sleep well?"

"Rather too well, I think. I'm sorry."

"What for?"

"Well—for not staying awake."

"Oh—that. Another time, maybe."

If he knew her better, he thought, he'd be able to gauge the extent of her irritation, which was undoubtedly there. She hadn't turned away from the mirror to speak to him and the movements of the brush in her hand had become noticeably more savage—

"There's coffee in the kitchen," she said.

"Thanks." Under the sheets, he was naked and his clothes were draped over the back of the chair on which Amanda was sitting. He lay still, wondering how to manage this—

"Well, go on. I'm not bringing it to you, if that's what you're waiting for."

Bravado was what was wanted here. He rolled out of the bed and strolled, as nonchalantly as he could, to the door. Was she looking at him? He had to know—

"Down here, is it?" he asked, turning his head to glance at Amanda.

"Yup." She was staring hard into the mirror. "You can't miss it," she said, ripping the brush across her scalp. "I mean, this isn't Hampton Court."

Standing naked in a strange kitchen, sipping coffee and looking out of the window over the slate roofs of Holland Park, was curiously liberating, Michael decided. It was something he ought to do more often. Preferably in this flat, sipping this coffee and looking out over these roofs—

"Puritanism is one thing," said Amanda, appearing suddenly at the kitchen door, "and so is awareness of the whole black/white thing—and behaving with mature circumspection is also something too—but not telling a person you're in the last stages of sleeping sickness is entirely another thing altogether."

"I'm really sorry. I guess I was exhausted."

"Well, you should have slept in the afternoon, like I did, shouldn't you?"

"You told me not to."

"Oh—well," said Amanda, sarcasm dripping from every vowel, "if you're going to do everything I tell you to do, what the hell is the use of you?"

The telephone on the wall next to him shrilled and Amanda crossed the small space between them and lifted the receiver. Michael made a small move away from her, to remove his nakedness from her immediate vicinity and Amanda shook her head at him and reached out her free hand and grabbed him by the wrist. "You stay where you are," she muttered and Lewis, on the other end of the line, said, "What?" loudly in her ear.

"Who is this?" said Amanda, holding tight to Michael.

"This is me. Is that you?"

"Lewis? Well, good morning. Did you sleep well?"

Lewis had taken three of Dr Beale's cautious little pills and had fallen into a dreamless sleep that had lasted, uninterrupted, until ten minutes before, when somebody clanking a bucket outside his door had pulled him from the depths.

"Not badly—not too badly at all. Are we ready for this?"

"Ready for what?"

"I'm sorry—is this Amanda Whitehall?"

"Yes, Lewis."

"Oh good. I thought for a moment I must have got the wrong number. What do you mean, 'Ready for what'? Ready for our little adventure. It has to be done today, because tomorrow's the play and I shall need at least twenty four hours to get over the emotion of today—and the next day we go home, so it has to be today and it has to be this morning."

"All right."

"I tried calling Michael but he's not at home, so it looks like it'll be just you and me."

"Lewis—"

"I must say, I'm rather disappointed in him. He agreed to help, after all."

"Lewis—"

"It wasn't so much to ask, was it? When you think of the money that agency has collected from me over the years—for doing precisely nothing, you know—"

"Lewis—"

"You keep interrupting. What is it?"

"He's here, Lewis."

"Who is where?"

"Michael. In my kitchen. He's standing next to me. Stark naked, drinking coffee."

There was a brooding silence from the Savoy Hotel. Then Lewis said, "I think, Amanda dear, that that is a smidgen more information than I really needed to know. Michael's breakfast preferences are nothing to me. He could be drinking a gin and tonic for all I care about it. What I really need to know is when can you both be here?"

"Half an hour, if we can get a taxi."

"I shall be ready. Goodbye."

Amanda replaced the phone. Then she turned and slowly ran her eyes up and down Michael's body. "Although I detest you," she said, "I have to admit you are probably the most beautiful man I've ever seen. If only for that reason, do you think, if you try very hard, you could possibly pull yourself together today and be in a fit condition later on so that we could consummate this affair?"

"I think I could manage that, yes. I could manage it now, but it looks like we don't have the time."

"No, we don't. You do pick your moments, don't you?"

"I'm sorry."

"You keep saying that. It's not good enough. And could you please put that thing away. It's very distracting."

Lewis refused to meet them in the lobby.

"No, you have to come up here," he shouted into the telephone. "There are things to be arranged."

They found him sitting on the edge of his bed. There was a matching pair of plastic laundry bags on either side of him, their bottoms bulging.

"Ah, Michael—you're dressed. What a relief. Now—I've got it all worked out," Lewis said, proudly. "It was Ossie who gave me the idea— well, you were there, weren't you?—you know, the prisoner of war thing, when they let the earth they'd dug dribble out of bags inside their trousers. I've got the bags—Giselle is divided fairly equally between the two and, if there is one a little heavier than the other, then I think Michael should have that one—good, Amanda, good, you're wearing exactly the right sort of thing for this and so is Michael at last, so that's one problem sorted out—and the cunning part is, you see, that if you turn the bags upside down, there's this plastic drawstring sort of thing, you see, which we can tie up so nothing comes out and then, once inside the shop, all you have to do is bend down—pretend you're tying your shoelaces or something—oh, I see neither of you have laces, so what could we do instead? Perhaps you've been bitten on your ankles by a mosquito and feel the need to scratch?—and then you loosen the drawstring, you see—just a bit—and then wander about without a care in the world while your grandmother dribbles out in a controlled flow, as it were—"

"Wouldn't it be easier," said Amanda, "simply to empty the bags—when nobody was looking—under a counter or something? All this dribbling sounds complicated."

"Yes, it would be easier," said Lewis, patiently. "However, that would not be *scattering*, would it? That would be *dumping* and Giselle specified quite clearly that she wanted to be scattered. If she'd wanted to be dumped, she would have said so."

"It won't work," said Michael.

"Why not?"

"We're too tall and the bags are too short. Besides, they're too fat—we'll look like we've got swollen ankles."

Lewis' shoulders slumped. "Well, it's the best I could come up with and now I'm too drained to think of anything else. Do you have any idea how distressing it is to divide Giselle into two equal parts and pack her in laundry bags? I'm an emotional wreck."

"Perhaps you could create some kind of diversion?"

"What did you have in mind?"

"Look, we're doing the difficult part," said Amanda. "The least you can do is think of the diversion."

"I can't think of anything at the moment."

"You could always sing something."

"Don't be silly. That's all I ask—don't be silly."

There weren't many people in Fortnum's, which was a relief. Only about seven customers were wandering the floor of the food hall.

"Where do you want her scattered?" hissed Amanda.

"On the floor," whispered Lewis. "That's all she stipulated. I see no reason to take it any further. And, I warn you, I'm having second thoughts about singing."

"Buy some jam," said Amanda, under her breath.

"I don't want any jam."

"Just make your presence felt. When you've been noticed, then you can start your diversion."

The laundry bags looked, at first glance, like any other plastic shopping bags and Michael swung his casually from one hand. He'd decided, if asked about the contents, to say he was carrying a cement sample for his architects. He had no idea what Amanda would say if approached and wasn't about to ask her; she'd hardly spoken to him on the way to the hotel and not at all on the way to Fortnum's, which could mean that any idea that they might work as a team was probably out of the question—

"What sort of jam?"

"It doesn't matter," Amanda growled. "Just make a big deal out of it. I'm going over there—Michael, you go somewhere else. We'll report back when we're done."

"Should I synchronize my watch?"

"Shut up."

Amanda walked away towards the pickles. Michael wandered in search of a space empty of other customers. Lewis scrutinized a row of jam pots and selected one. He took it to a dark-suited member of the staff—an older, friendly-looking man with a benign smile on his face—

who was standing by a till. Lewis said, loudly, "My dear fellow, are these real blueberries?"

The benign man smiled warmly. "Yes, they are indeed real, Sir Lewis."

"Ahah. You know who I am?"

"Of course, Sir Lewis. I'm a great admirer."

"Really? An admirer, eh? Of what, exactly?"

"Oh well—of everything, really, sir. I even have that record from the fifties, when you were in Las Vegas."

"You like my songs?"

"Very much, Sir Lewis."

"Well, I might sing one for you in a minute. Meanwhile, would you like my autograph?"

"Oh, no, sir. That won't be necessary. We do appreciate that people like their privacy."

Lewis waved the pot of jam in the air. "Yes, but look here. I don't want privacy. I want publicity. I crave it, in fact. Disgusting, I know—particularly at my age—but there you are. Do, please, accept an autograph. I shall be terribly upset if you don't."

"Oh, well—I wouldn't want to upset you, Sir Lewis."

The man, blushing, found a scrap of paper beside the till and produced a handsome fountain pen from his breast pocket. Lewis signed with a flourish, then looked around the shop.

"Anybody else?" he shouted. "Anybody else want an autograph? From me—Sir Lewis Messenger, playwright, novelist and songwriter? Yes, you, madam—in the blue hat—what would you like me to sign?"

Out of the corner of his eye, he could see the top of Amanda's head moving slowly down an aisle on the far side of the floor. He couldn't see Michael at all. The woman in the blue hat, looking embarrassed, was walking firmly in the opposite direction.

"Just form an orderly line," Lewis shouted. "I'll get to you all in time."

It wasn't working at all. You couldn't divert the English, Lewis remembered, too late. Not by shouting at them, anyway. The English, when faced with a spectacle that would cause every other race on earth to stand and stare, would do exactly the opposite—they would look in every direction except the one where the spectacle was taking place—on the other hand, there wasn't a soul in the world who wouldn't react to the sound of breaking glass—

Lewis raised the pot of jam over his head, peered myopically up at the label and then let the pot drop from his fingers. It shattered on the floor with a crash and the jam splattered across the tiles in a satisfying pattern.

"Oh, good heavens. How clumsy I am."

"Please don't worry about it, Sir Lewis—"

Lewis peered closely at the mess. "You know, I think you're right. They are real blueberries. I was prepared to swear they weren't, but I have to admit you were right."

"All our jams are of the highest quality, Sir Lewis."

He glanced quickly round the store. Now, all seven customers—and three new ones just inside the door—were staring at him. He grabbed another pot from a nearby stack.

"Now, can you say the same of your *strawberry* jam?"

"Indeed, yes, sir—"

Crash went the strawberry jam, the scarlet contents forming a charming abstract pattern over the darker blueberry beneath.

"Oh, dear, Sir Lewis—"

Lewis leaned close to the man's ear. "It's a *bet*," he hissed. "I shall pay double for everything and say nice things about the place to all my friends—just don't, on any account, have me arrested, I beg of you."

"Of course not, Sir Lewis—"

"Another part of the bet is a song. It's a very complicated bet, you understand and I lost it. Oh well, it could be worse, I suppose-it might have been two songs and only one pot of jam. All right, here we go."

Lewis raised his head so that everybody could see him. Then he called, "A song! That's what you're all waiting for, isn't it? Well, then—a song it shall be!"

He took a deep breath and launched himself, full pitch, into the first
verse of *Nora Isn't Nice*.

"Nora isn't nice, she has arteries of ice
And her heart's as hard as granite, damn her eyes!
She's rich, the naughty witch, and with every little twitch
Of her nose, the fellows cluster round like flies
Her yacht was got like Camelot
By gentlemen who give her pots
Of deutschmarks, sheckels, yen and dollars green
And Nora, gaily, spends them daily
On her Pekinese, Disraeli
And never never lets her grief be seen—"

Ah—that got them. He saw recognition in several pairs of eyes and
the woman in the blue hat was smiling with delight. Michael and
Amanda were nowhere to be seen. Now, if only he could remember the
second verse—

Amanda had found a display of canned fish, artfully arranged
around a pile of boulders. It was as good a spot as any she'd come
across—there were convenient crannies between the rocks where a little
gray ash could fall unseen—and she looked around, hearing Lewis
warbling on the other side of the store. Nobody was near. She ripped
open the neck of the laundry bag and turned it upside down over the
stack of boulders. Most of the ash slipped down between the cracks and
the rest Amanda swept into the nooks with her hand. Perfect. The
empty laundry bag was stuffed into her pocket, she took one more
quick look around to make sure she hadn't been seen and then walked
casually away. If Michael had done half as well as she had—

Michael was alone behind a market barrow laden with fruit. The
barrow was draped with mats of fake grass that reached almost to the
floor and Michael dropped to his haunches and peered underneath.
The space under the barrow was dark and empty. He opened the

laundry bag and pushed it into the cave and then took hold of one corner of the bag and shook it vigorously. A fine cloud of particles drifted out from the darkness. Michael pulled the laundry bag out, emptying the last few fragments onto the floor at his feet. With the side of his shoe, he swept them back under the barrow.

"How's it going?" said Amanda, appearing at his side.

"My half's under there. Where's yours?"

"There were these rocks. I hope she's satisfied. I don't know about you, but mine could only be called a dumping."

"Mine was a sort of layered strewing. We'd better rescue Lewis. *Nora's* long but not *that* long."

When Lewis saw Michael and Amanda walking towards him, both smiling broadly, he stopped in mid verse and hurried towards them. There was a scattering of applause.

"Thank you, thank you." He reached Michael and Amanda and seized their arms.

"Well, I hope you're satisfied," he hissed—and then, pitching his voice so that it reached the salesman, "I've fulfilled every part of the bet—two pots of jam all over Fortnum's nice clean floor and at least two verses of one of my songs—"

"You were supposed to sing all of it," said Amanda, severely.

"No, I wasn't. Shut up. Now, you have to honor your part of the wager. You have to pay this kind man for the jam and I promised him I would pay double, just for the nuisance."

"Really, Sir Lewis, that won't be necessary."

"Nonsense, I insist. In fact, I would like to buy to more pots of jam, one blueberry and one strawberry, and take them home to Orson. Amanda, Michael—pay the man, if you please."

An old couple approached Lewis and asked him for his autograph. They were American and effusive in their admiration.

"A real treat, Mr. Messenger. I mean, Fortnum and Mason's is so lovely and then, to have you—a legend in your lifetime and ours, too—perform for us, well—it's just made our trip."

"You're too kind."

Outside, on Piccadilly's pavement, Lewis said, "Well? Did you manage it?"

"We did," said Amanda. "I don't think she could complain."

"Well done. What a relief. Come back to the Savoy and I shall give you a present."

"Do I get a present?" said Michael.

"No. You get ten percent. The fact that you've finally *earned* it should give you spiritual compensation, which is reward enough, I think."

The present was a necklace—a heavy gold chain with a single big emerald suspended from it.

"The moment I saw you," said Lewis, pressing the necklace into Amanda's hands, "I knew this was for you. It belonged to your grandmother and I know she would have wanted you to have it. It was her favorite piece of jewelry."

"I'm not surprised," said Amanda, peering at the stone. "It's fabulous. How many carats is this?"

"I have no idea. Nine or ten. Don't be mercenary. Do you like it?"

"I love it. May I really keep it? I'll never wear it, of course, it's far too valuable for that—"

"Oh, but you must wear it. I insist you wear it. If you're not going to wear it, then you can't have it."

"It's just that I'd be afraid to lose it."

"Look, to keep me happy and to stop me taking it back and giving it to your mother—wear it tomorrow, at the show, would you?"

"All right."

"I should like that very much—in full view, on that long neck, together with a fairly low-cut, greenish sort of dress, with narrow shoulder straps and the skirt quite tight round the middle and the bust and then just flaring a little around the knees—you have such a thing, I hope?"

"I've got a green dress."

"Good, good. And your hair up, of course, with careless tendrils falling round your face. And pillar box red lipstick."

"Giselle, in fact, on a specific evening sometime in the past?"

"Heavens, no—what gave you that idea? No, no—I just think all that would go well with the necklace. You promise you'll wear it?"

"I promise, but you're up to something, I know."

"You're so suspicious. Not like your grandmother at all. Now, go away, the pair of you, I'm sure you have lots to do and I need some time to myself to contemplate the thought of Giselle lying in scattered state among the tins of caviar. Come and pick me up tomorrow evening at six."

Michael took Amanda back to the agency flat and they made love for the rest of the afternoon and Amanda decided that Michael wasn't quite such a fucking awful man after all and Michael decided that he was in love with Amanda and that he really ought to see a back specialist if they were going to continue playing such acrobatic games.

Chapter 13

Freddy was having the time of his life. He was in charge at last, emperor of his own empire, even if that empire consisted of just a few utilitarian rooms off a short, tiled passage. At the Park Place, his time and labor were dictated by legions of Managers and Under-Managers and Catering Managers and Personnel Directors, all of whom could, and did, exercise control over his working day. And then there were the guests, the customers, who came and went so fast, he never had time to establish any kind of relationship with any of them (not of the meaningful sort, at least)—none of which had mattered to Freddy until he'd come to Gladstones and discovered the joys of working in an actual house, where so much of your time was your own, where there were no intermediaries between you and your customers—and where your customers (apart from staying put) just happened to be two of the most wonderfully glamorous people in the entire universe (although Mr. Woodley's glamour was sometimes tarnished by his habit of tracking mud all over Freddy's nice clean floors—he'd have to have words about that when he'd cemented himself thoroughly into the fabric of their lives).

Yes, even with the mud, there was no doubt about it: seventh heaven, over the moon, a bed of roses—he was in all of them and, while he'd been perfectly happy at the hotel, the happiness was nothing to what he was feeling now. Now, he was the Manager and the Under-Manager and the Catering Manager and probably the Personnel Director too, not to mention the Transport Captain, the Receptionist, the Financial Officer and the Hall Porter, all rolled into one.

He had his own lovely little bedroom, which would be lovelier still when he'd got rid of all traces of Bella, especially the patchouli smell which seemed to have a tendency to linger; he'd got a dinky little bathroom, rather nicer than the one in Dollis Hill; this one had a bidet, would you believe? His kitchen—once he'd persuaded his gentlemen to spend a bit of money updating the appliances (which shouldn't be hard to do once he'd got them round his little finger)—was going to be smashing and he'd even got his own butler's pantry and scullery, too, which was more than he'd ever had at the Park Place; all he'd had at the Park Place was the Green Room, which was little more than a big cupboard and he'd had to share that with the maids. Here, at Gladstones, he even had a door in the scullery that led out to a fabulous little patch of grass which got the sun most of the day. Mr. Woodley hadn't pottered about, or even appeared, on the patch of grass at all, at least not since Freddy had arrived at the house, which led Freddy to hope that the little patch of grass was considered, by his gentlemen, to be the preserve of the housekeeper. If that was the case, then his very next purchase was going to be a nice sun lounger and one of those umbrellas in a concrete base.

Housekeeper. Freddy had decided to call himself that; after all, his gentlemen had put him in charge of the house, so that was what he was—the Housekeeper. Rather a grand title, really—like Mrs. Danvers in Rebecca, played by that wonderful Judith Anderson, so creepy she was—well, he was going to be the opposite of Mrs. Danvers; he was going to be a little ray of sunshine in his gentlemen's life, whether they liked it or not. He'd tried with Mr. Woodley already, who didn't seem all that keen, to be honest, on having a little ray of sunshine flashing about the place. Only that morning, at breakfast, when Freddy had done his Mary Poppins impersonation and clucked his tongue and pursed his lips at Mr. Woodley for taking too many pancakes, Mr. Woodley had said—quite sharply, Freddy thought—that, while he was grateful to Freddy for providing such a fine breakfast, he'd be obliged—while trying to eat it—if Freddy treated him a little more like an elder statesman and a little less like a flopsy bunny.

Mrs. Whitehall had choked on her coffee, which had softened the unpleasantness a bit but Freddy had decided to risk it and take a small umbrage and had said, quite tartly, that he'd only been trying to help and perhaps *somebody* needed a nap—and then there had been a moment of tense silence, while Mr. Woodley had decided how to react—finally breaking into crumb-spitting guffaws, which confirmed to Freddy that, while he had to be a little careful in these early days, the process of winding his gentlemen round his little finger had most definitely begun.

Dealing with Mrs. Whitehall was a different proposition, since the lady wasn't going to be a permanent fixture at Gladstones. He didn't have to work at getting her dependent on him, which made the relationship easier. Besides, Mrs. Whitehall was a very pleasant person, a very pleasant person indeed. She had lovely manners and always had a smile for him, which was nice. He could camp about a bit with her and roll his eyes, which made her laugh. Her situation—vis à vis his gentlemen—was terribly intriguing. Freddy had picked up a phrase here, a clue there—and had listened at the door enough as well—to understand the reason for her visit and it was too exciting, it really was, to be part of it all. She had shown him the ring that had belonged to Giselle Palliser and he'd admired it, exclaiming at the size of the ruby.

"You ought to wear it, madam. It's far too lovely to hide away in a box."

"I don't know, Freddy. It seems a little tactless."

"He gave it to you, didn't he? Seems a bit tactless not to wear it, if you ask me. I mean, if somebody gave me a ring like that, I'd wear it in my nose, just so everybody could see how lovely it was."

Later, at dinner, while Freddy was pouring the wine for the two of them, he noticed that Mrs. Whitehall was wearing the ring—although she was keeping the hand it was on in her lap most of the time.

Mr. Woodley was asking Mrs. Whitehall about the diaries and they were news to Freddy, so he lingered in the dining room, pretending to be busy with the decanter.

"How far have you got?"

"Not very far. Her writing is difficult to make out."

"No, well—it wasn't what her hands did best. Anything interesting?"

"Not terribly, I'm afraid. It's mostly about her hair at the moment. She seems to be having trouble with her hairdresser."

"Oh, she always had trouble with her hairdresser. Anything about me?"

"Some. But more about her hair."

"Vain little bitch. Sorry, but she was."

Later, while they were having coffee, Orson suddenly looked at his watch.

"Hah! Seven o'clock here—they're four hours ahead of us, so eleven o'clock there—curtain's just about coming down now. Long show, you know. Too goddam long, if you ask me. I wonder how it went?"

To Lewis' surprise, it had gone extraordinarily well. He should have known that Finlay would do a terrific job; despite all the pompous blather the man spouted these days, he was still one of the best directors of theater in the world, which was probably why he ran the National Theatre, come to think of it.

More surprising for Lewis, was how well *The Seersucker Suite* had stood up to the passage of time. Some of the sentiments it expressed were, perhaps, outmoded in these savager days and the slang placed it firmly in its pre-war period but, on the whole, the play still worked well and his songs—particularly the point numbers, with their clever rhymes—were still able to raise respectable laughs. The cast, none of whom he recognized, were wonderful without exception and the set was just about perfect, apart from the grand piano being white, which was a vulgarism his characters would never have allowed.

Because of some indecision by Lewis as to what he should wear, they had arrived at the theatre with only moments to spare before the curtain went up; they had been met in the empty foyer by a worried Front of House Manager, who had hurried them to their seats as the lights went down; only those seated nearby saw them come into the auditorium and it was only when the lights came up for the interval that people began to notice that Lewis was in their midst. Several members of the audience, on their way to a drink or the lavatories, stopped to say how much they were enjoying the show and Lewis, sitting in an aisle seat, was gracious with all of them. One of them called him 'Master'. Michael brought him a gin and tonic.

Then the lights went down again for the second half and Lewis settled back to enjoy himself. If the second half was as good as the first. He vaguely remembered there being three acts and two intervals—but somehow Finlay had managed to split the play in a very inventive way and Lewis wondered why he hadn't thought of doing it that way himself. It was certainly neater and allowed the audience to get out of the theater a good twenty minutes earlier which was, as far as Lewis was concerned, a good thing.

And then the final curtain fell and there was a moment of respectful silence before the applause and the bravos thundered out. Lewis found himself clapping and bravoing as hard as anybody as the cast took their bows and he went on clapping, even after the actors themselves took several steps forward, to the edge of the stage and began to bang their own hands together—which was odd, thought Lewis, unless the National Theatre had adopted the Russian custom of the performers showing their appreciation for their audience by returning the compliment—but then he realized that the actors were all staring and beaming at him and so was every member of the audience, those in front twisting round in their seats to look at him, those behind slowly getting to their feet—perhaps out of respect, perhaps just to get a view of him over the heads of those in front of them—either way, now the whole house was rising to their feet and clapping wildly and Amanda was holding his hand and kissing him on the cheek and Michael was slapping him on the back (a little too hard, in fact—it was almost painful) and Lewis was so caught up in the moment that he went on applauding until he realized that a little displayed modesty was, perhaps, appropriate for the occasion; he stopped applauding and slowly pulled himself out of his seat—pretending, for some reason he couldn't fathom, to be very much more infirm and elderly than he really was—and, once on his feet, he bowed in all directions and waved and mouthed 'Thank you, thank you'—and when the applause showed no sign of dying down, he bowed again and waved some more and then made shooing gestures and mouthed 'Go home, go home', which made everybody laugh and clap even harder than before.

"You know, I'm rather glad I came," he whispered to Amanda as they moved slowly up the aisle towards the exit signs.

"So are they, it seems," muttered Amanda, glancing round the auditorium; the audience were still standing and still applauding, refusing to leave before Lewis, as though he was a member of the Royal Family and not, as he said later in his suite at the Savoy, a mere scribbling tunesmith.

Out in the lofty concrete lobby, there were tables of food and waiters with trays of champagne and the promised string quartet, who started playing *Nora* the moment Lewis appeared in the doorway. A small line of dignitaries were waiting to receive him, none of whom he knew; they all seemed to be on the board of this organization or that and all seemed entranced to meet him. When he got to the end of the line, Tolly Utteridge was there, with Julian Whatever close behind him. Tolly offered him one limp, liver-spotted hand.

"Lewis. Great. Wonderful. Fabulous—"

"What, Tolly? The play or me? And what the hell are you doing here? You never leave New York, do you?"

"Only for something special. This is special. You remember Julian, don't you?"

"Yes, but not, embarrassingly, his other name."

Julian stepped forward, blushing, and mumbled a word which Lewis took to be his surname. It seemed to have cost Julian something to say it at all and Lewis felt it might be too much for the poor man to be asked to say it again, so he smiled and shook Julian's hand and said, "Well, I shall call you Julian," which made Julian blush more.

"Now, where's my chair?"

"Right here, Sir Lewis," said Julian, motioning towards a massive club chair in distressed, chocolate brown leather. The chair was set on a low dais which was positioned against a concrete wall and there was a small mahogany table set next to the table, with a full glass on a cork coaster; Lewis hoped it contained gin and tonic and was pleased to find, with the first sip, that it did. He stepped up onto the dais but didn't sit down; instead, he used the few extra inches to crane over the crowd. Michael and Amanda were hovering at the edge of the press of people who were gathering at his feet.

"I want them near me," he said to Julian, who was doing his own brand of hovering next to the leather chair. "Young Michael and the girl. Right by my side, if you could manage that, my dear chap?"

"Certainly, Sir Lewis," said Julian, and he began to push his way through the crowd.

So many people seemed to want to shake him by the hand. Some he recognized, most he didn't. Robert and little Peter were there, somehow at the front and Lewis stepped down to embrace them both. Peter looked smaller than ever, shrunken and wizened, like a gnome.

Robert said, "We thought you weren't going to come."

"Ah well, things change, Robert and I'm glad they do. Wasn't bad, was it?"

"It was wonderful, Lewis," squeaked little Peter. "Of course, we don't go out much these days, so we have nothing to compare it with but Bobby and I both had a lovely evening."

"Lovely," echoed Robert. "Such a change from *Coronation Street.*"

"Although we love that, too," said Peter.

"We do, we do," Robert sighed. "Come to dinner tomorrow evening—at eight o'clock, when it's over."

"When what's over?"

"*Coronation Street.* We can't miss that."

"Can't. Going back tomorrow."

"*Dommage*," said Robert and little Peter made a small grimace of sadness and then they were both swallowed up in the herd, that moved, like a restless sea, round the dais. The last Lewis saw of them was Robert's black cane, waving over the heads of the throng.

"Yes?" said Amanda, appearing at Lewis' side.

"Go and sit down on my chair," Lewis hissed. "Michael, you stand in front of her, like a Nubian slave or something—just hide her as much as you can. All right?"

"What are you going to do?" said Amanda. "Produce me like a rabbit from a hat?"

"Sit, sit!" said Lewis, hurriedly—because here, threading his way through a crowd that parted respectfully at his approach, came Finlay Ferguson.

He had aged greatly since Lewis had last seen him and, for a few seconds, Lewis could only stand and stare at the once familiar and yet utterly changed figure that came towards him.

Nearly all Finlay's hair had disappeared, apart from a narrow fringe of white that started just over each ear and ran to meet its fellow on the back of his head—but it wasn't the lack of hair that made Finlay look so different; when he was young, he'd plastered his then thinning locks flat to his head with brilliantine, so that there was never any attempt to disguise to the shape of his skull, which was narrow then and was narrow now; but what had changed his appearance was the fatness Finlay had gained over the years—pounds and pounds of the stuff, which hung limply on his small frame, bulging out his midriff and forming wattles of pink flesh under his chin, which the neat, white Van Dyke beard failed to hide.

He'd always been such a trim little man, Lewis thought—and, truth to tell, he was quite trim still, with his perfectly cut dinner jacket and his crisp white dress shirt—although his fatness now lent him a touch of untidiness, which the clipped and disciplined Van Dyke did its best to offset. Then, a second later, Lewis wondered how he must look to Finlay, who was at least ten years younger than him—and he raised his hand and touched his own shock of hair, just to make sure it was still on his head.

Finlay, eyes sparkling from his triumph, ran forward the last few steps and grabbed Lewis round his waist.

"Dear heart! Dear, *dear* heart! Lovely, lovely! To see you—to have you here—a treat! A positive treat!"

"The same to you, Finlay."

Flashbulbs were popping and Lewis felt Finlay pulling him into position next to him, so that they both faced out towards the photographers.

"This way, Sir Lewis! Lord Ferguson—over here, please, sir! Give us some big smile, gents!"

"*Gents?*" said Lewis, quietly into Finlay's ear, which was somewhere on the level of Lewis' top waistcoat button.

"Public conveniences, that's all we are, dear," said Finlay and he squeezed Lewis' waist.

"I think you did a wonderful job of directing, by the way."

"Thank you, dear heart. I did so want you to approve."

"I do, enormously. Everything worked splendidly, the actors very fine, the sets and costumes ditto—but do please get rid of that frightful white piano."

"That's all?" said Finlay, tearing his smile away from the photographers and gazing, enraptured, up at Lewis. "That's all that's wrong with it?"

"That's all, yes."

"Dear heart, it shall be done. Plain black—is that what we want?"

"It's what I want."

"Plain black it shall be and I don't care what the designer says. The Master has spoken."

"And less of that, please."

"All right—less of that—but more of you. We must have more of you. I want to do all your plays here over the next few years and I want you to direct some of them and we ought to discuss it—"

"I'm going home tomorrow, Finlay."

Finlay's eyes filled with tears. "That's what I heard—but you can't! You simply can't! Not after tonight! Everybody will want to meet you after tonight—"

"Yes, well—that's a very good reason for going. I'm delighted you want to do more of my old stuff and I absolutely refuse to direct any of them after tonight—I couldn't do it nearly as well as you—so that's really all we need to discuss, isn't it? I cannot change my plans and, besides, I've done what I came for. Well, almost. Just one more item on the agenda. I want you to meet somebody."

Lewis half turned his head and called out, "Rabbit! Come here and be produced!" Then, very quickly, he turned back to stare down into Finlay's face, determined to watch every millisecond of Finlay's reaction.

Finlay was smiling up at him, a little frown of puzzlement creasing his pink forehead. "Meet who, dear old thing? Hmm?"

Lewis felt Amanda arrive at his side, smelled the trace of Chanel she wore.

"This is Amanda, Finlay. Amanda Whitehall."

He watched as Finlay's eyes switched from his to a point six inches from his left shoulder.

"How do you do?" said Finlay, smiling warmly—which, to Lewis' infuriated surprise, was the only change in Finlay's expression. Lewis watched as they shook hands. Then, with impatience, he said, "You see the resemblance, of course?"

Finlay peered up at Amanda's face. "Resemblance to whom, dear heart?"

"To *Giselle*, Finlay."

Finlay tilted his head to one side and narrowed his eyes. "Giselle? Well, yes—there is a resemblance, I suppose—"

"You suppose? She's the spitting image, for Christ's sake."

"Well, now that you mention it—"

"Of course she is. Stop pretending, Finlay. She's exactly like her. Hardly surprising, since she's Giselle's granddaughter."

Finlay's face split into a wide smile. "Is she?" he said. "Is she really? Oh, but how wonderful! Giselle's granddaughter! Good heavens—I was married to your grandmother, you know."

"Yes, I know," said Amanda.

"Very briefly, of course. A wonderful woman. Oh, and good heavens, I see you're wearing the necklace I gave her."

"*You* gave her?" said Amanda, throwing a suspicious look at Lewis.

"Indeed, yes I did. I got it at Tiffany's in New York, when we were first married. I do hope naughty Lewis didn't tell you *he* got it for her?"

"Not in so many words."

"Not in any words at all," said Lewis.

"A hint would have been nice."

"Never mind," said Finlay. "It doesn't really matter who gave it to her. The important thing is that now you're wearing it and I'm delighted. It suits you so well. Oh, but this is marvelous! So, you're the daughter of Giselle's baby—what was her name, now?"

"Gloa," said Lewis. "Then, of course—not now."

"Gloa—yes! Such an odd name but there you are. Well, well. So you're Gloa's daughter?"

"Yup," said Amanda.

"And is she still—ah—with us, as it were?"

"Very much so," said Lewis. "You must meet her, too. Get to know each other—*at last*."

Lewis watched Finlay's face slowly lose its radiance. Finlay looked at him and said quietly, "Oh God. You're not going to start all that up again, are you. Lewis? Because, if you are, this is neither the time nor the place."

"There never was a time or a place for you," said Lewis, nastily.

Finlay, a broad smile still plastered on his face, said under his breath, "Perhaps we should go somewhere for a moment. Come to my office."

He turned to the crowd. "I'm going to steal him away for a minute. We have so much to catch up on. Please excuse us, won't you?"

He took Lewis' arm and began to thread his way through the people, stopping now and then to shake this person by the hand and exchange brief pleasantries with another—and Amanda and Michael folded in behind them. Soon they were clear of the crowd and Finlay led them to a door marked 'Administration' and then down a passage to another door, unmarked this time. He opened it and ushered them into a small, windowless room; an oval table, surrounded by chairs, took up most of the space.

"This is your office, Finlay?" said Lewis. "I'm astonished. I thought there'd be more of you in it."

"This is not my office, Lewis. My office is miles away, up countless stairs and I didn't think we should absent ourselves for the amount of time it would take to get there and back. Besides, nothing I have to say on this delicate and tiresome subject warrants my office, which is far too public a place anyway. All I have to say to you is to reiterate what I told you and Orson so very firmly all those years ago."

"Tell me again. I've forgotten."

Finlay sighed in exasperation. "No, you haven't, Lewis. You've simply refused to believe me for fifty years."

Finlay turned to Amanda and noticed, for the first time, that Michael was standing at her side.

"Before we go any further, may I ask who this is?"

Michael and Lewis opened both their mouths to reply but Amanda got in first. "My boyfriend," she said. "I want him to know everything."

Finlay nodded curtly. "Well, I'm afraid there's nothing to know. Giselle became pregnant at approximately the time that she left me. I hadn't the faintest idea then who the father was and I haven't the faintest idea now—but, all I can tell you is this: it most certainly wasn't me. I told Lewis and Orson that it wasn't me but they didn't believe me, which caused a certain friction between us—other than the friction already caused by their seduction of my wife—"

"We didn't seduce her, Finlay," said Lewis, mildly. "We simply made her laugh."

"For Giselle, that was pretty much the same thing. I, unfortunately, rarely made her laugh—but, at least she married me, which is more than either you or Orson can claim."

Finlay's whole body was quivering now and the pinkness of his cheeks had faded to a pasty white. He breathed hard in the silence that followed and then seemed to gather himself together, turning to Amanda and putting one small, plump hand on hers.

"I'm really very sorry I'm not your grandfather," he said, quietly. "I would have liked to be very much. But the fact is, I'm not. I know I'm not. I know beyond any reasonable doubt I'm not. That's really all there is to it. I'm sorry."

"Well, we're not either," said Lewis. "So who could it be, Finlay?"

"I have no idea, Lewis."

"How can you be so sure it wasn't you?"

Finlay stamped his foot down hard on the carpet and the pallor in his face flooded to red.

"I just *am*, all right? As sure as you're standing here, Lewis—an event I'm rapidly regretting that I arranged—I was not the father! Not, not,

not! I refuse to discuss this any further! It's been fifty years, for God's sake! Why can't you let it go? I mean, fifty bloody years—"

He subsided, staring down at the carpet. Then he said, "We ought to be getting back."

Amanda felt a flood of compassion for this small, round man—and a sense that he was, probably, telling the truth. His denial—while an angry one—held none of the outrage you might expect from a liar; to Amanda, it seemed to hold only sadness She said, "It's all right, you know. I believe you."

"Thank you," said Finlay, still staring at the carpet. Then he lifted his head and smiled at her—looking, Amanda thought, like a diminutive Santa Claus. "That's rather a relief," he said. "Just so long as you believe me, it doesn't really matter about all the rest of it."

Lewis said, "Finlay, you ought to understand that we are currently being visited by Gloa, who received a letter from Giselle just before she died. Gloa—Amanda's mother—is obviously interested in knowing who her father is. She assumed it was either me or Orson. We, naturally, told her the truth—or rather, the truth as we have always understood it. You mustn't be upset if you're still a prime suspect."

"I'm not upset at being a suspect, Lewis. I'm merely upset that I'm still not believed."

"Well, here's why not, Finlay. You see, once Giselle came with us, Orson and I were with her all the time. All three, together. We slept in the same room at the Algonquin for several months. We were never separated for a moment. Neither of us touched her in that time. We had a pact not to and watched each other like hawks. The only occasions when Giselle was out of our sight were a few brief visits she made to you; and Orson and I waited for her outside your apartment every time. So, when Giselle announced she was pregnant—and that you were the father—what were we to believe?"

"Why not believe *me*?" said Finlay. "I wasn't the liar in the group. Giselle was the liar."

"True," said Lewis. "But even liars have to have opportunities. Giselle had none."

"It was one of you," said Finlay. "It has to be."

"Impossible."

"*Impasse*, then, as always, Lewis. And when one reaches an *impasse*, the best thing to do is step round it and pretend, at least in public, that it wasn't there in the first place. And we are in public, Lewis. There's about a thousand public out there wondering where the hell we are. Can we please go back now?"

Chapter 14

It was hard to read with Freddy prattling at her, so Olga pushed the diary away from her and leaned back in the lounger and closed her eyes against the sunlight.

"All I'm saying, madam, all I'm saying is, he ought to be swimming. That's all I'm saying."

"He doesn't like swimming, Freddy."

Freddy rolled his eyes. "It's not a question of like, madam, is it? It's a question of health. Mr. Woodley could do with a bit of exercise and swimming's the best sort. I know, I've been through it with my old Mum. After she had her stroke, the doctor—well, he was a physiotherapist, really, only I didn't tell Mum that because she'd never have taken any notice of him if I had—the doctor told her she had to get off to the public pool at least twice a week and give it a good old ploughing, too. Up and down, up and down and no sitting about in the shallow end. And that's what she did, with a bit of pushing from me, of course. 'I'm off to swim the Channel', she'd say and away she'd go with her pink rubber cap and her stretchy bathing costume, happy as Larry, she was. Until she died, that is."

"Another stroke, was it?"

"No. She drowned, poor old bat."

"Freddy."

"Oops. That was naughty. Slap wrists. Shouldn't joke about the dear departed, should I? No—what happened was, she had this coronary all of a sudden and dropped down dead sitting in her recliner watching the wrestling on ther telly. Sad, but there you are. The point is, madam, that the swimming brought her right back to life, until she died."

"Mr. Woodley won't go swimming, Freddy. You know that. It's no good nagging him about it, either."

"Me, nag? Never, madam. Well, all right—just a bit. It's for your own good, I said and he said swimming makes me sick and I said not as sick as you could be if you don't take some exercise and he said if you don't shut up I shall get all the exercise I need chasing you around the house with meat cleaver and I said we're not at home to Mr. Grumpy, thank you very much—"

"I'd drop it if I were you, Freddy."

Freddy sniffed and squinted up at the sun. He was wearing his nicest floral Hawaiian shirt and a pair of his white polyester trousers and his feet were bare—a new sensation for Freddy, who had only gone barefoot once before, in Frinton, when the weather had got hot enough for it. He'd burnt his soles on some hot tarmac that year and had never done it since; but here, where most of what you trod on was made of cool, white marble, the feeling was fantastic and Freddy had decided—unless his gentlemen made some sort of objection to it—to go barefoot most of the time. Maybe even swapping his trousers for a pair of his polyester shorts, if the circumstances felt right—

"When are they getting back?' said Olga.

Freddy looked at his watch. "Not long now, madam. They ought to land in half an hour. I just hope that driver knows what he's doing. I offered to pick them up myself, but no—Mr. Woodley wouldn't have it. He said he didn't want me to have the responsibility. I know to what he was referring—that little ding in the Mercedes wing, which was not my fault, as I pointed out to him—that manky cyclist came out of nowhere and it was just a miracle nobody was hurt, that's all I can say. I just hope that driver knows where to go at the airport. I've no faith in him myself, I don't mind telling you, madam."

"It's a very small airport, Freddy. I mean, he can't get lost there, can he?"

"Hoo—'can't' is as good as a nod to a blind horse, madam. Well let's hope for the best and plan for the worst, as my Auntie Kath used to say. I'd better get on—it's been lovely chatting but some of us have work to do. I'll let you go back to your book. Interesting, is it?"

"Some of it. Some of it is quite boring."

"I kept a diary once. When I was on tour with John Hanson. Mine wasn't boring at all. Of course, I could never let anybody read it. I was a bit of a rapscallion, I don't mind telling you. Quite a scamp, I was. I had a little bonfire in the back yard when I got home. Ooh, look at the time—I've got some bougainvillea cut for Miss Amanda's room and if I don't scamper, it'll droop."

Freddy went off in the direction of the kitchen and Olga picked up the diary again. She'd reached the period in New York, when Giselle was first married to Finlay Ferguson. Giselle appeared to do very little with her time, other than wander about the city while Finlay was busy directing some play or other. She shopped frequently and wrote exhaustively about the things she'd bought; she talked on the telephone, too and every detail of the conversations were reported; Olga was struck by how lacking the conversations were in anything more profound than the price of a pair of shoes at Bloomingdale's. Giselle, Olga had decided, was as shallow as a saucer.

"How far have you got?"

Olga turned. Orson was standing at the edge of the terrace, where the marble gave way to a grassy path that led out into the garden. He was wearing his old straw peasant hat and the knees of his corduroy trousers were stained with earth.

"She's in New York. With Finlay Ferguson. She doesn't seem to be having a very nice time. All she writes about is shopping."

"I don't think she liked New York. She thought Americans disapproved of her. Well, they did, rather. Except for me, of course."

"She hardly mentions Finlay."

"No, well—that marriage was hardly made in heaven. Tiffany's, more likely. He bought her, really—which was why we didn't feel too bad about taking her away from him. Shouldn't they be here by now?"

"We think about an hour."

"We?"

"Freddy and I."

"Ah, Freddy. I wonder—do you think there's the remotest chance we might wean him from this godawful habit he has of singing 'I've got a luvverly bunch of coconuts' at the top of his lungs every time he sees a palm tree?"

Olga laughed. "None at all, I'm afraid."

"No, I didn't think so. Well, I won't keep you. Got a bit of clipping to do."

Orson waved and turned away down the path. Olga began to read again.

January 7th. Rained all day. Finny was home. Told me all about rehearsals. He's having trouble with the girl. I told him to slap her silly face but he won't of course. Went to Maisie and Doug's for drinks. Doug told a funny story about Elsa. We all shrieked! Home and bed.

Much more of this, Olga thought, and I shall give up on her.

Orson was cutting back an unruly hibiscus. It was hot work and he paused to rub the sweat from his eyes. There was a low stone bench by the side of the path and he decided to rest for a few minutes. The hibiscus could wait.

New York. His favorite city, more so even than London or Paris. Anybody who was brought up in Buffalo wanted to get out of Buffalo as soon as possible and go and be in New York and he'd gone there as a very young man, to a bad art school on 48th Street. He hadn't learnt anything at the school, which was why he'd eventually left the place and gone to Paris—and Paris was lovely because that was where he'd met Giselle and Lewis—but not as lovely as New York.

He'd met Monica in New York. That was years later, of course, well after the war, in 1949 in fact, when he and Lewis were in their late forties and Giselle not far behind them. He'd come up to New York from Saint Marta's, alone for once, because Lewis had invited what seemed to be the entire cast from one of his shows to stay at Gladstones and neither he nor Giselle could get away.

The gallery that handled his stuff—the one on 5th Avenue (*what was its name?*) was having a retrospective of some of his work that had failed to sell in the past and had thought that perhaps sales might be brisker if Orson put in an appearance on opening day; so Orson had flown up to Manhattan at the gallery's expense and had put in his appearance, wearing his old black Bohemian hat just for the fun of it and later, when his time was his own again, he'd gone walking the night streets, revisiting those landmarks from his youth.

There had been a small, smoky nightclub he remembered, somewhere between 7th and 8th, on 42nd Street and he turned towards it, not thinking it would still be there, of course—not after all these years—but it would be pleasant to walk the same sidewalk and he had nowhere else he particularly wanted to be.

The club was still there. The red neon sign was new but the six steps down to the basement area were the same worn stones he'd walked down so many times—and inside, too, little had changed. It was still dark and smoky; the carpet was still sticky underfoot; the tables still had their gingham cloths; the Chianti bottles, with dribbles of wax encrusted on their necks, still doubled as candlesticks. He sat at the bar and drank a whisky and soda and watched as the four-piece band began to assemble itself on the small stage at the far end of the room. Somebody tapped him on the shoulder.

"You're Orson Woodley, aren't you?"

Orson swiveled on his stool. She was (as far as he could tell in this dim light) beautiful, with high cheekbones and a long, narrow nose. Her small head was tilted on her impossibly elegant neck and she was smiling expectantly at him. She looked, Orson thought, like an Ethiopian princess—or, at least, what an Ethiopian princess ought to look like.

"I am, yes."

"I was at the gallery today."

"Really? I didn't see you."

"Ah, but I saw you. You were busy and anyway, I only came in to buy something."

"Something of mine, I hope."

"Sure. That little drawing of the boy with the chickens. It was the only one I could afford."

"I like that one."

"So do I. That's why I bought it." She held out one slim-boned hand. "Monica Bassie. I really love your stuff."

"Thank you, Monica Bassie. I'd probably love yours too, if I knew what it was."

"Are you sticking around for a few minutes? If you are, you'll see my stuff. You've got a good seat, too. I wouldn't move, if I were you."

"I won't."

She glided away into the shadows. Orson drank another whisky. The band began to play, softly and the woman appeared in a single spotlight and started to sing. She had a musky, velvet voice and she sang the kind of songs that Orson liked—*Smoke gets In Your Eyes*, and *Stardust* and even *Blues In The Night* which was one of his favorites.

When she'd finished, she came back to him at the bar.

"Well?"

"I like your stuff. Better than I like *my* stuff, in fact."

They talked and then had a bad dinner together at the club. Monica asked if he was married and Orson said that he wasn't, which was true but misleading. He went with her in a taxi, back to her apartment in Greenwich Village and, when she got out, she kissed him lightly on the cheek.

"Can I call you?" he said, leaning out of the taxi window.

"Sure, why not?"

The affair started after their third date and Orson telephoned Saint Marta's and said that he wasn't going to come back right away, as arranged, because the gallery had all sorts of plans for him and several Broadway producers were interested in him designing sets for their forthcoming productions and, really, he ought to be around for discussions for the next couple of weeks.

"He's having an affair," said Giselle to Lewis, over breakfast on the terrace. All the guests had gone two days before, except for a young American actor called Murray, who was Lewis' friend at that time. Lewis had invited the entire cast simply to camouflage the evidence of their relationship, which was more erotic than sentimental and therefore entirely satisfactory, as far as Lewis was concerned. Murray was due to go back to New York the next day. Meanwhile, he was sitting at the table with them, eating toast.

"What? An *affair*? Why on earth do you say that?"

"Because I know he is," said Giselle, cutting—more savagely than usual—into a mango.

"Who with?"

"I don't know. Some woman."

"Well, yes—obviously some woman. Are you sure?"

"No, of course I'm not sure. Not without catching him in the act— like you did with us at Neuilly. Lewis walked right in on us, Murray. You should have seen his face. Of course, he wasn't queer then. Well, not very, anyway."

"The Queen of Tact, that's what you are, dear."

"Didn't you suspect anything *before* you walked in on us?"

"Yes, I did."

"There you are, then. So do I, now. The thing is, I don't want to catch him in the act, because that would be frightful. I'd rather you did."

"Did what?"

"Catch him in the act. Then you could do all the remonstrating. You could wag your famous finger at him and tell him he was being a beast and that he was to come home immediately and I could pretend I didn't know anything about it, which is what I'd rather do, if you don't mind."

"You mean, you want me to go up to New York. Find him and drag him home?"

"Please, sweet."

Lewis looked at Murray and Murray looked back at Lewis—both thinking that it would be good to continue seeing each other for a few more days. They could stay at Murray's apartment…

Orson found out about this conversation because Lewis told him all about it a week later. Lewis didn't catch him and Monica Bassie in the act, because the affair was conducted in Monica's Greenwich Village apartment and Lewis didn't feel he could break down the door without causing more of a scene than he was prepared to cause on Giselle's behalf; he simply asked Orson about it the second night of his stay in New York and Orson, shamefaced and sotto voce, admitted everything.

"Who is she?"

"A singer. You ought to see her. We'll go tonight."

Lewis said that he didn't want to see her, particularly, but Orson insisted they listen to Monica Bassie sing. So Lewis called Murray and told him that they were all going to a seedy nightclub on 42nd Street and Murray said, "Not Club Pellicano?" and Lewis said that yes, he thought that was the name—and Murray said that there was a marvelous singer there called Monica Bassie and that he'd been dying to go to Club Pellicano for ages—so all three went that evening and, after Monica's set, Lewis was glad that he'd given in. She had an extraordinary voice and was very beautiful, in an exotic, tribal way and later, when Orson took them all out to dinner at Sardi's, Lewis found that she was also delightful company.

When Monica went to the bathroom, Lewis wagged his finger in Orson face and said, "She's lovely but you've got to stop this. You've got to come home."

"I know. Stop wagging that thing at me. I know."

"So does Giselle, unfortunately."

"You said she was guessing. She doesn't know anything, does she?"

"No, she doesn't—but Giselle's guesses become, as fast as you can blink, Giselle's certainties. You know that."

Orson sighed. "You're right, I guess. OK. We'll go home tomorrow."

"No," said Lewis, shaking his head. "No—you'll go home tomorrow. I'm going to stay on for a few days. It's not fair that you have all the fun. Murray and I deserve some too, don't we Murray?"

Murray nodded, grinning.

"We shall see some shows," said Lewis. "And go to some concerts. And feed the squirrels in the park. All the things we can't do on Saint Marta's."

"And several things we can," said Murray.

"Hush. *Pas devant les heteros.*"

"Huh?"

Orson spent his last night at Monica's apartment and, when he began his breaking-it-off speech, Monica kissed him and said, "I know. It's OK. You go."

"You don't mind?"

"No. We had fun. And I knew there was somebody else."

"You knew? How?"

Monica smiled her Gioconda smile. "Because it's written all over your face."

He'd come back to Gladstones the next day, leaving Lewis and Murray in New York. Giselle had been very loving at his return and had never said a word about her suspicions, which made him love her even more than before, if that was possible. It clearly was.

There was the sound of a car horn on the drive and the rattle of a diesel engine. Orson pulled himself to his feet. The hibiscus was looking better but there was still a lot he could do to it. He'd do it tomorrow.

He went by the terrace, but Olga wasn't there any more. The French windows were open and he saw Lewis, dressed in his overcoat, with his homburg pushed back on his head, slumped in one of the sofas.

"You're back, then."

Lewis waved one languid hand. "So it would seem. Is it me, or is it frightfully cold in here?"

"The air-conditioning is on, if that's what you mean. No, it's not frightfully cold at all."

"I've been cold for the last forty eight hours. The airplane was freezing, so were both airports and the Savoy was positively arctic. London was hell but not, cruelly, in a hot way. How anybody lives there is past belief."

"You had a good time then?"

"Bits of it were all right. The show, surprisingly, was one of them."

"Scatter Giselle, did you?"

"Yes. I'm very tired. All these questions."

There was a pause, then Orson said, "We had a quiet time of it. I gave Olga all Giselle's jewelry—"

"Good. But not quite all of it, actually. I gave Finlay's necklace to Amanda."

"So that's where it went. And we found the diaries in the safe deposit box, too. Olga's been reading them. I don't know where she is."

"She said hello and then scurried away. A little distrait, I thought."

Michael and Amanda came in through the front door, carrying suitcases. Amanda dropped her bags and went to Orson and kissed him on both cheeks. Then she stood back and ran her eyes over him.

"I was hoping Freddy might have cleaned you up by the time we got back. My hopes are dashed."

"You shut up, creature. I'll have a little respect, if you don't mind."

Freddy threw open the door in the side wall and stood, posed like Judy Garland trying to get home from the Emerald City. He clasped his hands under his chin and gazed earnestly up at the ceiling. Then he clicked his heels together three times and said, "There's no place like home. There's no place like home!"

"Hello Freddy," said Amanda. "You didn't manage it, I see."

"He starts out clean, Miss Amanda," said Freddy. "In the morning you could eat your breakfast off him. I can't be held accountable for what he gets up to the rest of the day. Welcome home, Sir L. You look a little peaky. Can I get you anything?"

"A coffin would be nice," said Lewis, faintly.

"Oh, Sir L—you are a card. Here, give us your titfer, we can't have you sitting about like the Godfather." Freddy saw that Michael was about to start up the stairs with the bags and he ran forward and took them out of Michael's hands. "No, let me take the suitcases, young sir. You sit down and take the weight off. Anybody needs me, I'll be upstairs unpacking."

He staggered up the flight and disappeared into the corridor. Orson sat down opposite Lewis and Amanda and Michael flopped into a pair of armchairs.

Orson said, "Did you see Finlay?"

Lewis told him about the meeting and Orson shook his head. "Lying asshole."

"I think I believed him," said Amanda.

"So do I," said Olga, walking slowly in through the French windows.

"Hello," said Lewis. "What do you mean—so do you? You weren't there."

Olga held a leather-bound book in her right hand. She looked apprehensive, Amanda thought—but it was an apprehension tinted with an almost invisible wash of amusement. She watched her mother walk to the group and stand awkwardly in front of them, the book clasped now in both hands and held, defensively, over her stomach.

"It's something I read in her diaries," said Olga. "1938—the year before I was born."

"What happened in 1938?" said Lewis.

"Perhaps this isn't the right moment—you must be tired after that flight—"

"I'm near death but I can still listen. What happened in 1938?"

"I don't know how to tell you, really, other than show you the passages."

"I never could decipher her writing," said Orson. "Why don't you read it to us? I like being read to."

Olga paused for a moment, looking from Lewis to Orson and then back again. Then she said, "All right. That way, at least they'll be her words and not mine."

She sat down between Amanda and Michael and opened the book. "It starts here—January 15th, 1938. They're in New York, she and Finlay Ferguson—'*Finny thrashed about all night, making silly noises. I couldn't sleep a wink. Nearly bashed him with an ashtray. Lunch with Thelma. I had a salad. Home. Finny said he had a fever. Bed.*'

"Riveting," said Lewis.

"Next day: '*Finny wouldn't get up. Said he had a pain. Wanted to see a doctor. Called doctor. Doctor came. Prodded Finny about, said he had influenza. Finny said bugger that, he had something a lot worse than influenza. Doctor said he didn't. They had a row about it. Frightfully idiotic, Finny thinking he knows best. Too bloody opinionated for words. He felt much worse later, which serves him right for arguing. Poor old Finny. Too funny, really.*'

"What a callous thing she was," said Orson. "I had the 'flu once. She wouldn't speak to me until I was better."

Olga turned over two pages. "There's nothing for a couple of days—and then this:

'*Not so funny after all. Finny in hospital. Doctor said he's got Meningo-something-itis, which is something awful to do with his brain and all because of mumps, which is a silly thing to get at his age. Doctor says he'll be all right after a long recuperation. Cocktails with Thelma and Bugs. Home alone, boohoo.'"*

"Thelma and Bugs," said Lewis, ruminatively. "Weren't they one of those American couples we met that evening?"

"Quiet, Lewis," said Orson.

"There are another two blank pages and then this: '*Went to hospital, saw Finny. Looked much better. Doctor came in and said he wanted a word. Went out into corridor with him. Doctor rather sweet with a little blonde moustache. Then—thunderbolt! Mumps very, very severe and Finny now completely sterile! No wigglies at all! Would I tell him? No I wouldn't. Told sweet doctor to tell him. His job, after all. Cried a bit in taxi on the way home. Don't know why—rather relieved, in fact. No bloody babies! Dinner with usual crowd at Twenty One. Why does Louise wear her hair like that?*'

There was a silence. Olga looked up from the book. She said, "That's it. Oh, and there's this."

She held up a small sheet of paper, creased in the middle. "I don't know why she kept but it was sandwiched between these pages. It's some sort of medical report, from a Doctor Morgenthal, confirming it all. Finlay Ferguson got a severe attack of mumps in January 1938 which made him sterile. Apparently it's rare for that to happen but in his case, it did. Anyway—the fact seems to be that Finlay Ferguson couldn't have been anybody's father after January 1938. Which means he wasn't mine, you see. He's telling the truth. Sorry."

"What have you got to be sorry about?" said Lewis. "The mystery wasn't of your making, was it?"

"No."

"Well then."

Amanda reached forward and put her hand on the diary on Olga's knees.

"Haven't you got any further with it?"

"No. Well, it was rather a stunner. Enough to stop me in my tracks, anyway."

Amanda said, "May I?" and slid the book from under Olga's limp hands. She frowned down at the book, skimming the words and then turned the page.

Lewis cleared his throat. "I'm not surprised it stopped you. It would have stopped the most voracious of readers. Certainly would have stopped me. What a puzzle it is, to be sure. Not Finlay, after all—and us spending all this time thinking it was. Question is now—if not Finlay, who then?"

Orson shook his head. "Why would she do that? Why would Giselle do that? She always insisted it was Finlay Ferguson's, there was never any question about it and we accepted it, didn't we?"

"Absolutely," said Lewis. "Just goes to show how gullible even reasonably intelligent men can be."

"I'm sorry," said Olga, staring hard at her empty hands. "I just cannot see what you found so wonderful about her. She seems so—so—oh, bugger it, she seems so pointlessly cruel. Like somebody pulling the legs off a spider. I mean, to lie about something like this. Why? What for?"

Lewis spread his hands wide. "She often did things for which there was no rational explanation. Mind you, they were trivial things, certainly more trivial than giving birth and then lying about the child's paternity. I have no answer for you."

"Then what did you *see* in her?"

"Well, now. What did we see in her? I know what I saw in her. Ossie? What did you see in her?"

"Oh," said Orson, vaguely. "You know."

"So succinct. What though, can you expect from a painter? I shall tell you what we saw in her. Rooms brightened when she walked into them. Funerals she attended turned into cocktail parties. Ferocious guard dogs would lick her hands. Confirmed old bachelors found themselves in love and wondering what they'd missed. When she walked in the park, it never rained. Or, if it did, we never noticed. You had to be there, you see, to understand. You're right, of course—she was awful, really. She was everything frightful that you imagine her to be. But what you can't imagine is that, no matter what she did or said or even thought, everybody always forgave her. They couldn't help themselves, you see. Whatever dreadful thing she did, the only possible reaction from those who knew her was instant, unconditional forgiveness. Ossie and I were no different. Perhaps, because we were so familiar with her, our expressions of forgiveness were delayed by a few minutes but they always arrived long before Giselle could begin to feel any remorse. We made sure of that. We spent a lifetime in a state of uncomplaining forgiveness and, to us, the only truly unforgivable thing Giselle ever did was to go and die on us."

Unnoticed for the last few moments, Oscar had congealed, slowly, into a state of rigid immobility. There was a spreading pallor beneath the ruddy tan of his face and his eyes stared, unfocused, at a point only inches from the end of his nose. Nobody saw his stillness; they were staring at Olga, who refused to meet their eyes, instead looking steadfastly down at her hands that lay, palm upwards, in her lap—almost as though the book that Amanda was currently flipping through with concentrated haste was still in her own hands and her eyes were still making out the words. She felt their gazes boring into the top of her head and she muttered, "Sorry," again.

"Ahah," said Amanda, stabbing suddenly at the diary.

"What?" said Lewis.

Amanda was staring down at the diary. "Here's something interesting."

Oscar shook himself out of his trance and said, "Hold it, creature. I'd rather you didn't."

"Rather she didn't what?" said Lewis.

"Tell you it was me," said Orson and he said it so quietly that, at first, nobody other than Lewis appeared to have heard him. Certainly, and for several seconds, neither Olga's nor Michael's eyes swiveled in his direction, and Amanda continued to squint down at the book, her eyes darting fast across the writing. Olga and Michael seemed wrapped in some private deliberations of their own.

"Tell me it was you *what*?" said Lewis.

"Tell you it was *me*, Lewis. The one responsible. Mind you, in case you think I've been hiding it all these years, I've only just realized the possibility. The window of opportunity, as it were. I assume that's what she's found—the creature, I mean."

"What has she found?" said Lewis, his voice dangerously low.

"Something," said Amanda. "I don't know how telling it is. Dated May 12th. She wrote—'*Horrors. Darling old O has been and gone and put me up the spout. What am I to do? All is lost. Shan't tell anybody. Will claim virgin birth.*' She looked up at Orson and said, "How many darling old O's did she know?"

"Several," said Lewis. "But only one biblically." He glared stonily at Orson. "You're right up shit creek, aren't you?"

"I rather think I am."

"And utterly paddle-less, too. When? That's all I want to know. When? When did you choose to break the pact?"

"There was this one time. I guess that was enough. We didn't tell you. We didn't want to upset you."

"I'm extremely upset right now. *When?*"

"We were still in New York, at the hotel—"

"I didn't ask where, I asked when? I mean, for Christ's sake, this was precisely why we had a pact. We agreed that we were emotional partners and, until the matter was properly resolved, there was to be no hanky panky by either of us. You agreed to keep your sticky fingers off her until things became clearer and things did not become clearer until we came to Saint Marta's, which was when the pact was officially dissolved, if you remember?"

"I remember. Do shut up."

"I won't. Exactly when, please?"

"Does it matter?"

"Yes, it bloody does. When was this window of opportunity?"

"Hardly a window. More like a peephole. You went down to the lobby to get some cigarettes."

Lewis exploded like a small firecracker. "You shit! You old *shit*! Oh— a real quickie, was it? Oh, how nice—particularly for Olga, to know that she was conceived during a nanosecond of nicotine withdrawal." He stopped abruptly, breathing hard. Then he said, "I don't remember this at all. I don't remember going down for cigarettes at all."

"Well, you wouldn't, would you? An inconsequential act like that—"

"It wasn't inconsequential at all though, was it? It had consequences coming out of the woodwork, didn't it?"

"I mean, it's not peculiar that you don't remember it and I do. Our act was, dare I say it, more memorable than yours."

"And, dare I say it, if only for the astonishing alacrity in its performance. I mean, how long could I have been gone, for Christ's sake?"

Michael said, "Wow," quietly and it was as though a referee had stepped between two boxers. Orson and Lewis stopped glaring at each other and looked, instead, towards Michael who, with a flick of his eyes, directed their gaze towards Olga, who was still staring blankly down at her hands. Orson sighed. "I think, Lewis, that we should stop bickering about the event and pay some attention to the result instead." He coughed and Olga looked up.

"I'm sorry," he said. "Are you very upset?"

"No. No—how could I be?" She was twisting her hands together now and her eyes seemed unable to meet Orson's. "It's just—I feel guilty, somehow, for forcing you to confront this issue—I didn't mean to—"

"I don't see why you should feel guilty," said Amanda. "I don't."

"Well, you wouldn't," said Orson. "You're just this creature."

"Who apparently just happens to be your granddaughter, don't forget that."

There was a long silence. Then Orson said, "I feel really peculiar. Does anybody else feel peculiar?"

A second, more awkward silence—broken suddenly by a high-pitched squeal from above, raising all eyes to the head of the staircase, where Freddy stood, hands pressed against his cheeks.

"What is it?" said Lewis, wondering, for a second, if Freddy had found something loathsome in one of his suitcases.

Freddy took his hands away from his face. "But—it's the most wonderful news!" he cried. "Don't you think? We ought to be celebrating."

"What news?" said Lewis.

"What news? *What news*? Madam's news, of course! Mr. Woodley's, too. And young Miss Amanda's. Honestly, Sir L, I don't know what I'm going to do with you. All of you, actually, sitting there like you're at the Queen Mother's funeral."

"Oh, you heard, did you?"

"Yes. Well, I couldn't help it, could I? I was stuck up here, not knowing whether to stay up or come down—so I stayed up, out of the way and—oh—I couldn't be happier for you all, I really couldn't, not even if I'd won the football pools—and I don't care what you all say, I'm opening champagne, that's what I'm doing and if you don't want any, I'll drink it all by myself."

Freddy was coming down the stairs now and the great, tooth-baring grin across his face and the sight of his Hawaiian shirt tails flapping out behind him and the sound of his bare feet slapping rapidly on the stone steps seemed to break the collective paralysis, so that eyes at last were prepared to meet other eyes and mouths that were thinned by embarrassment now softened into smiles—and words that had seemed impossible to form a moment ago now began to tumble out in a stream—beginning with Olga saying that she was finding it ironic, to say the least, that in this present climate of Political Correctness she found herself indebted for her very life to the tobacco industry—and then Amanda joined in and said, loudly, that she was either going to start smoking again or, at the very least, was going to be joining Freddy in some champagne because, as far as she was concerned she was delighted to have Orson clean or Orson dirty—it really didn't matter—as her grandfather—and Michael kept muttering 'wow' to himself—and slowly the pinkness was returning to Orson's face and a small, tentative smile was curling up the edges of his mouth and he managed to stammer out that if everybody was happy then so was he, because he really couldn't imagine a better daughter for himself than Olga and even the creature would do, at a pinch, for his granddaughter—

And only Lewis remained sober and watchful, his eyes darting coolly, like a judge at a dog show, from one celebrant to another.

Chapter 15

Lewis was the only member of the party who went sober to bed that night. The rest drank too much champagne before dinner and too much wine during—and when they left the table, Orson insisted on several shots of brandy, which made him unsteady, so Freddy had to help him up the stairs at midnight. Lewis had announced that he was exhausted from the long flight and intended to be in bed by nine o'clock; he'd left them straight after dinner. His absence was hardly noticed; Orson, sprawled in a sofa, (with Olga and Amanda on either side of him, their hands clutched firmly in his) insisted on a detailed history of the Whitehall family and, when that was done, he regaled Olga, Amanda and Michael with rambling, inconsecutive stories about Giselle and their lives together—until Freddy appeared from the kitchen quarters and said it was time for bed and that he wouldn't be held responsible for the way Mr. Woodley was going to feel the next morning and, when Orson replied cheerfully that he didn't expect more than a slight hangover, Freddy said that he'd be the one with the slight hangover, thank you very much but Mr. Woodley was going to be positively migrainic if he didn't stop tossing back the Courvoisier and go to bed this instant. Amanda said that she was tired—exhausted, actually, what with the plane and the ancestor thing and rather more liquor than she was used to. She kissed Orson and took herself up the stairs, with Michael close behind her. Orson watched them go and then said, mistily, that it was good that they were such friends and Olga began to say that she thought they were rather more than friends—but Freddy was fussing about Orson, chivvying him out of the sofa and Orson didn't hear her.

He woke, as usual, at six the next morning. The headache, tucked tightly into his skull just behind his right eye, was small but steady and he knew it would be there all day. He rolled over, closing his eyes against the early sunlight that slanted through the shutters on the window but he knew it was hopeless trying to sleep. There were too many thoughts crowding his mind, each thought worming its way past the headache to pop, unannounced, into his consciousness, like latecoming guests at a party— for, no sooner had one thought occupied his mind but the doorbell would ring again and he would have to drop that thought and open the door (which separated his conscious from his unconscious mind) to the new one. Fleeting visions of Giselle at the Algonquin—*buzz*—Finlay at the apartment, his distress mixed with obduracy—*buzz*—Lewis holding Giselle's hand in the hotel lobby as they paid the bill—*buzz*—Giselle's face dissolving, effortlessly and with remarkably little change in the features, into Amanda's—*buzz*—what were they going to do about Freddy (if anything because, after all, he was very nearly perfect if you discounted his Mary Poppins impersonation)—*buzz*—Lewis' uncharacteristic reserve last night, while everybody else seemed to have taken the news so tremendously well (and it was wonderful news, so long as you didn't mind finding yourself responsible for what could be the start of a dynasty and, right now, Orson could find no reason to think the idea anything but rather fun, because, after all and at his age, surely he wouldn't be expected to do very much about the situation other than sit back and watch the developments?)—*buzz*—that hibiscus ought to be looked at again, he'd left it kind of raggedy-looking—*buzz*—a sudden chill as he realized why Giselle had insisted the child was Finlay's and not his: if she'd admitted it was his, there was a distinct possibility that he'd have insisted they keep the baby and Giselle had made it plain from the moment the diaper question arose that that idea was out the window—so she'd told them that the baby was Finlay's simply to ensure they wouldn't feel bad about giving it away—yes, that was the awful truth about her, she was quite capable of such a terrible thing and that image of her had to be banished from this party as soon as possible because it was as an unwelcome guest as it was possible to be, so please let that doorbell ring again—*buzz*—oh, thank god, here's the hibiscus again, definitely time to have another whack at the hibiscus—*buzz*—Giselle—*buzz*—the hibiscus—

The hibiscus was winning by dint of Orson's effort and now seemed to be standing in the doorway, demanding all his attention like a neighbor come to complain about the noise and Orson rolled over onto his back and opened his eyes and stared up at the ceiling hoping that perhaps a third, less demanding, thought might flush out both the hibiscus and Giselle—but, though Giselle faded into the background, the hibiscus refused to go away, so he sighed and heaved himself off the bed and went to brush his teeth. He thought of having a bath but decided there was little point if he was going to get stuck into the hibiscus; a bath could come later. He pulled on his gardening clothes and left the room, padding as silently as he could in his socks down the corridor and then, less silently, down the stairs. He thought he heard a sound coming from the kitchen area, so he opened the door and shuffled down the short passage and found Freddy at the stove, humming something from *Brigadoon*. Orson coughed and Freddy turned and looked at him with narrowed eyes.

"Bit of a throbby, have we? Behind the eyes, I suspect. Well, never mind, Mr. O, join the club, I'm taking care of mine right now with a couple of Speedy's fizzies, you just hang onto the table for a sec and I'll see you to rights—it was all in a good cause though, wasn't it? I mean, what a discovery, you must be over the moon—and what an early bird you are, aren't you?—I didn't think we'd see any surfacing before nine at the soonest and here you are at the crack of dawn, lot on your mind, I expect, what with all the ramificazziones, I'm sure I wouldn't have slept a wink if it had been me—going to do some gardening, are we?—because that's the only explanation I can think of for those horrid manky old trousers, and the only *excuse* come to that."

Orson sank into a wooden chair and held his head in his hands while Freddy rattled about the kitchen, putting first a fizzing glass of Alka Seltzer in front of him, followed by a cup of wonderful coffee and two slices of toast and marmalade, which Orson chewed reluctantly because he didn't feel up to eating anything at all—but Freddy was not to be denied.

"You have to have something in your tummy, Mr. O, if you're going to exert yourself. Besides, we need it to soak up all that alcohol we consumed last night, don't we? How's the noggin now?"

The noggin seemed to be feeling better. Orson pulled himself to his feet, patted Freddy on the top of his head and shuffled out of the kitchen. He found his gardening shoes outside the French windows, stamping his feet into the mud-caked leather. There was a touch of cool dampness in the air and the he took several deep breaths, which cleared his head even more. The hibiscus, he thought, was in for a shock.

The secateurs were where he'd left them, next to the pile of clippings. He began to snip at the stems, scientifically at first and then, as he thought more about what Giselle had done, with a kind of haphazard indignation, until the hibiscus was little more than a few ragged twigs protruding only inches from the earth of the flower bed.

He was sweating now but his ire had died away and he was beginning, as always, to search for extenuating circumstances, so that his inevitable forgiveness of Giselle's rotten behavior could be justified. The choice Giselle had made, he decided, was at least merciful to the child; Giselle would have been a lousy mother and, perhaps she'd known that and had abdicated her responsibilities for altruistic reasons and not for selfish ones at all—yes, that was the answer, of course, it had to be, for the sake of Giselle's memory, if for nothing else. And the woman had turned out well, after all. She was a little old to be considered a daughter—a new father, surely, had the right to expect that his offspring's face be as yet untouched by time—but, apart from the few wrinkles round the very attractive eyes and a slight pouchiness developing under the equally attractive chin, Gloa—*Olga*—was as nice a looking middle-aged daughter as a man his age and stoutness had the right to expect. And the other one, his *granddaughter* would you credit it—well, that was something else again. Apart from the startling resemblance to Giselle, the girl—the *creature*—seemed to have the brains and the beauty and the goddam spunk to make any grandfather just about as pleased with the final product as a grandfather could be. All in all, rather a wonderful outcome—so long as nobody got too mushy about it, or expected him to do anything very paternal all of a sudden. It was far too late for that and, besides, he didn't think any such behavior would be particularly welcome either. Friends, that's what they'd all be. Good friends, with that dash of familiarity that only ties of blood can achieve.

It was a pity about Lewis' reaction but, no doubt he'd get over it in time. Orson seemed to remember that Lewis had taken himself off to bed quite early the night before—and silently, too, which was unlike him—so it looked like there was going to be some sulky brooding in that quarter, for several days at least. Well, the hell with him. He was probably jealous.

His body was aching and sticky with sweat, so he dropped the secateurs onto the pile of clippings and trudged back towards the terrace. He paused there for a moment, tucking himself behind the big green sunshade and peering round it to look up at Gomorrah's window, in the vague hope that the creature might appear there and, if she did, then he could wave at her in an approving, grandfatherly way, which would be a good, tone-setting start to the day—and suddenly, there she was in the window—or at least the top half of her was there and the top half was naked and Orson saw that her breasts were just like Giselle's had been when they were young—and then he realized that he shouldn't be seeing this, not at his age and certainly not now that he was actually related—so he stayed quite still, hoping Amanda wouldn't catch sight of the top of his head, which was the only part of him that would be showing from behind the sunshade.

She was looking straight out over the terrace, at the sea below. Orson wondered how long she was going to do that, because he couldn't stay hidden here all morning and, if he moved—however nonchalantly—out from behind his cover, even with his eyes fixed on the ground, the creature might suspect that he'd been having an ogle at her and that would never do; that was not a grandfatherly way to behave and the tone would be ruined for the whole day and, possibly, for ever.

The silly girl was just standing there, like some Praxiteles statue, lovely but irritatingly immobile. Surely she'd seen enough of the sea by now? Surely her toothbrush and her face cloth were calling? His back was hurting—

And then two brown arms circled Amanda from behind and two brown hands slipped up to cup her breasts and Orson saw the creature smile and lay her head back, pressing her cheek next to the face that had appeared from the gloom behind her—and the face belonged to Michael—and Orson, possessed by the most frantic agitation he'd ever experienced in his long and frequently agitated life, stepped out from behind the sunshade and shouted up at the window, "Stop that! Stop that at once! Dou you hear me? *Stop it!*"

Two heads jerked in his direction, eyes wide—and then the figures were gone, swallowed up in the darkness of the room. Orson stumbled through the French windows and up the stairs. Panting, he ran to Gomorrah's door and began to pound on it.

"Michael! *Michael*! Come out of there at once! You hear? Get your sorry ass out of there this instant!"

Muffled words from behind the door, the rustling of clothing—

"Michael!"

The door opened and Michael stood there, a hurt, embarrassed look on his face. He was wearing the clothes he'd worn last night, and they had been dragged on hurriedly, so that half a shirt tail was flowing over the waist band of his jeans. Amanda's pale face hovered over his shoulder. She was wrapped in a sheet.

Michael said, "Look, I'm sorry—I didn't think—"

'No, you didn't, did you? Come on, out of there. This is appalling. Dreadful. This must never happen again. In fact, Michael, I think the best thing would be if you went straight back to New York—yes, on the first plane out of here—because, you see, this situation cannot be allowed to continue—not on any account—no, no, never *mind* about your shoes, you're not to go back in that room, you hear me—in fact, I want you to go straight to Sodom and start packing—"

Lewis and Olga opened their bedroom doors almost simultaneously— Lewis in a midnight blue silk dressing gown and Olga in a pair of extraordinary pink flannel pajamas with pictures of cowboys all over them—which momentarily drew all eyes to her, standing in her doorway with a look of anxious query on her face—and then Lewis dragged his eyes away from the cowboys and fixed them sternly on Orson and said, "What's going on?"

"This is what's going on!" Orson shouted, waving passionately at Michael and Amanda. "Under our noses—these two—God knows what but you don't need much imagination, not when they have no clothes on—I saw them from the terrace, just happened to look up and there they were, in the window, buck-assed naked for Chrissake—Michael, I told you to go to your room—"

Michael said, "I'm very sorry. It was wrong of us, I guess—we should have asked if it was all right—"

"Asked? *Asked*? Asked what? That you could screw her?"

"No. I mean, like, under your roof—"

"What the fuck's my roof got to do with it? It's got nothing to do with my roof!"

"Then, what *has* it got to do with?" said Lewis, mildly. "They're having an affair, Ossie. People do, you know."

"An affair?" said Olga.

"It started in London. I thought you all knew."

"Well, we didn't!" shouted Orson. "In fact, are you telling me *you* knew?"

"Of course I did. And I think Olga knew too." Lewis turned to Olga. "Didn't you?"

"I guessed they were."

Lewis regarded her gravely. "And do you have any objections?"

"Not to the affair, no. But, obviously, they should have behaved more tactfully—"

Lewis raised his eyebrows. "Hard to behave tactfully when you're sleeping in rooms called Sodom and Gomorrah. I mean, the names alone give one a green light to behave immoderately, I would have thought. And, indeed, over the years, innumerable guests have flitted, nightly, back and forth between Sodom, Gomorrah and Zeboiim, without the slightest objection from Ossie, I might add—which begs the question, Ossie—why are you objecting now? I can't believe it's because of some misplaced sense of paternal responsibility, I really can't."

Orson seemed to shrink beneath his clothes and he lowered his head and swung it from side to side, like a disgruntled grizzly. "I just don't like it, that's all."

"No, no, Ossie. That won't do at all, you know it won't. Come along now, let's have it. Spit it out, before it chokes you. You're turning an unhealthy shade of red and we can't be doing with an apoplexy, not at this godawful hour of the morning."

Orson gulped a couple of times, his eyes darting warily between Michael, Amanda and Lewis. Then he muttered, "I'd like a word in private, Lewis."

"No, Ossie. You've upset far too many people, all of whom deserve an explanation and, in fact, we're all going to stand here until you come up with one. Michael, don't move. Amanda, come out of there, you look like a nervous gopher. All right, Ossie—out with it."

Orson took a deep breath. "All right. But you're not going to like it. Any of you." He paused and took another breath. "See, the thing is—the creature here is my granddaughter—we've established that, I think—and this other creature here—well, he's—um—well, not to be beat about the bush—not to put too fine a point to it—well, goddammit—he's her goddam uncle."

The smile that Lewis had been trying to control broke free and twisted up both corners of his mouth. He looked up at the ceiling and said, "*Is* he now?"

"He's her *what?*" said Olga.

"My *what?*" said Amanda.

"I'm *what?*" said Michael.

"Her uncle!" Orson shouted, his face shading to purple. "Uncle, uncle, *uncle!*"

"Such a ludicrous word, don't you think?" said Lewis. "Particularly when repeated like that. *Uncle.* Uncle, uncle, uncle. Bizarre. So, how do you figure this, Ossie?"

"I've no intention of figuring it," said Orson, his eyes refusing to meet Lewis's. "Suffice to say that he is and, as such, this—this relationship must stop immediately. Michael, will you please go to your room and start packing. I'll find out when the next flight is—"

'No, no, Ossie. This won't do, you know. We deserve more than that."

Orson stood, panting heavily, chewing his lips. Then he took a deep breath and let it out in one long shuddering sigh.

"Oh God. All right. But not here. Maybe we could all meet on the terrace in five minutes—"

"Is five minutes enough for you to get your story straight?" said Lewis.

"Shut up, Lewis. I was thinking about these two getting themselves decent and I daresay Olga will want to change out of those peculiar pajamas and, while you look very distinguished in that robe, I for one have seen enough of it. Five minutes. On the terrace."

Orson turned away and retreated back down the corridor and down the stairs. Lewis raised his eyebrows and said, "What an exciting time we've been having, don't you think? All these revelations, all these skeletons leaping from their closets." He looked sideways at Michael and Amanda. "Oh, do stop looking so stricken, you two. Everything will be all right, you know. I guarantee it, in fact. Why don't we all get dressed—although, I must say, I *shall* miss those pajamas, Olga. Wherever did you get them?"

Ten minutes later they gathered on the terrace, a silent group apart from Lewis, who seemed to be deriving amusement from his careful placing of them round the patio table. "Now, you sit there, Olga—and Michael over here and Amanda next to him—no, perhaps not—yes, that's right, you come over here and sit next to me and *what* a pretty outfit, although I think I preferred you in the sheet—and yes, Ossie, you sit there at the top end, like the chairman of the board. Good. We can all see you and, if you speak up, we can probably all hear you, too. Ah, and here's Freddy, who appears with almost theatrical precision at exactly the most dramatic moments, how do you do it?"

Freddy was standing in the French doors, his arms folded disapprovingly across his chest.

"Oh, it's brekkie out here, is it?"

"I think just coffee, Freddy. Food might, or might not, be needed later. If anybody wants any, we'll all come in later."

Freddy sniffed. "If you'd just told me, Sir L—"

"He's telling you now," snarled Orson.

"Somebody got out of the wrong side of the bed this morning—"

"Not now, Freddy," Lewis said, gently and Freddy—ever sensitive to the mood of his employers—lifted one eyebrow and disappeared into the house. They waited in silence until he came back with his tray and Freddy served them without a word of his customary running commentary. Something, he thought, was up and whatever the Something was, obviously they wanted to keep it to themselves, within the family as it were and, while he thought of himself as pretty much part of that family, his years of discreet service—and the pride he'd taken in it—overcame the disappointment of being excluded. Anyway, he reasoned as he poured the last cup, he'd find out soon enough.

"Well, I'll leave you to your cogitations. Give us a shout if you need anything."

They watched him walk back into the house and Orson, twisted in his seat, waited until he saw him go through the service door.

Lewis rapped once on the table top. "We're all ears, Ossie."

Orson wiped his hand over his face, leaving a smear of dirt on his cheek.

"All right. Jesus, this is difficult. I don't know where to start. OK—I had this affair and Michael's the result. That's all there is to it."

"You're my father?" said Michael, slowly and with an air of amused disbelief.

"Yes, I am. I don't know why you think it's so extraordinary. Somebody had to be. Sorry you didn't know earlier."

"Well, well," said Lewis, smiling up at the sky. "First Olga, now Michael. Are there any more of your progeny scattered about the cosmos, or is that it?"

"That's it," growled Orson. "Don't enjoy this too much, Lewis."

"My mother said my father was dead," said Michael. "Why did she say you were dead?"

"It seemed right at the time, Michael. I'm very sorry you had to find out like this."

"But—who's his mother?" said Amanda.

"I shall answer that," said Lewis. "Orson would have us believe that Michael's mother is Monica Bassie, an extremely beautiful and charming woman with whom Orson had a bit of a ding-dong back in 1949, I think it was—"

"It wasn't a ding-dong, Lewis," Orson muttered. "You were the one for the ding-dongs, not me." He looked, reluctantly, into Michael's eyes. "We had a passionate love affair for a short time and then she let me go.

Back to Giselle. Later I learned she was pregnant. I offered to marry her—but she wouldn't have it. She never showed me a moment of rancor about the break-up, not a moment of resentment—in fact, she behaved with extraordinary grace and dignity throughout the whole thing and I don't regret even a second of it. In fact, it was a privilege just knowing her, Michael, I want you to believe that."

"I do," Michael said. "She's my mother. But, I still don't get why—"

"It was because of Giselle. Your mother understood the strength of our relationship and decided not to get in the way of it. She also—wisely—understood the dangers of fame and the traps that can befall those that suffer from it. If the truth was known, by even a small number of people, then inevitably Giselle would have found it out and your mother had no intention of ruining our lives. A remarkable woman."

Everybody was watching Michael now, wondering how he was going to take this. Michael himself was gazing levelly at Orson, his face and body still, as if he was holding an interesting hand at poker and was determined his opponent should know nothing of it.

"I won't call you pop, even if you go down on bended knees."

"Thank you very much—I had no intention of doing that."

"It's unlikely that he *could*," said Lewis, still gazing serenely up at the sky.

There was a short silence and then Michael smiled. "*Half* uncle, really. Does that count?"

"This is so muddling," said Amanda. "Who *is* everybody?"

Orson sighed. "It's perfectly simple. I, with all the irresponsibility of youth, fathered two children by two separate women, although, in my favor, I only knew about one of them. The children are Olga and Michael. Michael is your mother's half brother, which makes Michael your half uncle—and yes, Michael, it *does* count, it counts like hell, what do you think this is, Mississippi or something?"

Lewis said, "You don't seem all that surprised, Michael. Either that, or you're exercising a positively Anglo Saxon sang froid."

Michael shrugged. "Well, I never really believed the death story. It seemed too convenient—and kids fantasize a lot. At least, I did. I guess I hoped that my father was either President Kennedy or one of you guys and, as I got older, I dropped the Kennedy idea—"

"You've been *fantasizing* about us?" said Lewis.

"Not obsessively, no. But enough that it's not really a big surprise, that's all. My mother inadvertently dropped hints all my life, too. She didn't know she was doing it but I picked them up. Little things—like if one of you was in the news, she'd be—I don't know—*differently* interested."

"How flattering," Lewis said.

"How is she?" said Orson.

"Very well. She sends her regards to you both, by the way."

Orson cleared his throat noisily. "I did pay for you. I don't want to think I left you entirely high and dry. I did the schools and everything and there was money sent regularly. I dropped a word in Tolly's ear, too—although you don't seem to have needed any help there, he says you're terrific—"

"Tolly knows?"

"No. If Tolly had known, then everybody would've known. No, he thinks there's just a sort of avuncular interest, because we were fond of your mother."

Michael nodded and settled back in his chair. He looked at Olga and smiled. "Well—now I know how you feel. Weird, isn't it?"

"It is rather," said Olga, smiling back. "What are we supposed to do?"

"I have no idea," said Michael, cheerfully.

"You don't have to *do* anything," said Orson. "Other than stop the incestuous business, of course. We can't have that. This house may have seen some imaginative couplings in the past but we must draw the line at this, I'm afraid."

Lewis got up and wandered to the terrace balcony. For several moments he stood there, leaning on the balustrade, staring sightlessly out to sea and ignoring the muted conversation behind him. Michael's reaction had been interesting—hardly what one might expect and certainly not what he'd have written in a play—but the boy himself was interesting, of course and how clever of him to turn the tables on them, so that the real surprise for everybody lay in his composure, rather than in the startling news itself—even if the news was so dazzlingly wrong—

Lewis turned from his contemplation of the Caribbean and strolled back to the table. There was a momentary lull in the conversation and he said, "I want you all to go away for half an hour and leave Ossie and me alone. There are things we need to discuss. Would you all do that, please?"

"What's to discuss?" said Orson. "Everything's out in the open now, nothing left to be said, we all know who we are—what's to discuss?"

"Things," said Lewis.

Amanda stood up abruptly. "I'm going for a swim," she announced. "Michael—*Uncle* Michael—you come too."

Olga said, "I don't think—"

Amanda pointed her finger at her mother and said, "And you come too. You can be our chaperone and get to know your brother. Besides, if these two have things to discuss, imagine what *we've* got to talk about. Come on."

She walked into the house and Michael and Olga followed her.

"What?" said Orson, irritably.

"Wait," said Lewis. "Wait until they've gone to the beach."

Orson grunted and Lewis sat down next to him and wondered what he was going to say.

When they saw the last flash of Amanda's yellow bikini disappear down the path, Lewis took a deep breath and said, "I've always known about him, you know. About Michael."

"You knew? Good God. Why didn't you say anything?"

"Some things are better left unsaid. There were complications. Wheels within wheels."

"I don't know what the fuck you're talking about. How did you know?"

"Oh, come on, Ossie."

"Did Giselle know?"

"Of course she did."

Orson jerked round in his chair. "What?"

Lewis put his hand on Orson's arm. "Now, do calm down. It's essential you keep calm, otherwise I won't keep on with this."

"But, neither of you ever said anything to me about it."

"No, well—you had your little secret and we had ours."

"Oh yes? What was yours?"

"Ours was knowing all about your little secret. As long as you weren't prepared to divulge yours, Giselle and I were buggered it we'd reveal ours. It was, I think, the only secret Giselle was ever able to keep and she probably only managed that because she knew I'd slit her throat if she ever let it out."

Orson stirred with a new thought. "Wait a minute—if you knew—and I don't know how you did—if you knew Michael and Amanda were blood relations, then how the hell could you let them start an affair?"

"Oh, don't be silly, Ossie. That would be like Caligula whipping the English Channel because it wouldn't let him across—a pointless exercise. They were at it like knives the moment they set foot in London. What was I to do? Interpose my body? I'd have been cut to pieces. Besides, it's rubbish."

"What's rubbish?"

"The whole thing. The blood relation business. It's rubbish. It's not your fault, but it's rubbish."

"It is most certainly not rubbish. Those two are closely related and cannot be allowed to continue their relationship and, if you can't see that, then your laissez faire attitude has reached new heights of aberrance—"

"Well, that's rather the point, you see. The fact is, they're not related at all."

Orson snorted. "Yes they goddam are!"

"No, Ossie."

Lewis and Murray had taken Orson to the airport and had waved him off. Orson, who'd been subdued in the car, had managed a mournful "Have a good time," before disappearing through the gate and Lewis had called after him, "You, too," which had been thoughtless, because Orson—rigid with contrition—was going back to Giselle, who might or might not give him a horrible time about Monica—if she chose to know about it, of course.

Once Orson was out of sight, they'd driven back to Murray's West Side apartment. The apartment had begun to depress Lewis because Murray's ideas about housekeeping didn't match Lewis's; the boy didn't seem to understand what the sink in the kitchen was for and Lewis had found himself, all too frequently, up to his elbows in soap suds, washing dishes that should, had Murray the smallest interest in hygiene, have been dealt with several days before. Murray himself was turning out to be a disappointment; back on his home turf, he didn't seem to be quite as nice as he had been back at Gladstones.

"I think, "said Lewis, on the following morning, drying his hands on a foul dishcloth, "I think we should check into the Plaza for a few days."

"What for?" said Murray, who was beginning to think that his apartment had never looked so nice.

"Because I don't like it here."

"What's wrong with it?"

"It's squalid, Murray."

"Squalid?"

"Squalid and fetid."

"You Limeys. So fucking la-di-da."

"Quite," said Lewis, dropping both the dish cloth and Murray with startling ease.

He moved, alone, into the Plaza and spent two dull and lonely days wondering when it would be tactful for him to go home. He knew Orson and Giselle would need several days alone together to sort everything out and, besides, he had no intention of being around them while they did—so, how to occupy his time, that was the question? Unlike Orson, art galleries held no interest for him at all—there were far too many examples, from every period of history, of what he had long ago dubbed 'That Bloody Family'—museums bored him rigid, he hated going to the theater alone and, for some reason, all their New York friends seemed to be away on vacation, so there were no little dinner parties to look forward to either.

On the third night, on an impulse he hardly understood, he went back to Club Pellicano.

"You *saw* her? What for?"

"I don't know. I was lonely, I suppose. Everybody we knew was out of town. I liked her. She was beautiful. She sang nicely. How many reasons do you need?"

"What happened?"

"What happened? Well, let me see—well, eventually, I went to bed with her."

Orson made a strangled sound in his throat and turned, slowly, to stare at Lewis.

"You did what?"

"I went to bed with her. Well, she did that thing with her earrings—"

"What thing, for Chrissake?"

"That thing. You know. Didn't she do it with you?"

"For a wordsmith so proud of his pithiness, you're being irritatingly oblique, Lewis. Do *what* thing?"

"Taking her earrings off. Didn't she do that with you?"

"I don't know. Maybe—probably. I can't remember noticing."

"Oh, you'd have noticed this. It was a slow, languorous little performance, during which she never took her eyes from yours, watching you watch her as she slipped the earrings off each ear with those long slim fingers of hers and—still without looking anywhere but in your eyes and with that enchanting, sleepy smile of hers—placing them quite silently on the coffee table by her side—"

"No, she never did any of that—but, wait a minute, wait a minute—you went to *bed* with her?"

"Several times, in fact."

"But—for Chrissake, Lewis—you're a *homosexual*, for Chrissake—"

"Your point being?"

"You don't like women. Not in that way."

"Oh, Ossie, stop it. Don't you remember *anything*? I liked Giselle."

"Yes, but—"

"Look, I admit I was surprised by Monica—but then I worked it out. I'm attracted to the same people that attract you. I always have been. If you like them, so do I. If you want to go to bed with them, so do I. And, of course, Monica made it so easy."

"Do you mean to tell me that, only hours after she was sleeping with me, she was sleeping with you?"

"Not hours, Ossie. A few days. Monica was cheerfully promiscuous but she wasn't a tart."

"And you *liked* it?"

"Very much. It made a nice change."

"Good God. I never thought you'd surprise me again. So, let me get this right—you jumped straight into the same frying pan that I'd just been persuaded to get out of by one of those goddam finger-wagging lectures of yours. Talk about hypocrisy, Lewis. How could you?"

"Remarkably easily, in fact. I wasn't being unfaithful to anybody, remember—unless you count Murray and, by then, I didn't."

"And where, if I might ask, is all this leading?"

"Well, Ossie—it's leading to the fact that Michael isn't your child. He's mine."

Orson went very red and blinked slowly several times.

"Fucking crap."

"Not fucking crap."

"Michael is *mine*, Lewis. He's always been mine."

"No. You've always *thought* he was yours. There's a difference."

"I don't know where you get these fucking dumb ideas, Lewis. Let me tell you, he's *mine*. Goddammit, Monica said he was mine."

"That is, indeed, what she said. We thought it best."

"*We? We* thought it best?"

"Yes. In retrospect, perhaps it wasn't such a good plan. We thought—Monica and I—that it might be embarrassing for the boy if he ever found out that his father was a notorious old queen. If we'd known how the climate would change—I mean, nowadays, it's almost de rigueur to have at least one gay parent—we'd never have bothered. Also, we thought you might like it. Being a parent. I mean."

"Oh, you did, did you?"

"We thought you'd make a good one. Better than me, anyway. And, you were—apart from not being there, of course. In all other respects, you've been exemplary."

Orson shook his head. "I don't know why you're doing this, Lewis. It's far-fetched beyond belief and you can't expect me to buy it. It's ridiculous—"

Lewis sighed. "We had a blood test done, Ossie. Obviously there was doubt, so we had one done. Why do you think Monica was so adamant about not marrying you? Because the child wasn't yours, that's why. And, of course, there was no question of marrying me—that would have made us both miserable. If you like, we'll do this new DNA thing, just to confirm it—and you can telephone Monica, too. I'll get you the number—"

"I know the fucking number. Shut up. Let me think."

They sat in silence, gazing out over the terrace towards the horizon. Then Orson thumped one fist down on the arm of his chair.

"Goddammit—I paid his fucking school fees!"

"*We* paid his school fees, Ossie. The common purse, remember?"

"This is really true?"

"Yes, Ossie."

"And, I suppose Giselle knew about this too?"

"Yes, she did. It was one of the few things she and I shared exclusively. You had her physically, I had her in the shared secret of *your* secret, which wasn't yours at all, only you didn't know that. Giselle took delight in noting your little cover-ups over the years. They afforded us endless amusement, I'm afraid."

"I bet they did. But, why would Monica do that? Why would she let me believe he was mine for all these years. Why would you, for that matter?"

"Well, apart from the perfectly good reasons I've already given you— it's History repeating itself, Ossie. It's what Giselle did, wasn't it? And, in all the world, Monica was the woman most like her—apart from being black, of course. Which was why we both fell for her. Not the black part, you understand."

"But, godammit, Michael's got my nose—"

"Michael's nose is entirely unremarkable, as are both of ours, Ossie. Let it go, there's a good chap."

Orson grunted and said, without heat, "If this is all true—"

"It is, Ossie."

"—then, all I can say is, you both behaved with unmitigated beastliness. And so did Giselle, if she really knew—"

"Which she did—"

"And I don't know if I can ever forgive you. Any of you. To let me believe, for all these years, that I was a father, when I wasn't—"

"Ah, but you *were*, weren't you? And for many more years than we led you to think. So you'll be able to forgive us after all."

"Huh. Fat chance."

"Look at it this way, Ossie. You thought you had a son and now you discover you haven't—but what you *do* have is a daughter and a granddaughter, both delightful, which is a fair swap in my book. You really can't complain about that, can you? I mean—*two* for *one*. As for me—for years, I had to pretend to have nothing in the way of offspring, which rankled a bit, particularly when I detected whiffs of parental

smugness wafting off you. Now, here we are, both admitted fathers—
and in your case, a grandfather, too—of children who, for all the neglect
we showed them, have still never been to prison, which is more than
some parents can say these days—and one of yours and one of mine are
in love with each other and might—the coincidence is almost
supernatural, but then all the best ones are—they just *might* produce a
grandchild for me and—and this will irritate you—a *great* grandchild
for you."

"Oh, Jesus Christ—God forbid."

"Why? You could dandle it."

"What the fuck is dandling?"

"I think that's what we did with Gloa, wasn't it? Bouncing her about
on the knees, if I remember. And you liked that, didn't you?"

"It was OK."

"Well, there you are. Something to look forward to."

"It won't live with us, will it?"

"No, but it might visit if we're nice to it."

"And we won't have to do its diapers?"

Lewis smiled to himself. Orson had accepted the situation. There
would be some sniping, of course, but he could always duck. "Perhaps
we're jumping the gun a little, Ossie. All we've got here is an affair,
remember. They'll probably break up any minute."

Orson nodded slowly. "Meanwhile, they're down on the beach,
carefully avoiding any sort of physical contact. We ought to put that
right, don't you think?"

"But, who's going to tell them?"

"Well, it's your news, Lewis. You tell them."

"I couldn't."

"Well, neither could I."

"Perhaps, in unison? Like a barbershop duet?"

"We'd have to rehearse that."

Lewis scratched the side of his jaw. "What's Michael going to say, do you suppose?" he said, a trace of nervousness in his voice.

"God knows, Lewis—but let's hope he hasn't used up all of his remarkable sang froid. With any luck, his delight at being able to put his sticky paws on the creature again will overcome any distaste at discovering he's your son and not mine."

There was a discreet cough behind them. Freddy was standing in the French windows and, for a moment, both Lewis and Orson wondered if he'd heard them. They glanced at each other, and Orson shook his head. There was a good twenty feet between them and the French windows and their voices had been muted.

Freddy coughed again, with a hint of impatience this time and said, "I was wondering how much longer you expect me to stand about in the kitchen, waiting to see who wants what? I mean, I wouldn't mind, only I've got the cooker on, ready to go with whatever's ordered, and it's getting like the Black Hole of Calcutta in there. I'm half cooked myself, if the truth be told. You could have me on toast."

Lewis and Orson turned slowly to look at him. Then Lewis said, "A small favor, Freddy. Would you pop down to the beach, where you'll probably find a subdued little party of three splashing about in the lagoon—"

"And, if they *are* splashing about," said Orson, "we want you to stand on the shore, cup your hands around your mouth and yell 'Shark!' at the top of your voice. That should get their attention."

Freddy's eyes widened. "It'll do more than that, Mr. O. It'll give them seizures, that will."

"We have Valium if they need it," Lewis said. "And champagne."

"Ooh—something to celebrate, is there?"

"You could say that, Freddy," said Lewis.

"And, when I've frightened them half to death—?"

"Ask them if they would come up here."

"Righty ho. I'm completely in the dark, of course—as *usual*—but righty ho."

They watched as Freddy trotted off down the path. Then Orson said, "Perhaps we could reveal it all in the form of a song? One of yours, Lewis? Adapted of course, with a few changes? *Nora* might work. Let's see now—how would it go?—

'*Lewis* wasn't nice, he indulged in every vice,
and he even humped his best friend's paramour,
he got her in the club and blub-blub-blub-blub-blub'—"

"Yes, all right, Ossie," said Lewis. "You were never any good with words. You'd better leave them to me."

"Happy to. What should *I* do then?"

"You could paint them a tableau, illustrating the whole business, Ossie. A picture being, apparently, worth a thousand words. Not of mine, of course. For a thousand of *my* words, they could expect a veritable comic book of illustrations from you. Now, *there's* an idea. You as Captain America, Monica as Wonderwoman, Giselle as Batgirl—"

"And you as The Flash, I think," said Orson, grinning fiercely.

"If you like, Ossie," Lewis said, with an air of exhausted dignity.

Then they were still and silent for so long that Lewis wondered if Orson wasn't perhaps brooding himself into another small flash of resentment. To break the unnatural inertia, Lewis waved his right hand to brush away an imaginary mosquito and was pleased when Orson, a moment later, flapped his own hand at the illusory insect.

Then Orson said, "Perhaps, Lewis—under the circumstances—we ought to think about sticking together for a bit. What do you think about that?"

"Sticking together? Well, I think that's a very good idea, Ossie. At least for a bit."

"Yes. I think that would be the right thing to do. If only for the chi-" Orson stopped suddenly and feigned a small choking fit. When the fit subsided, Lewis said, "If only for the what, Ossie?"

Orson pointed irritably down in the general direction of the sea. "For them. You know—*them*."

"Oh, *them*. Absolutely. If only for them. For the kiddiewinks. Yes, Ossie."

"I mean—easier for them if they want to *visit*, you see."

"What—just coming to the one place?"

"Right. Rather than two separate places, if we were to split up—"

"Oh yes. Much easier for them."

"And cheaper, too."

"Oh, much."

Lewis felt one of his too-broad smiles coming and, to cover it, he pretended that the mosquito had returned to land on his knee. He slapped down at it hard. "Missed, dammit," he muttered, his eyes following the fancied flight of his creation.

And what was rather wonderful was that Orson, three seconds later, slapped himself viciously on the cheek and—examining the palm of his hand (which was quite unadorned with the corpse of anything)—said, with obvious satisfaction, "Hah! Got the little bastard *that* time."

"Oh, well done, Ossie," said Lewis, allowing the too-broad smile full access to his face. "Well done. The last thing we need is any more visitors."

* * *

About the Author

Ian Ogilvy is a writer and an actor. As an actor, he has appeared extensively in Theater, Television and Film. As a writer, he has two previously published novels to his name—Loose Chippings and The Polkerton Giant—both published in the United Kingdom. He lives in Southern California, with his wife Kitty and his two stepsons.

9 780595 010073

Made in the USA
Middletown, DE
18 January 2022

59079655R00163